"OH LIEUTENANT, THANK GOD YOU'VE come!" May Wrede cried out. There were heavy shadows under her eyes and she trembled slightly.

"What's the matter?" Norah asked as she entered the main floor of the duplex.

"It's Mr. Isserman. He hasn't come down in three days. We haven't seen him. He hasn't picked up the food, not his tray and not hers. Neither one of them has had anything to eat for three days."

"It's all right, Mrs. Wrede, I'll go up."

The place reeked of neglect. Norah noted the array of expensive medical equipment installed behind the bed; it was as dusty and neglected as everything else. With a deep sigh, she turned to the bathroom. The door was closed. Before opening it, Norah got out a fresh handkerchief and covered her nose and mouth. Then she went in. . . .

CASUAL AFFAIRS

Lillian O'Donnell

FAWCETT CREST • NEW YORK

PROLOGUE

The phone rang in the night.

As on all the other nights for the past month, Helen Arnow fell into a sleep of emotional exhaustion as soon as she turned out the light. The gray, featureless days had followed one upon the other, indistinguishable in a chain of anxiety and sorrow. Sleep was her only easement; surprisingly it came to her without the aid of drugs. Yet it took only one ring of the telephone to dredge her up into instant alertness. In forty-two years of marriage she had never been separated from Bert more than a couple of days at a time. Now, in her lonely bed, eyes wide in the half-dark, Helen Arnow knew that on this night she had not fully loosed her grip on consciousness, but had been waiting. Before the phone rang a second time, her hand was on the receiver.

Automatically, she noted the illuminated digital display of the clock-radio beside the bed: 3:41 A.M.

She picked up the receiver. "Yes?"

"Mrs. Arnow? This is Dr. Benning at Chazen-Hadley."

She knew. There was only one reason for the hospital to call at this hour. "Yes."

"It's about your husband. I'm sorry, but Mr. Arnow has passed away."

1

She sighed. "When?"

"At two forty-five this morning."

There had been no nightmare, no intuitive flash to shock her into wakefulness so she might say later: *Yes, I sensed it. I knew.* Only the mundane sound of the telephone—like the other time. It had been her turn to entertain the ladies' duplicate bridge: twenty ladies, five tables. She'd been holding thirteen points and a five-card heart suit headed by the king, queen—a legitimate opening bid. Her partner had supported the hearts and then, before she could carry the bidding further, the phone call. It was the police. There'd been an accident. Her son, her only son Jack, had been killed outright. A fine young man, twenty-seven years old, with his whole life ahead of him, Jack Arnow had swerved to avoid a drunk heading straight at him on the wrong side of the road. He crashed through the barrier and plunged over high cliffs to the Hudson River below. Helen Arnow had been forty-eight and Bert sixty-three, but it was Bert who supplied the strength for both of them. He had encouraged her, supported her, saved her sanity. By the time they buried their son, Helen Arnow's hair was as white as her husband's and she was emotionally the elder.

"Mrs. Arnow?" The doctor, kind but impersonal, recalled her to the present.

"Yes. Yes. Will tomorrow . . . I mean, this morning . . . will that be time enough to make the arrangements?"

"Of course. I'm very sorry, Mrs. Arnow."

"Yes. Thank you. Good night."

She hung up. It was over. She hadn't asked how it happened. She didn't need to. It didn't matter. She was just glad it was finished. She hadn't turned on the light, and she didn't need to do so now. She knew exactly where she had put the container. She pried off the top, shook a couple of tablets out and palmed them into her mouth. The glass of water to wash them down was easy to find. Helen Arnow swallowed, hesitated, then took two more.

The administrator sent for the resident to question him and get an explanation.

The office of the administrator was a small bright room,

taking its country motif from four high, elegantly arched windows overlooking the hospital's enclosed garden. The vista showed a square of lawn bordered with proud red and yellow tulips, and dotted with modest clumps of purple crocus. While the May sun shone cheerily, patches of leftover snow were reminders of a late April blizzard. The sun illumined the resident's haggard face, accentuating every line and furrow, emphasizing the dark shadows and the unshaven jaw. Clyde Benning was underweight. He had slept only six hours out of the last thirty-six, but that wasn't unusual. He was also young, healthy, and eager to excel in his chosen profession; he would bounce back. At the moment, anger and frustration kept him going and staved off exhaustion.

"He extubated himself!" Benning spoke low but with intensity as though the offense had been against him personally.

Vincent Wadman passed a freckled hand over his pale blue eyes, shielding them for a moment from the bright sunlight and from the resident's demanding stare. It was not the first time a patient on a respirator had managed to pull out his breathing tube—most of them tried—but it was the first time anyone at Chazen-Hadley had died as a direct result.

"I want to know how he got free to do it," Benning went on. "I want to know who untied him and left him untied in the middle of the night."

"Do you expect anyone to step forward and admit it?"

"No, of course not," Benning sighed, some of his truculence assuaged.

"Who was on duty?" Wadman asked.

"Lavarette. She's been at Chazen-Hadley five years. She's got a good record. She's reliable, dedicated. She—"

"I know Kate Lavarette," the administrator broke in. "What does she have to say?"

"She was working on the charts."

"Who else was on duty?"

"Romano. She was on a break. But there was an intern." He paused. "He was at the station updating case histories."

In Intensive Care the patient is monitored constantly—which doesn't mean someone is at his bedside every moment. Unit 3A was small, consisting of four beds with an alcove serving as the nurse's station. It was common practice for interns, residents, attending physicians, and nurses of every grade to do paperwork at the counter in the alcove. Every member of the IC staff was instinctively attuned to the beep of the cardiac monitors and the rasp of the respirators; any variation instantly alerted them.

"Lavarette heard the alarm but it indicated no more than an ordinary intermittent high-pressure reaction caused by accumulation of secretions. She was due to suction in a few minutes anyway, so she waited. When the alarm increased in intensity and steadied, she went in. She saw what had happened and yelled for the intern to page Emergency, then started to bag the patient manually. When the lungs failed to inflate, she inserted oxygen, but still couldn't get a reaction. The crisis team arrived promptly, but were unable to save him. His heart couldn't stand the strain."

Wadman sighed again, this time with relief. Apparently they were dealing with no more than an unfortunate accident. Bertram Arnow had tried to relieve himself of the irritating endotrachial tube. Managing somehow to free his hands, he had removed the source of his distress without any idea of the damage it would do. Wadman leaned back in his chair. "It appears that Lavarette was tardy in responding."

"She followed established procedure."

"Perhaps that procedure should be reviewed. We'll take that up at the next staff meeting."

Benning waited. "That's it?"

"By no means, Doctor. I will interview Lavarette, the intern, and the crisis team. If there was any . . . carelessness, I promise you I'll find out."

Vincent Wadman was forty-two, six feet tall and carried about ten pounds more than he should, but he was solid, as strong and compact as biweekly workouts on the Nautilus machines could make him. His light brown hair was thinning and his blue eyes, deceptively mild, could dissect with clinical ruthlessness. He had set out to be a doctor, but in the middle of his first year at Cornell his father died, leaving a domino lineup of debts that made it impossible even to consider the long years of study and internship. The memory of his father's financial irresponsibility was an ever-present caution for the administrator, while his first choice of profession made him particularly sympathetic to the problems of the medical staff. It was a good balance. Yet he was not pleased to have had his night's sleep disrupted, particularly since he could deduce no real cause for alarm. He resented having to rush out into the night, shirt unbuttoned, tie in his pocket, no breakfast. His stomach was sour from too many cups of coffee. It was barely eight-thirty, and he was already dragging. Maybe he could get away early. Then he groaned: there was that damned dinner party of Joyce's tonight.

Meanwhile, Benning hadn't moved.

"Don't you think we'd better find out what happened, exactly what happened to Mr. Arnow, before his wife gets over the initial shock and starts asking questions?"

"Why should she ask questions?" Wadman snapped, giving in to the irritation of lost sleep and a lingering anxiety. "The patient was seventy-seven years old." He glanced down at the file in front of him. "He came in with all the symptoms of poor circulation due to arrhythmia. The emergency administration diagnosis was confirmed. While here he experienced two seizures and was twice resuscitated. What more can she expect?"

"The truth. The truth!" Benning exploded. His pale face was covered with sweat, his dark, lank hair saturated, his thin frame trembling with intensity. "Bertram Arnow's principal problem was pneumonia, but he was *recovering*. He had a chance. He did. Damn it, he had survived the two previous arrests without brain damage. He was sentient. We were weaning him off the respirator. We were getting ready to move him back to his room."

Wadman scowled. "Maybe he didn't want that. Maybe . . ." The administrator looked deep within himself before finishing. "Maybe he wanted to die."

Clyde Benning caught his breath.

Wadman knew Benning's father had been a small-town doctor, knew that Benning had learned to consider the whole patient, not just the disease. It was Vincent Wadman's job to know such things. It was one of the reasons Dr. Benning had been selected from the long list of applicants for residency at the small but highly regarded hospital. Now was the time for Benning to learn pragmatism. "If, as you insist, Arnow was sentient, than he knew what he was doing. The intermittent alarm suggests that he extubated himself gradually, so as not to alert the nurse until the last moment, till he was beyond help. It suggests a well-thought-out plan—more than that, a frightening determination to die. Is that what you want me to tell Mrs. Arnow?"

Benning groaned, then slowly shook his head. "No sir, I wouldn't lay that on her." Discouraged and depressed as he was, and feeling the leaden weariness at last, Clyde Benning nevertheless pulled himself straight and leveled his gaze at the administrator. "I still want an answer. Who made it possible for Arnow to kill himself? Who untied his hands?"

Wadman waited till the resident was gone, then leaned back in his chair, closed his eyes, and gave in to despondency. He'd looked for a solution to spare them all—the personnel on duty, the hospital, and Mrs. Arnow. He knew now it was not possible. He couldn't pass it off as an accident. The general perception of a patient on life support was that he was unaware of his state and felt nothing. True, if the patient was in a coma. But a patient even partially conscious, like Arnow, was at best uncomfortable, if not in outright pain. Immobile, he had to lie in one position until a nurse had the time and inclination to turn him. He felt the needle of every injection. The worst was the damn breathing tube down his throat that made it impossible to eat or to speak and communicate his needs and feelings. It scratched his throat till it became raw and ulcerated. The occasional swallow of ice water, grudgingly allowed, did little to soothe. The one overwhelming desire was to yank it out. That was why his hands were tied. And being tied, not only couldn't he pull out the tube, he couldn't scratch an itch, cover himself if he was cold, uncover himself if he was hot. A conscious patient chafed at the restraints; pain and frustration were almost beyond endurance.

Perhaps somebody had pitied Bertram Arnow and untied his hands merely to give him a few moments' respite. Nurses were compassionate. Patients and their families pleaded to have their hands freed. It was not unusual. But to untie a patient like Arnow in IC and leave him unattended during the night? No, no responsible nurse would do it.

Wadman rubbed his brow with one hand, then raised his head. He swung his chair around to look out the window at the sunlit garden and considered the alternative.

CHAPTER ONE

It was the Rose Ball, the last major social event of the New York season. Roses don't bloom in the East till June and it was only the seventh of May, but none of the festive crowd cared. They were there because everyone who mattered, or thought he mattered, was there. By the usual standards the second floor ballroom of the Plaza Hotel was small for such an affair, but selectivity was part of the mystique. The limited capacity made it a privilege to pay the one-thousand-dollar-per-person ticket price in the name of charity.

The decor consisted principally of roses, of course. An abundance of red and pink blossoms spilled from baskets and bowls. No trellises or hanging garlands here; everything was understated. The scent of flowers was intensified by the warmth of the room and the bodies that crowded it. In the soft glow of the lighting, each sconce and every bulb of the massive central chandelier and the single lamps on each table muted by a pleated silk shade, the women's complexions were unflawed yet their jewels sparkled. At the changeover, Phil Sutton's Society Orchestra slid into a bland mix of show tunes. Couples dancing apart came together; those who had been together drew closer.

Sarah Hoyt nestled her head against her husband's chest. She was small and slim, with a fragile look. Her face was pointed, features finely chiseled, hair cut short in a dark cloud around her head. Tiny unflawed diamond earrings glittered against it like stars. She wore white satin, one shoulder bare. The thin white shoulder added to the impression of vulnerability. Sarah Hoyt had a fixed smile on her face as she and Justin moved slowly around the dance floor; she wasn't enjoying herself. She hadn't wanted to come, but Christina Isserman, chairman of the ball, was her sister and had made an issue of it. As usual, Christie had won. It wasn't a bad party of its kind, Sarah thought, just meaningless. The people here were the same people she and Justin saw everywhere. She did like the old Plaza, though. This ballroom was as familiar to Sarah as a local restaurant might be to someone less privileged. Having grown up in a mansion with its own private ballroom under a stained-glass conservatory-style dome, Sarah was not easily awed. She felt comfortable here. There were memories, good memories.

The Gardner School, a private school catering to girls who lived in mansions, with or without ballrooms, had held all its functions here—Saturday afternoon dancing classes, Christmas parties, commencement exercises. Here Sarah had taken prizes for English and Drama when she graduated from the eighth grade. She had been elated till Christie was called up for Science and Math. Her father, Theodore Sexton, proclaimed himself equally proud of both his girls, but Sarah knew it was the Science and Math awards he valued.

Theo Sexton was the scion of legendary barons of the railroad industry, dating back to his great-grandfather Anatol's investment in the Hannibal and St. Joseph Railway, a small line that hauled into Kansas City in the 1870s. Through that holding the immigrant Sexton was able to buy into the Missouri Pacific Railway System. He amassed a fortune, not in the class of the Goulds and the Vanderbilts, but a base on which succeeding generations could build.

It was Theo's grandfather who built the mansion in New York—though not on Millionaires' Row, as the length of Fifth Avenue from Sixtieth to Ninetieth was known at the turn of the century. David Sexton preferred to break new ground and erected his castle on Madison Avenue, where the Villards and others like them soon followed suit.

Theo Sexton inherited more than money, he inherited his grandfather's individualism, adding to the family fortune by steering Sexton Industries toward the future: television, airlines, and just before his death—space. Sexton put his money into a satellite business-communications network and was part of a consortium to promote experimental drug production in the gravity-free environment 22,300 miles above Earth.

Sexton's wife, Anna, died when Christie was ten and Sarah six. He never remarried. Nurses and governesses raised the girls with Sexton maintaining close supervision. He was scrupulous never to show preference, and Sarah had not realized till the day of the awards, here in this room, that her father loved Christie more. Christie was smarter, more beautiful, more popular; she deserved to be the more loved. Yet it hurt. Sarah believed that while she could never outdo her sister, she might match her scholastically at least. She tried. She studied long hours, but she couldn't excel, not in the fields that mattered. And now that they were adults, Sarah mused, it was Christie who led the idle life; a life of meaningless activity with the occasional gesture toward good works, like this charity party. She, Sarah Sexton Hoyt, was the business success. As she rested her cheek against her husband's chest and drifted dreamily around the dance floor, she wished Dad had lived to see it.

Sarah had had both her engagement party and wedding reception here; by then the mansion had been torn down. Christie, opting for more size and flamboyance, had celebrated one marriage at the Waldorf with five hundred dear friends. When she married Walther Isserman, both ceremony and reception were held on the 170-foot Sexton yacht as it circled Manhattan. It was considered a graceful compliment to the background and interests of the groom, even an indication of the way Sexton investments might turn as a result of the union. Certainly that was Walther Isserman's own interpretation, and it only intensified his later disappointment. Sarah had known better from the start. Theo Sexton was no more enthusiastic about this latest of Christie's men than he'd been about the others. At best, he was cautiously optimistic. At worst, he considered Isserman an improvement over the Delaware playboy; certainly preferable to the gardener's son—though most had forgotten Mario, including, probably, Christie.

Sarah opened her eyes, searching for her sister. The committee members, their guests, and the largest contributors sat at tables located on a mezzanine two shallow steps higher than the main floor. The tables were further distinguished by cloths of a slightly deeper shade of rose and somewhat more elaborate centerpieces. Christina Isserman and her party commanded the center. Christina held court.

She wore black velvet. In studied contrast to Sarah's white satin? Why not? Sarah thought. Christina's blond hair was pulled up into a sleek coil at the crown of her head, making her long, slender neck seem infinitely graceful. Always full-bodied, she'd recently put on weight. Her normally serene face was marred by a deep frown, a frown so frequent lately it would soon become a permanent disfigurement. Still, Christina was the most beautiful woman there, her sister thought. Sarah felt no pang of envy; the familiar ache had passed a long time ago. Passed in fact, when she'd found the right man. Sarah Sexton Hoyt raised her lips to Justin and they kissed lightly.

Almost everyone was dancing but Christina Isserman remained seated, blond head high on that white column of neck, with only one of her guests in attendance—Frank Veloney, chairman of the board of Sexton Industries and an old family friend who had known the girls since birth. Frank talked to Christina earnestly, making every effort to draw her attention to himself. She wasn't listening; she watched her husband, following Walther with her eyes as he guided an awkward young member of their party around the dance floor.

Isserman was a man whose looks captured attention—and who had the wit, education, and social graces to hold it. He was tall, slim, aristocratic. His fresh complexion, combined with thick dark hair sprinkled with touches of premature gray, made people misread his age. That some thought Isserman older than his thirty-nine years—or younger—was a reflection of their own point of view. Walther Isserman was born in Italy but did not consider himself Italian. In fact, his parents were

Austrian. His grandfather, Rudolf, was a papal count. His grandmother, Eva, was one of the Milosevic family, owners of the premier shipping company of Trieste, the Lowe-Milosevic Line. As Trieste before World War I was the only access to the Adriatic for the Austro-Hungarian Empire, the Milosevics enjoyed great power. When Trieste was ceded to Italy, however, it became, along with Venice, Genoa, and Naples, just another port on the Italian coast. The Milosevic interests suffered. Lowe-Milosevic became Lowe-Adriatica and then, anonymously, Linea Adriatica.

What remained of a once proud dominance was finished when the airplane became a dependable means of transportation. The Isserman fortunes, entwined with the Milosevic, were wiped out. Rudolf Isserman salvaged enough to retire to the hills of Opicina, where he and Eva lived in gentle regret but always great pride. The couple did not allow themselves to forget who they were. The clean mountain air sustained them into their early nineties, she going first and he a scant two months after.

During World War II Trieste was occupied first by the Nazis and then by the Communists. In the current climate of democracy, with the Russian presence only a spasm away at the Yugoslav border, terrorism became a part of daily life. Feeling they were under constant surveillance, Dieter Isserman, Walther's father, considered it prudent to drop the title, to forego the use of the coat of arms on notepaper and linen. But he didn't forget either, nor did he permit his son to forget.

That wasn't enough for Walther. It was his intent to restore the family fortune and position. He envisaged a return of luxury passenger travel by sea. When Walther came to New York, he met Christina Sexton. She was rich and beautiful; an heiress whose money came from the railroads—transportation. It seemed to Walther an omen; the two families were meant to unite. But Theodore Sexton had long since divested himself of the last sentimental vestiges of his railroad holdings and shifted into airlines. An indication of flexibility, Walther reasoned. He wished his grandfather had done the same.

At the table, Veloney continued to talk earnestly to Christina, but she'd given up even the pretense of listening. "The next meeting's Monday at ten. The board will be delighted to see you again. And we can have lunch afterward. What do you say?"

"I'm sorry?" She turned to him at last with barely masked irritation.

"You used to take such an interest in the business. You were good at it."

"It pleased Dad."

"It would please him still."

"You don't need me."

"Of course we do. One of these days I'm going to retire. You have to start to give some thought . . ."

"Not yet. Not for a long time, Frank." She patted his hand and turned, searching again for her husband among the dancers.

"At least have lunch with me, Christie," Veloney urged. "I need to talk to you about some of your holdings. They should be closed out and the proceeds reinvested."

"If you mean those old bearer bonds of Dad's, no. I told you, I want to keep them."

"That's sentiment, not good business. Your father would have been the first to tell you not to form attachments to an investment."

"I don't want to talk about it. Not now."

"All right, but . . ."

"I don't want to sell. That's it, Frank." She turned her back to him. Her dark eyes narrowed as they settled on Walther again. "Will you tell me what he sees in that girl?"

Veloney followed her gaze. "Claire Meese? You can't be serious. He's only dancing with her out of courtesy. You know that."

"How about some courtesy to me?" Christina half rose in her chair.

Veloney put out a restraining hand. "I think the set's about finished."

Sarah saw her sister's movement from the dance floor. She observed Veloney's gesture and Christie's resulting flush. The jealousy's beginning to show, Sarah Hoyt thought—but in this case it was misdirected. Christie was, as usual, drinking too much. Walther, for all his social skills and graces, couldn't hide his concern. His partner wasn't having a good time either. Claire Meese had come with her parents. There were only a few single men at the dance and none of them had sought her out. Claire was plain, last year's debutante—not that that kind of thing mattered anymore. Sarah was shocked at herself for applying the label, but unfortunately it stuck easily on Claire. She had little else but social birth to recommend her, and was painfully aware of it. At this moment she was very conscious that Walther, though charming, was performing an obligation. Isserman's very sophistication betrayed the fact that his interest was mere formality. Every time he smiled and murmured something in Clair Meese's ear, the poor girl blushed. And Christie, observing from her table, glowered. Mercifully, the set ended at last and Walther escorted his partner back to her place.

Before he could get Claire seated, Christie complained. "Aren't you going to ask *me* to dance?"

Walther hesitated, looking over his shoulder at the dancers leaving the floor. "The music's stopped."

"How convenient for you." Christie glared, then turned and bestowed an icy smile on the girl. "Did you enjoy dancing with my husband?"

Claire bent her head so that an untidy fall of drab brown hair hid her embarrassment. "Oh yes, Christina, very much."

"Smooth, isn't he?"

Claire kept her head down. "Yes."

"That's what all the women tell me. I haven't danced with him myself in . . . how long is it, darling? How long is it since we've danced together? I wonder why we bother to come to these affairs."

Walther didn't reply. He bowed slightly to his erstwhile partner, who was still blushing, nodded to Veloney, and last to his wife. "Please excuse me."

"Where are you going?" Christine demanded. "Where are you going now?"

"I need a breath of air." He was formally polite.

"And I want to dance," she topped him, her voice rising to the edge of stridency. Unsteadily, Christina Isserman got to her feet. As she pushed the chair back it toppled, but the floor was carpeted and there was no noise; no one noticed. "I want to dance," she announced more loudly and, turning, stumbled from the table to the wrought-iron railing and down the two steps to the dance floor.

Walther hurried after her. Veloney got to his feet. Both were too late; Christie had already started across the empty dance floor. Once in the center she swayed slightly and moved toward the bandstand.

"Let's have some music. I want to dance. Well, come on. What are you waiting for? I said I want to dance."

Reaching her, Walther took her arm and warned Veloney with a look to keep back.

"Ah, here you are at last, darling." Christie bestowed a sarcastic smile on him. "A waltz, Maestro, please. My husband is very good at waltzing the ladies, aren't you darling? Let's show the people just how good you are."

The scene caught the attention first of those at ringside, then of the other guests. Conversations subsided, finally stopped altogether. With the exception of a few nervous gasps, the ballroom was hushed. The bandleader, Phil Sutton himself, appeared from backstage, where he'd been having a smoke. Baton in hand, he rapped his men to attention.

"We shall have music!" Christina proclaimed. Arms outspread, she began dancing alone. Quickly, Walther stepped in and enfolded her while Sutton gave the downbeat and the band began to pound out sound and rhythm, loud and fast.

Sarah and Justin were about to return to the table but resumed dancing instead. Veloney took Claire as his partner. When one or two others joined in, it seemed the scene was over. Till Walther tried to steer his wife from the floor.

"Where are you going? Where are you taking me?"

"It's time to go home."

"I don't want to go home. It's too early. The party's just started. I want some more champagne."

"You've had enough. Come on now." He tightened his grip on her arm and led her toward the coat room.

"No. No!" She pulled back. "I don't want to go. It's too

early. I want champagne. Waiter. Waiter. Champagne!" She was flushed, her eyes wild, her color high.

"Christie, please . . ."

"Christie, please . . . ," she mimicked.

"Everybody's looking at us."

"Who cares?"

"Christie, please, be a good girl and let me take you home."

"Christie, please, be a good girl and let me take you home," she parroted. "Let me take you home and dump you so I can go and fuck Lucine. That's why you want to get out of here, isn't it? Isn't it?" she yelled.

Walther Isserman's lean, handsome face froze. His aquiline nose and high cheekbones seemed sculptured. Only the pulses throbbing at his temples indicated his anger. He kept his hands rigid at his sides, using every effort of will to keep from reaching out and striking her.

"You think I don't know about you and Lucine?" she taunted. "I'm not stupid. You think I believe those excuses about late-night business meetings? What business? You don't even have a job." Her face was mottled, swollen by drink, distorted by frustration. "You think everybody doesn't know? What nobody knows is what you see in her. She's old and she has no money."

Walther clenched his jaw.

"Where is she tonight, anyway? How come she's not here? She turns up everywhere we go. It's a little late for discretion."

Before anything more could be said by either, Sarah and Justin Hoyt, along with Veloney and Claire Meese, closed about the couple. The music blared to the brink of distortion, and Christina Isserman was carried off the ballroom floor of the Plaza Hotel as by a flying wedge—crying, laughing, shaking—all at the same time.

The next morning Walther Isserman got out of the house early. As his wife had taunted, he didn't have a job, but he did have an office. The office, though small, was prestigiously located and impeccably decorated. Isserman also had a topflight secretary whose only duties were to answer the phone, keep track of his luncheon appointments, and pay the office rent and other business expenses. She was much too capable to waste her talents in this manner, but Isserman paid well for her boredom. The listing on the building directory was "Isserman Enterprises." Certainly Walther Isserman was involved in all kinds of deals, but none ever reached fruition, or hadn't so far. Days went by when he didn't put in an appearance, and others when he looked in for about an hour at noon to dictate a few letters before leaving for lunch. Sometimes he called to say he wouldn't be back to the office; most times he didn't bother.

On this bright May morning, Tuesday the eighth, Isserman surprised the staff of the Fifth Avenue duplex by appearing in the breakfast room at eight. He wanted only coffee along with his usual brioche with sweet butter and natural honey. He read the paper in less than his customary leisurely fashion and was gone by eight-thirty. He strode down Fifth Avenue admiring the white and pink of flowering cherry and magnolia trees in the park. At Fifty-seventh Street he turned and walked over to Madison Avenue. At nine precisely, Isserman entered the Trump Tower along with hordes of workers whose numbers he had heretofore never suspected.

Striding through the tiny reception room to his only slightly larger private office, Walther Isserman advised Elsie Schubart, his paragon of a secretary, that he didn't want to be disturbed and closed his door. He placed a series of transatlantic calls to Rome, Paris, Zurich. At 1:15 P.M., as he was considering lunch, Elsie Schubart buzzed him.

The Issermans had long since stopped breakfasting together. That ritual had lasted only one week of their marriage. Within a month Walther moved to a separate bedroom—so he wouldn't disturb his bride when he got up to go to work at Sexton Industries. Not that Christina slept all that much later, not in those days. She followed her husband into the office on lower Broadway within an hour, never more than two. Though she didn't stay long, she never failed to put in an appearance—and she also knew exactly what was going on. That was while Theodore Sexton was alive. Though Walther didn't like it, he didn't object. After the old man died, he didn't have any reason to; Christina stopped the practice. As Frank Veloney had remarked, she'd lost interest. She slept late, then later, and was served breakfast in bed. On the morning after a big party, Christina Isserman rarely rang for breakfast before eleven.

On the Tuesday morning after the Rose Ball, May Wrede was in the kitchen waiting. She had the tray set, coffee ready to be plugged in, bread in the toaster. As the hands of the electric wall clock neared twelve she began to worry. "Should I go up and knock?" she asked Maggie McCullough.

The cook shrugged. "Leave her be. From the black look of himself I'd say they had another battle royal last night."

"Oh, they did. I heard them." May sighed. There was no need to elaborate. The encounters were frequent and followed a pattern familiar to both.

"There you are then. She probably had a couple too many and knocked herself out. Poor lamb."

They exchanged knowing glances. McCullough was a comfortably plump woman of fifty-five whose only affectation was dying her snow-white hair a flamingly incredible red. An old retainer, she had been with the Sexton family over thirty years, going back to the old mansion and the summer place in the Adirondacks. Also in her fifties, May Wrede was a relative newcomer hired since the marriage—a scant six years. She had never been in domestic service before. When her husband died after a long illness that had wiped out their savings, she had been forced to look for work in the only field in which she had any experience—housework. The agency reluctantly sent her on the interview only after their most qualified candidates had been turned down. They were as surprised as she when she got the job. May was grateful, and quickly became as fiercely devoted to Christina as the longtime employee. Neither liked Isserman. It wasn't because he had neither hired them nor paid their salaries. And it wasn't because he was a foreigner, though both were intensely prejudiced. They thought he treated Christina badly. Both of them knew the marriage was failing, and they put the blame on Isserman.

By twelve-twenty McCullough was fidgeting too. She plugged in the coffee and pushed the bread down into the toaster. "You'd better go up and make sure she's not sick or anything," she told Wrede.

It was the "or anything" that was on both their minds. Without another word, May Wrede made her way through the pantry into the dining room and out to the main entry hall of the duplex. That was the fifteenth floor of the building; the gracefully curving inner staircase led up to the sixteenth floor, which formed the second floor of the apartment. The master bedroom was just to the right at the head of the stairs. Wrede stopped at the door, hesitated, took a breath, and knocked. No answer. She knocked again. Still not getting any response, she went to the railing and looked down at McCullough, who was waiting.

"What should we do?"

McCullough was already lumbering up. She passed Wrede and went directly to the closed door. She knocked loudly, urgently. "Miss Christie!" she called out. It was a formality, a necessary formality, but neither woman any longer expected an answer. Even as she called, McCullough had her hand on the doorknob, barely pausing before turning it. She pushed the door partially open and, with Wrede at her shoulder, the two of them peered inside.

As usual the shades were pulled down so the morning sun would not disturb the sleeper. All the two of them could make out was a form under the rumbled satin blanket cover. By common consent they crept close. Christina Isserman lay on her stomach, head nestled in the crook of her left arm, turned away from them.

By right of seniority McCullough took charge. "Miss Christina?"

Nothing. No sound, no movement.

"Child?" Maggie McCullough entreated. She moved around to the far side of the canopied bed to look into Christina Isserman's face. Tears brimmed from the old woman's eyes. "She's sleeping," she told May Wrede, and the tears ran down her raddled cheeks. She leaned over and gently shook her employer. "Miss Christina? Wake up, Miss Christina. Wake up."

Still no reaction. After a moment of hesitation, McCullough grasped the sleeping woman by both shoulders, rolled her over so she was face up. "Wake up, Miss Christina. Wake up," she begged, shaking her like a rag doll. Finally the old woman raised her hand and slapped Christina Isserman's face.

She didn't even blink.

McCullough sobbed. May Wrede was crying too, but she was the one who pulled herself together. "I'll call the mister," she said.

The call forced Miss Schubart to disregard her boss's instructions.

"I'm sorry to disturb you, sir, but Wrede's on the phone. She's nearly hysterical. I think you'd better speak to her."

Isserman picked up the receiver. "All right, Wrede, pull yourself together. What's the problem?"

"It's Mrs. Isserman, sir. She won't wake up."

Walther hesitated. He sighed deeply. "She had quite a lot to drink last night. She's sleeping it off. Don't worry."

"No, sir, no. It's not like the other times. She's hardly breathing. Should I call an ambulance?"

"No!" Walther snapped. "For God's sake, woman, how do you think she's going to feel when she wakes up and finds herself in an emergency room? Embarrassed and humiliated. Just leave her alone and let her sleep it off." He slammed down the phone.

Wrede looked helplessly at McCullough. Again, there was no need for words between them.

CHAPTER TWO

Norah's first inkling that this was to be more than a casual gathering of a few friends and relatives for a couple of drinks came when she saw the sign in Vittorio's window: CLOSED FOR PRIVATE PARTY.

Jim Felix and his wife had offered Norah a ride uptown from One Police Plaza. It had struck her as odd that they caught every red light, lagged behind every truck and bus, and that Inspector Felix, normally an impatient driver, showed a great deal of restraint. Now Norah knew why.

She walked in to a round of applause. Twenty-five minutes earlier Norah Mulcahaney had been one of sixteen newly appointed lieutenants to step up to the podium and shake hands with the mayor and the police commissioner. Now friends and relatives drew near—smiling, congratulating, shaking her hand to show their joy and pride in her. The Sophisticates, a five-piece combo wearing tuxedos and red bow ties, belted out swing and society music in their version of big-band style—if not sound—and a place had been cleared for dancing. The bar was going strong. From the table settings Norah could tell it was going to be a full sit-down dinner. The entire Capretto clan was there, starting with her late husband's mother and his seven sisters. Counting husbands and children, uncles and aunts, nieces, nephews, cousins, they nearly filled the restaurant all by themselves, but there were plenty of others. Norah had been asked for a list and, thinking it was to be no more than a few drinks at Lena and Jake's house, had put down the twenty men in her new command as well as friends from other times and other cases. Some, like herself, were in uniform, having come directly from the ceremonies; others were in civilian clothes. But with the exception of the men on duty they were all there, every one. Norah was touched. Through all the years of her marriage to Joe Capretto, and even since his death, she had been overwhelmed by the sheer number of Joe's family. When they gathered she seemed to be absorbed, to lose her individuality. Not today. Lena and Jake DeVecchi, who had organized this, had made sure. Norah Mulcahaney Capretto's dark blue eyes misted: this was truly *her* day.

She looked over to Joe's mother, Signora Emilia, the matriarch, ensconced in a special chair Vittorio had provided. She was eighty-eight, mentally alert, physically active, and most definitely interested in all family matters. Joe had been her only son, a police officer; and it had taken Signora Emilia a long time to accept Norah as his wife and a police officer too. At this very moment, the old lady held court in the midst of her children and grandchildren. She did it as a matter of course, and Norah no longer resented it. In fact, she realized with a rueful twist of her full lips and a softening of her blunt chin that she was doing exactly the same thing herself.

Norah Mulcahaney stood her full five-eight, straight and proud in the uniform she seldom wore except for ceremonial occasions. It was one of the mystiques of making detective that you go out of your "blues" and into plainclothes, and Norah had been a detective for nearly ten years. Yet it felt good to be wearing the uniform again, and she knew she looked well in it. She was thirty-seven and at her most fit. Norah's white skin glowed; her deep blue eyues were alert, shining with pleasure at everyone and everything around her. Her dark hair coiled at the nape of her neck, lustrous as a skein of silk. In this moment of happiness, the square cut of her jaw, which sometimes made her look obstinate and at the very least determined, was barely noticeable.

It had not been easy to achieve this state, and Norah wasn't thinking of her promotion—though she was proud of that, very proud. In the past year and a half she had lost both father and husband. Patrick Mulcahaney had lived a full, in fact lengthy span, but Captain Joseph Capretto had been taken at the height of his vigor. She had to think of Joe now. How could she not think of him? Married six years, they'd had their hard times, disappointments—principally not being able to have children. But it had been a good marriage, a strong marriage. They'd complemented each other, and in the last months the early ardor had been rekindled. But Joe was killed in the line of duty: shot while attempting to stop a rape and then run down. He'd been caught in the get-away car's undercarriage and dragged through the streets of Chinatown till he was unrecognizable.

Norah quit the force, or tried to. Her boss, Jim Felix, refused to accept the resignation and suggested a leave of absence. Insisted on it. Norah learned then that the job was almost as much a part of her life as Joe had been. She learned not to run away from memories but to cherish them. She made her accommodation with loneliness, learned to fill the void—well, at least to fill the time. She went back to work. She could laugh again and honestly enjoy herself. Sometimes, though, at the end of the workday and the companionship it brought, when she was at home and by herself, Norah had to admit she still missed Joe deeply, probably always would. But the pain was less acute.

The new lieutenant, however, was not allowed to stand to one side for introspection too long. A stream of new arrivals milled around her, shook her hand, congratulated her, joked, laughed. Sally Felix came up and kissed Norah. Despite the long-standing friendship between Sally's husband, Inspector Felix, and Joe Capretto, the wives had little social contact. Sally had been an actress and was still active in community theater. Their worlds didn't touch, yet there was a strong bond between them, an empathy, a warmth of understanding that didn't require weekly lunches, bridge games, or gossipy phone calls. Each stood ready to sustain the other. Sally had shown the depth of her caring at Joe's death; now she showed joy in Norah's achievement. Felix broke in.

"Care to dance, Lieutenant?"

Head of Homicide, Jim Felix had himself been promoted recently from deputy to full inspector. He was fifty-three. His hair, once a curly rakish roan mixutre, had gone completely white. He'd put on weight, but it was so evenly distributed over his tall frame that he looked big rather than fat. His long, lean face had filled out, but his green eyes were the same—penetrating, perceptive, and at this moment sparkling with pleasure. Norah moved into his arms to the accompaniment of a round of applause that started from a few people nearby and spread through the entire room.

"Have I told you how pleased I am by your appointment?" he asked as they moved out on the dance floor.

"Thank you, Jim."

"And I know how proud Joe would have been."

Tears sprang into Norah's eyes for a moment. "Yes."

"So I'll give you a piece of advice for the two of us. Okay?"

She nodded.

"You're going to have a much wider field of responsibility; it will reach past the number of men you command. Don't try to do everything yourself. Trust the people working with you as you always have. Don't change."

"I won't."

"Good. And I'll add one more thing for myself: if in doubt, ask. If you need help, don't be shy. Don't be proud. Don't wait till your back's up against the wall."

"I hope I've learned that much."

Roy Brennan cut in.

"Congratulations, Norah."

"Thanks. I hear congratulations are in order for you too."

He grinned. "Yeah. Grace is pregnant again."

He didn't need to say how happy he was; it was all over him. Norah had known Roy as long as she had Felix; both had been Joe's friends originally. Roy had already been a detective working out of the old Homicide North when she was just a rookie. In fact, he'd been her immediate boss at one time. With his experience and ability he could have gone, could still go, a lot higher. Never lazy, he had simply been satisfied; a man who'd found his niche. A confirmed bachelor. In that respect, very much like Joe, Norah thought, smiling reminiscently. At forty-two, with his life pattern apparently set, Roy Brennan met *the* girl and in three months he was married. From a man without animation, Brennan had turned, if not outgoing, certainly mellow. He became a family man. No more hanging around with the guys for a couple of beers, or more, after the shift. Again like Joe, Norah mused, except that her husband had started as a swinger. And of course Roy had an infant son as well as a wife to go home to. Now there was to be a second child and Roy Brennan seemed to be getting younger.

Ferdi Arenas was next to cut in. Though he'd recently made sergeant, Arenas still treated Norah with the deference he'd shown when first assigned to work for her, according her the respect he would a teacher. Despite the years and the cases, despite the real affection, there was a formality between them. Just as there was between herself and Inspector Felix, Norah mused, and always would be. As Ferdi put his arms around her for the dance, his smile was easy. Ferdi had gone home to Mayagüez, Puerto Rico, last summer where, after years of mourning the death of Pilar Nieves, the policewoman he'd intended to marry, Ferdi had met someone who made him live in the present again.

"I hear Concepción is coming up for a visit this summer," Norah said.

"Yes." His eyes were shining. "To see if she'd like to live here permanently."

Before the number was over, Gus Schmidt presented himself. He too was an old friend working out of the 20th, a seasoned cop on Norah's team. Graying, comfortably overweight, bespectacled, Gus was everybody's uncle. Under the mild exterior, however, behind the bemused pale blue eyes, was a tough cop who'd been around thirty-one years, going for forty. He could still disarm a young punk, score in the top five of the precinct on the rifle range—but he'd lost some speed when it came to a foot chase.

"Wonderful occasion, Norah. Wonderful party."

Even Captain Manny Jacoby had come, Norah noted, though he didn't appear to be really enjoying himself. He was trying too hard. He wanted to let down the barriers, but he was too loud, working at it too obviously. She liked him for the effort, and at the end of the dance, Norah parted from Gus and walked over to Jacoby to introduce him to Inspector Felix. The captain was more comfortable in an upward relationship. He knew how to handle the brass.

Then the family moved in. Literally. Lena's husband Jake and after him Rosa's, Bianca's, Isabella's, and Carlotta's all took turns cutting in and twirling Norah in exuberant style till she gasped for breath. Celeste and Ron had come the farthest, from Boston, so Ron insisted she had to do an extra turn with him just for the distance. Norah, flushed and perspiring, begged off.

Looking for a place to sit, her eyes lit on Gary Reissig over at one end of the bar. She excused herself and joined him.

"Hi. You don't look like you're having much fun."

"Sure I am. It's a great party."

"You're the only one who hasn't asked me to dance."

"I didn't want to butt in."

"You know better than to say a thing like that."

"Sorry." He took a breath then smiled. "Care to dance?"

She smiled back. "In fact, no. I'd rather just sit here with you."

Vittorio himself came over to serve her. "What'll it be, Lieutenant?"

"I can't get used to being called that. White wine, Vittorio, please."

"You will," Reissig said.

Norah looked at him hard. "What's wrong, Gary? What's the matter?"

"Nothing. Just . . . I feel a little strange. I mean, everybody here knows everybody. You all go such a long way back together."

His hand was on the bar toying with his highball. Norah put her own hand over it. "You belong here as much as anybody. I couldn't have done it without you."

"Come on."

"That's right. You encouraged me. You pushed me to take the exam. You supported me, helped me to prepare, drilled me.

Oh, those drills—over and over. Relentless. I'll never forget them."

"You would have made it without me."

"Well, maybe. But it wouldn't have been as much fun." Impulsively, Norah leaned over and kissed his cheek. He responded with a look so strained, so sad, she knew instantly she shouldn't have shown even that much of her affection. Gary's feelings for Norah were deeper than hers for him, much deeper than she wanted to acknowledge.

But Reissig recovered quickly. He managed a smile. "Gosh, I've never been kissed by a lieutenant before."

From then on Gary Reissig tried hard to enjoy himself, or at least to give the appearance. In fact, he was surprised by his own reactions. What Norah had said was true: he had urged her to go for the promotion; he had helped her to study and get ready. He was happy for her, happy she'd succeeded. So what was eating him? Reissig was thirty-one, blond, stocky, tanned—a tan he never completely lost because he lived at the shore. A widower with two small children, both handicapped—Robin was retarded and Anna deaf—he thought he'd made his own accommodation with what life had dealt him. Till he met Norah. Now he wanted more.

There was a core of depression, an anxiety inside Gary at this moment he couldn't explain. Eating and drinking, dancing, finally he asked himself how he would be feeling if Norah hadn't made the grade and he was instantly ashamed to even wonder. He was a detective himself, in Queens. He'd worked with Norah on a big case. He'd been able to handle her higher rank then.

The party broke up at midnight. Gary took Norah home.

"Don't you want to come in for coffee?" she asked as he started to pull away at the door.

"Thanks, but it's late. I've got a long drive. Besides, you must be tired. It's been a long day for you."

She knew about the drive. Why did he think he had to apologize? "Come on in. For a few minutes. I'm all charged up. I need to unwind. A cup of Sanka and that's it. Okay?"

"I can't say no to a lieutenant."

The smile that went with it should have taken the sting out of the remark, but it didn't. She was making too much of it, Norah chided herself, and decided to ignore Gary's comment. She took off her coat and hung it in the hall closet. She kicked off her shoes. Meanwhile Gary headed for the kitchen.

"How about Ovaltine? It'll help you sleep."

"Good idea." Norah flopped down on the sofa. They'd met only that past summer, she and Gary Reissig, while working on a series of brutal slashings of young single women. The first murder had been in Central Park, Norah's jurisdiction. The second had been out in the Rockaways, his. Putting them together, comparing them to subsequent stabbings, they'd found a common denominator—the Ladykiller. They also discovered they had a lot more to share than the job. When their schedules coincided, Gary came to the city two or three times a week to see her. Listening to the clink of cups and saucers as he prepared their drinks, Norah realized how comfortable they'd become together—and acknowledged that she took the companionship Gary provided very much for granted. Putting her stockinged feet up on the coffee table in front of her, Norah mused on how large a part of her life Gary—and his children—had become. Robin and Anna were as cheerful, outgoing, and loving as any children she had ever known. Her visits with them were important and happy events. As Gary came out of the kitchen carrying a tray with two mugs, she smiled up at him. Whatever was bothering him, this was a good time to have it out. "Gary . . ."

He stood stock-still in front of her, the tray in his hands. "Will you marry me?"

"What?"

The cups and saucers rattled. "Will you marry me?" he repeated.

Norah stared at him for several seconds. "I don't know what to say. It sounds Victorian, but honestly, this is so unexpected."

"You must know how I feel about you."

She took a deep breath. "I'm not sure. I thought we were friends, very special friends."

"So that's my answer?"

"No. What I mean is—I can't give you an answer. It's not even a year and a half since Joe died. I haven't thought about marrying again. I can't think about it yet. I may never be able to."

"That's it then."

"No. But it is too soon." Her deep blue eyes held his light gray ones. Now that the question was asked, they both knew a bridge had been crossed. There was no going back to the way it had been, yet Norah tried.

"Why did you have to ask me tonight of all nights? Why couldn't you have waited?"

"I thought later I might not have the courage."

"Because of my promotion?"

"That's part of it, yes."

"Why? What difference does it make?"

"I don't know. I feel uncomfortable."

"You didn't feel uncomfortable when I was a sergeant. We got along fine. Nothing's any different. Maybe if we worked out of the same command, but we don't. You're way out there in another county. And if it really bothers you, all you have to do is take a couple of exams yourself and we'll be even."

"Play catch-up ball," he muttered bitterly.

"I didn't expect a remark like that from you."

"I didn't expect it from myself. I'm sorry." He picked up his topcoat from the chair on which he'd laid it.

"Will I see you again?"

He hesitated. "There's no point, is there? Norah, look. I love you and I want to marry you, but you're not giving me any real encouragement to wait. I can't go on as we were." He paused. "Anything less than marriage wouldn't be right for either of us. I need a wife. My children need a mother. So I have to find someone else, someone who's looking for what I have to offer."

"I'm sure you'll find her." It surprised Norah how much it hurt to say that. "Suppose I'd said yes?" she asked suddenly. "What would you have done?"

Startled, Reissig met her gaze. "I don't know."

Norah sighed. "You knew I wouldn't say yes. That's why you asked at this particular time."

"That's not true! No." But his indignation was not convincing. "We could have made it work."

"On whose terms?"

They looked at each other one last time, then he turned and walked out. When he was gone, Norah followed and locked the door.

She would miss Gary. Through him and his children Norah had participated in the kind of family life she'd always wanted. She cared for Gary deeply. Tears sprang to her eyes. Be honest, she chided herself: she'd been enjoying the benefits without the responsibilities. Norah came back and stood in the arch of the large quiet room with its eclectic assortment of furnishings she and Joe had chosen so carefully, and with so much shared pleasure. Somehow, Gary had fitted. They might have continued for a long time as they were, she thought. Indefinitely. But for the promotion. It was the promotion that had forced him to make his declaration.

Norah picked up her handbag from the console table where she'd laid it and took out the newly issued ID case. She stared at her own photograph and her name: LIEUTENANT NORAH MULCAHANEY with the gold shield beside it. Would she consider giving up the appointment?

The answer was no.

So she must content herself with casual relationships, not focus on anyone in particular. Stay loose. Stay free.

CHAPTER THREE

When Lieutenant Mulchaney entered the squad room of the Eighty-second Street station house the next morning, hardly anyone looked up. A couple of the detectives grunted as she passed their desks. Lou Logan, dark hair long at the back but balding in the front, was propped on the rear legs of his chair and frowning at the ceiling. He gave her a sideways glance and a casual wave. Sid Grundlach, dapper as a pimp—he had recently been transferred from Vice—smiled as he lit a cigarette then squinted through the smoke at the keyboard of his battered manual typewriter. Well, Norah thought, she couldn't expect the congratulations and festivities to go on forever. Actually, though the formalities of her appointment had been celebrated yesterday, she had started the new job a week ago and was already moved into her office. It was the typical corner partitioned by wallboard and frosted glass, but it was hers; it had a door. The word HOMICIDE on the glass was faded, the last two letters flaked to illegibility, but in the lower right-hand corner her name glistened in freshly painted black. Norah allowed herself a barely perceptible break in stride to admire it.

The furnishings were inherited from her predecessor—a battered desk and three dilapidated wooden chairs, a metal locker, two file cabinets, a glass-doored bookcase—all standard PD issue.

Lieutenant Bruckner had cleaned out the desk, removed his personal effects: family photos, a bowling trophy so assiduously polished its thin silver finish had worn down to the underlying copper, an assortment of pottery ashtrays collected on his one trip abroad, to Mexico. He had not touched the filing cabinets. They were full, stuffed, seemingly as he had found them. The drawers were so jammed Norah had to brace herself each time she tried to yank one open. Sometime she'd have to go through them and clean house. Probably she'd be able to get rid of most of the stuff. Start fresh. Meanwhile, Norah did as Leon Bruckner had—she put out a few pictures: Joe in his captain's uniform, smiling proudly; her father leaning on his cane only slightly as he stood in front of the West Side Democratic Club, of which he'd been a district leader. She had a photograph of each of her brothers: Pat, Jr., with his blonde wife and two blonde girls in front of a Spanish-style stuccoed house with a terra-cotta roof in Albuquerque; and Michael with his brunette wife and only son in a lush garden of azaleas and rhododendrons in New Orleans. But the desk became quickly cluttered and the pictures were already pushed to one side.

When she opened the door on this clear Tuesday morning in May, Norah turned to the right toward the locker. She had her coat off and a hanger ready when she literally did a double take. On her desk was a vase of red roses. How could she have missed it? The scent alone should immediately have caught her attention. Its sweet sultriness overcame the stale air and acrid tobacco smoke seeping through the gaps in the partition. She bent to inhale the perfume and when she straightened, she looked into the beaming faces of those detectives who had not been able to attend her party.

She looked at them one by one. "Thank you. I can't tell you how much this means to me. Thank you."

"Mulcahaney. I'd like to see you. Now."

The voice came from the back and dispersed the group immediately. Norah followed Captain Jacoby to his larger but not much more comfortable office. Jacoby was heavyset, medium height, balding. He'd been commanding officer at the Two-Oh for a year and was still trying to prove himself, though he didn't need to. Still leaned heavily on his authority, though that wasn't necessary either. When she'd been a sergeant, Jacoby usually let Norah stand; now he waved her to a chair. Or was the courtesy in recognition of having attended her party? Norah wondered. Was there to be a new, easier, more social relationship? The captain's deep scowl belied that.

"What do you know about Christina Isserman?"

Norah thought quickly. "Only what everyboby else knows, I suppose. I read in the papers recently that she's in a coma."

"Right. She's been that way for about a week." Without a change of expression, Manny Jacoby picked up the top sheet from a pile on his desk. "On the night of Monday, May 7, Mrs. Christina Sexton Isserman attended the Rose Ball, of which she is the sponsor, at the Plaza Hotel. She drank heavily and apparently took sedatives later at home in addition to the alcohol. She went to sleep and Tuesday morning, when her maid entered her bedroom, she did not respond to attempts to awaken her. Mrs. Isserman was transferred to Chazen-Hadley Hospital in a comatose state. Since then her condition has not changed. It was assumed the drugs were self-administered. Now her sister, Sarah Sexton Hoyt, has gone to the DA. She claims the husband, Walther Isserman, deliberately introduced drugs into his wife's drinks. She wants him charged with attempted murder."

The Sextons were American aristocracy on a par with the Kennedys and the Rockefellers. Having married the daughters, Justin Hoyt and Walther Isserman were regarded as consorts and accorded equal recognition by the public, and only a little less adulation. Like their distinguished counterparts, the Sextons valued privacy and for Sarah Hoyt to seek help from the public prosecutor indicated an overwhelming conviction her sister had been criminally assaulted.

"Here's a copy of the complaint." Jacoby pushed it across the desk. He didn't need to tell Norah the situation was delicate. The sweat on his face did that.

* * *

Chazen-Hadley was a small private hospital on Central Park West catering to the rich and famous. The rooms resembled those of a good hotel, the hospital appointments being disguised as much as possible. It was famed for its discretion and its amenities—the visitors' dining room was particularly well regarded—rather than its medical services. Yet the care was expert at Chazen-Hadley. Those who were patients merely took that for granted and were more concerned with being shielded from publicity. The illnesses these celebrities sought relief from were usually self-inflicted—alcoholism, drug overdose, drug reliance, obesity. All due to self-abuse or lack of self-control, Norah thought. She was not inclined to be philosophical about the self-destruction of the privileged. She cared about those who wanted to live, who had something to offer life but were brutally and cold-bloodedly prevented from fulfilling their promise. Into which category did Christina Isserman fit?

Norah Mulcahaney drove her gray Honda past the canopied entrance and around to the back service area, where she found a parking space. Then she returned on foot to enter the front. The lobby was fully carpeted, softly lighted, dominated by a tasteful and expensive arrangement of fresh flowers displayed on a gilt console and reflected in a floor-to-ceiling mirror. Muzak played in the background. Norah went up to the desk.

"Mrs. Isserman, please."

The receptionist didn't need to punch up the name on the computer. "Mrs. Isserman is not receiving visitors," she reported with cool disdain.

"I'm not a visitor." Norah displayed her shield.

The woman behind the desk was neither young nor glamorous; the patients at Chazen-Hadley had all they wanted of that on the outside. She examined Norah's ID, focusing instantly on the rank. Then she examined Norah. The dark red linen pants suit fitted very well, but it was by no recognizable designer. Anyhow, pants suits were *out*. Norah's dark hair was tied back with a matching ribbon, the style also passé. Nevertheless, the receptionist recognized authority. "Mrs. Isserman is in Suite 32, Lieutenant. That's on the third floor. Mr. Wadman asked to be notified when the police arrived." She switched a lever on the small hospital board.

Norah didn't wait. "I'll go on ahead." She made for the elevator.

As soon as she got off she was intercepted by the floor nurse. Again, the shield did the trick and she was directed to the Isserman suite.

Actually, Norah had expected the patient to be in Intensive Care. When she learned she was not, Norah instinctively minimized the gravity of her condition. The rich had a tendency to overreact, she thought. They demanded the attention and attracted the publicity they claimed to shun. But she'd been wrong, Norah admitted as soon as she entered. Once past the small vestibule, she was confronted by the standard battery of life-support equipment. A special nurse sat beside the bed. Norah's job was homicide investigation, had been from the beginning of her career as a detective. To say she was accustomed to viewing death by violence would imply she was hardened. She was not, but she had taught herself to observe, to consider the violated bodies as clues. Also, when she approached a victim, Norah already had some advance knowledge of the crime that made it easier for her to aniticipate what she would have to deal with. She had encountered victims of brutal abuse, even torture, who had managed to survive. That was even more difficult. But this was the first time Norah had ever seen anyone in a coma.

Christina Isserman lay like a bloated jellyfish washed up on the shore. Her skin was blue, her eyes closed. She lay on her right side, knees raised slightly in a crouch—the precursor, Norah later learned, of the fetal position comatose patients ultimately assumed. Christina Isserman was being fed intravenously, but she would eventually waste away to a bag of brittle bones and atrophied muscles. The tubes and wires that sustained her seemed to grow out of her body like malignant weeds. A respirator drum that rasped as it expanded and contracted her lungs, the beeping cardiac monitors, and the green dots that jumped on the screen were the only signs the woman in the bed was alive. Alive, Norah thought, this victim could tell her less than others dead and brutalized.

Victim! She had no right to label her that. Not yet.

"I'm Lieutenant Mulcahaney," she told the nurse. She noted the name on the ID card pinned to the pocket of her uniform. "Miss Philbro, I'm just going to take a look around."

"Yes, ma'am." The nurse set aside the baby booties she'd been knitting. "I was told to contact Mr. Wadman when you came."

"He's on his way."

Norah moved to the head of the bed. It was hard to reconstruct a sentient image of the woman in the bed. It was not a question of seeing her in a state of temporary unconsciousness: Christina Isserman gave no indication of life. Norah had seen photographs of her, had seen her on live television—blonde, regal, proud. She summoned up those images and tried to superimpose them on the creature in the bed. She couldn't.

"Lieutenant Mulcahaney?" A tall, slightly overweight man with thinning brown hair held out his hand. "I'm Vincent Wadman. I wanted to meet you and to offer my assistance."

"Thank you."

"This is a very distressing business and we're very anxious to get it cleared up."

Norah nodded. "What was the drug? And how much of it did she take?"

"Valium. But it's not the amount that matters. In combination with alcohol the effect is totally unpredictable."

"The amount could indicate intent."

"A person who is heavily reliant on tranquilizers and sleeping pills has a tendency to lose track of how many he has actually taken. In fact, alcohol increases tolerance and, as the tolerance grows, the patient takes more and more till he finally overdoses."

"According to the patient's sister, the drug was not self-administered. That's why I'm here."

Wadman sighed. "The amount was massive. I'll see to it that you get a copy of the lab report."

"What is the prognosis for Mrs. Isserman?"

Wadman frowned. "Our doctors feel, and her own physician concurs, her condition is irreversible."

Norah sighed.

"Adding to the problems inherent in her case, this accusation against Mr. Isserman . . . well, it puts the hospital in a difficult position."

"In what way?"

"Well, Mrs. Hoyt, Mrs. Isserman's sister, has demanded that we bar Mr. Isserman from visiting his wife. We can hardly do that. So I thought maybe you could put a guard on her door?"

"You're suggesting a possible second attempt?"

"I'm not suggesting anything, Lieutenant. It's to placate Mrs. Hoyt."

"And to protect the hospital."

"Well, yes, I admit that."

"We haven't yet established a first attempt, Mr. Wadman," Norah pointed out. "We don't know that a crime has been committed. As for Mrs. Hoyt wanting her sister's husband barred from visiting, that's a matter for the lawyers."

The administrator looked disappointed.

"I really don't think you have anything to worry about, Mr. Wadman. I see there's a private nurse in attendance and I assume someone is with Mrs. Isserman around the clock."

"Of course."

"Then no one has anything to worry about."

"I just wanted to make my own position clear."

Norah looked at him hard. "In fact, Mr. Wadman, you've thrown doubt on it. Is it that you don't trust your own security system?"

"Not at all." He was shocked.

"Is it that you don't want to keep Mrs. Isserman here and you're looking for an excuse to remove her?"

He hesitated. "It's the notoriety," he blurted out. "Chazen-Hadley has always protected the privacy of its patients."

"A guard on the door won't do anything for you there, Mr. Wadman.

There was no doubt Vincent Wadman was deeply worried and that he was hiding the true cause of his concern. As administrator, Norah assumed he was competent, pragmatic, and probably not overly imaginative. Therefore, he must have a good reason for anxiety. She could have pressed him harder, but she sensed it would only shore up his resistance. She'd need to know more to get the leverage to open him up. So she left him to brood and headed across the park to Fifth Avenue.

The Isserman apartment was a corner duplex. Every window overlooked either the park or Eighty-second Street toward the Metropolitan Museum. A uniformed maid admitted Norah to a hall as large as most apartment living rooms. It was nearly noon, but Walther Isserman was at home.

"I've been expecting you, Lieutenant Mulcahaney."

Was he letting her know he had contacts who could inform him of what the police were doing—or was he complaining that he'd been kept waiting? By reputation, Walther Isserman was an intelligent man. He was also very much the European aristocrat. The marriage of the elder Sexton daughter had been covered in depth by newspapers, magazines, and television, so Norah knew his background had been thoroughly researched. He was extremely handsome, his features finely chiseled, though his eyes were a bit too close and his nose was slightly hooked. Nevertheless, there were plenty of aging, handsome men, foreigners too and of noble birth, available to a woman like Christina Sexton. There had to be something more to attract one of the most beautiful and richest of American heiresses. On her part, Norah had no need to impress Isserman.

"I went to the hospital first," she told him. They'd had no appointment, and if he wanted to assume she was apologizing because he'd waited, that was fine.

"Of course. How is she?"

"The same, I'm afraid."

He sighed. "I'll be going myself this afternoon."

He was stating a duty to be done. Whatever grief or pain he felt, he hid it effectively, Norah thought. Also, she had to admit he was making no attempt to charm or influence her to his side. Either he was secure enough that he didn't think he needed to bother or he was using reverse psychology.

"I'd like to take a look at the bedroom, please."

"Of course." Isserman nodded, then led the way up the marble staircase to the duplex's second floor. He opened the door nearest the landing and stood aside to let Norah precede him. It was a large airy corner room decorated in French provincial, with a fireplace and a delicate crystal chandelier. An oversized canopied bed dominated one side. A shallow alcove serving as dressing room offered a wall of mirrored closets, and the bathroom had an oversized tub. Norah noticed a small door cut in the wood paneling.

"You have separate bedrooms?"

"Yes."

"Perhaps it would be easier if you told me what happened."

"I don't know what happened."

"As I understand it, you and Mrs. Isserman attended a party at the Plaza Hotel on Monday, May 7. There was a quarrel and you had to remove her. What was the cause of the quarrel?"

Isserman pursed his lips, a thin white rim of displeasure outlining them. "I prefer not to go into that."

"Your sister-in-law has already given her version."

His eyes narrowed; he swept a hand through his thick mass of hair. "Christina had had too much to drink. She took exception to my dancing with the daughter of guests at our table. Then she transferred her jealous resentment to a lady who wasn't even present."

"What happened when you got home?"

"As I said, she was very drunk. She couldn't walk unassisted. Paulson, our chauffeur, had to help me get her out of the car and upstairs. Between us, we brought her directly to this floor in the house elevator; there's a separate entrance—actually, we have two apartments with two elevator stops and two private entrances, one downstairs and this one. The staircase was put in to connect them. Well, when Paulson left, I tried to get her to bed, but she was abusive. She ordered me out of the room and I went."

"That's the last you saw of her—conscious?" *Alive* was what she'd almost said.

"Yes."

"Where was she? I mean—on the bed, in a chair, standing?"

"She was fixing herself another drink, which I told her she didn't need." He indicated a small ornate cabinet. "There wasn't supposed to be any liquor there. I'd given orders, but . . . her orders superseded mine." He shrugged.

"Is your wife habitually a heavy drinker?"

"She's become one."

"Why do you think she's taken to drinking?"

With studied nonchalance Walther Isserman reached to his inside pocket and withdrew a slim gold cigarette case, which he politely opened and extended to Norah. She declined. He couldn't hide the tremor of his left hand as he lit up. "You should ask her psychiatrist," he replied at last. "Dr. Jeremy Kuhn. I hold him responsible for what's happened to Christina. He's the one who put her on Valium. I tell you, Lieutenant, I blame that man. He was supposed to be treating her for alcoholism, but he merely switched her from one drug to another. In the end she became dependent on both."

"It's your contention she took the drug herself, mixing it with alcohol?"

"Of course."

"Were you ever present when she took it?"

"On other occasions, yes, many times."

"And did you try to stop her if she attempted to take the drug when you knew she'd been drinking?"

"Yes. Yes, of course."

"But you didn't see her take Valium that night?" He shook his head. "So you were here with your wife in this room when she fixed herself a nightcap. You told her she shouldn't have it, but she ignored your advice. Then what?"

"Then I left."

Norah glanced toward the connecting door.

He hesitated. "Yes, I went to my room but I didn't stay there. I was restless. I went out. For a walk."

"It must have been well after midnight."

"I was upset."

"Go on."

"That's it. That's the last I saw of Christina that night. I got back home around one-thirty and went straight to my room and to bed. I got up the next morning and went to work."

"You didn't look in on your wife?"

"No. It's not my custom. She's a late sleeper. There's no point in waking her."

"When did you first learn something was wrong?"

"Wrede, the housekeeper, called me just before lunch."

"According to the complaint, you didn't show up at the hospital till four in the afternoon."

"I didn't take it seriously. My God, Lieutenant Mulcahaney, it wasn't the first time she'd abused herself into such a condition."

Norah was taken aback, and showed it.

"My dear sister-in-law didn't mention that? I'm not surprised. How about the hospital? Nobody said anything either? Well, this has happened twice before. Twice before, Christina went into coma; the last time she was out for four days. We thought it was the end. But she resurfaced. She will again."

"The doctors say no."

"That's what they said before."

"And in spite of these previous incidents your wife continued to use the Valium in conjunction with her drinking? Being well aware of the danger?"

"She didn't believe there was a real danger. They never do—the addicts."

He didn't like applying the label, and Norah gave him marks for that. "And her doctor?"

Isserman shrugged. "He stopped prescribing Valium. I suppose she got it from someone else."

"So in your opinion she overdosed accidentally?"

"If you're asking me was she trying to commit suicide, the answer is definitely no. There are people who apparently have everything in life and yet seek death. Not Christina. I've analyzed it. What such people lack, or think they lack, is power. Christina *has* power."

"You mean because she controls Sexton Industries?"

"Yes. And in her personal life."

That was a surprising admission, Norah thought, but she let it pass. "What is your position with Sexton?"

"I'm no longer connected. A matter of a difference in direction."

Norah filed that away also. "How about the Sexton money? Is there a will? Or perhaps a marriage settlement?"

Once again Isserman's lips puckered into that thin white line. His entire face was pinched. "I realize you are doing what you believe is your job, Lieutenant. However, I resent this line of questioning and I wonder if I shouldn't consult a lawyer."

"Perhaps that would be best," Norah agreed. "So far we don't know that a crime has been committed, but if you have any anxieties about incriminating yourself, you're not required to answer any more questions."

"But you'll go and get the information elsewhere, and that will make me look bad."

"Not necessarily."

"I might as well tell you. It appears complicated, but it really isn't. If Christina were to die right now, I would receive her personal fortune, but her shares in Sexton Industries representing control of the company would be divided between her sister and the present officers. If we remain married for ten years and then she dies, I receive the fortune and the shares. I put the present worth of Sexton at three and a half billion and Christina's personal worth at five million. We have been married six years. So you can see that if I intend to get rid of her it would be very much worth my while to wait a bit longer."

Norah smiled. "As far as I'm concerned those figures are unreal, Mr. Isserman. Five million or five billion are equally beyond my grasp."

"Those extra zeros represent power, Lieutenant. You will find out that I have my own company and that there are problems. But there are also great expectations. I intend to succeed, perhaps not to the size of Sexton Industries, but I intend to make Isserman Shipping the premier luxury passenger line in the world." His eyes gleamed; his whole being came alive.

He denigrated power, yet he was chasing it, Norah thought. "I appreciate your cooperation, Mr. Isserman. Now, may I take a look around?"

"You'd like me to leave?"

"No. It's simply that I don't have a search warrant. I'll need your permission."

"You have it, Lieutenant." He held out his hand and when Norah gave him hers he raised it to his lips with a slight bow, looking directly into her eyes. This was a glimpse of the man who had wooed and won an American heiress over an international field of competitors. Dazzling. Then Norah remembered that in all his fulsome explanation Walther Isserman had not once expressed love for his wife or regret for her condition. Not once had he expressed sorrow for their estrangement.

Then Isserman left. Was it an indication of innocence or of self-assurance and complete confidence that what he had allegedly done could never be proved? Norah walked around the sumptuous room examining this ornament, that piece of furniture, a painting, a bronze figurine on the mantel, not knowing exactly what she was after. She was intrigued briefly by an antique manicure set displayed on the dressing table. It consisted of three sizes of scissors, nail files, and a cuticle shaper. The handle of each piece was of rosy yellow gold shaped as a bird, fish, or flower, the working end of finely forged steel. Norah was well aware it was a full week since Christina Isserman had occupied the room and that it had since been thoroughly cleaned and vacuumed. Certainly the glass from which she'd drunk that night had been washed. Nevertheless, Norah opened the cabinet Isserman had indicated. The elegant piece had been transformed on the inside into a modern bar unit with a refrigerator on one side and shelving on the other. It held half a dozen heavy cut-crystal glasses, but no liquor. According to Isserman, there had been liquor available when they came home from the Rose Ball.

Idly, Norah looked around through the drawers of the bedside tables. She found a sleep mask and ear plugs, items that should have got little use in view of the heavy sedation by drugs and alcohol. Suddenly it struck her: where were the pills? Norah searched the bathroom. All the usual health aids and nostrums were there, but no Valium. Not even an empty container. She checked the wastebasket. Of course it had been emptied. Back in the bedroom she located the call button and pressed it.

May Wrede appeared in moments. She was a small, middle-aged woman. The dress she wore was a dark brown silk, all tucks and pleats, totally unsuitable for a dumpy woman in sensible shoes. Behind thick lenses of gold-rimmed spectacles, her protuding eyes were abnormally magnified. Her small pouty mouth hung open from a sinus condition.

"You rang, ma'am?"

"Are you the housekeeper?"

"Yes, ma'am. I'm Mrs. Wrede."

"Hello. I'm Lieutenant Mulcahaney. Who else do you have here in help?"

"The cook, Mrs. McCullough; she lives in like me. Ellie's day help for general cleaning. I take care of Miss Christie's personal things. We have a cleaning team that comes in three times a week for the heavy work."

"I see. Then you can tell me where Mrs. Isserman keeps her medicine?"

"It used to be in her night table, but then Mr. Isserman said she wasn't to have it anymore and took it away."

"She wasn't supposed to have liquor either," Norah observed.

May Wrede's round face showed her concern. "Yes, ma'am, I know. We all know. But if she orders it, how can we say no?"

"I understand. On the night of the Rose Ball, was there liquor up here in the cabinet?"

"There was never liquor available. She had to ring and ask for it."

"And did she that night?"

"Yes, ma'am. Earlier in the evening, before they went out."

"Did you remove the liquor after she and Mr. Isserman left for the ball and bring her more later when they returned?"

"Yes, ma'am. It was Mr. Isserman's orders that no liquor should be left around. She rang as soon as they got home."

"And was the bottle empty the next morning?"

"When we found her we didn't give a thought to an empty bottle, ma'am."

The bottle would have been thrown out as a matter of course, Norah thought. If the drug had been introduced into the bottle, there was no way it could be proved.

CHAPTER FOUR

Where had Christina Isserman hidden her supply of Valium? With the help of May Wrede, Norah went through drawers, the pockets of every item of clothing in the wall-length closet. She opened the various stacked boxes of cashmere sweaters, silk scarves, leather gloves, and assorted expensive jewelry, the real carelessly jumbled with the fake. Nothing.

"How long have you worked for Mrs. Isserman?" Norah asked the housekeeper.

"Since they first got married, six years ago."

"How is she to work for?"

"She never takes her upsets out on the help."

"And Mr. Isserman?"

She hesitated. "The same."

"Would you say they were happy?" To encourage her confidence, Norah went on. "So far, what I've heard is largely gossip. I'm hoping to get the truth from you."

"They were very happy at first. Not lately. Not since Miss Christie started drinking. Or maybe she started drinking because she wasn't happy. I don't know."

"Did they quarrel frequently?"

"Yes, ma'am."

"Did he ever strike her?"

"Oh no, ma'am!" She was genuinely shocked. "Mr. Isserman never so much as raised his voice." She paused, then almost in spite of herself, "It drove Miss Christie wild."

Norah knew exactly what she meant—cold self-control could do that. "What did they fight about?"

May Wrede shook her head. "I didn't listen."

"Sometimes one can't help hearing."

The little woman pressed her lips tightly and shook her head.

"What can you tell me about the night of the ball?"

"Nothing."

"Were you up when the Issermans returned?"

"We're not required to wait up. Both Mrs. McCullough and I retired at our usual time. I was asleep."

"Does that mean you didn't hear them come in? Or that you were awakened when they did?"

The mouth fell open farther, the bulging eyes fixed on Norah. "I don't know what to do. I want to do the right thing, but I don't know . . ."

"Tell the truth, Mrs. Wrede. Just tell me what happened."

In fact, May Wrede had already made up her mind. She'd discussed it with Maggie McCullough and they had both reaffirmed where their loyalty lay. But she wanted to be urged, to be able to justify what she was about to do.

"Take your time, Mrs. Wrede," Norah said.

The housekeeper sighed. "They woke me. Our rooms, Mrs. McCullough's and mine, are on the first floor in the back. Mr. and Mrs. Isserman came in by the upstairs entrance. They often use it when it's late and they're going to retire right away. Ordinarily, I wouldn't have heard them, but that night they made a terrible commotion. They were shouting at each other, that is, after Paulson left."

"The chauffeur?"

"Yes. I've never heard Mr. Isserman yell at Mrs. Isserman before. Maybe it was because he thought nobody could hear, but it worried me. I thought if he really lost his patience he might . . . I don't know, hurt her. I heard the two of them go down the corridor and into her room."

"How do you know they both went into her room?"

May Wrede scowled. "Because I only heard one door open and shut."

"How do you know it was her room and not his?"

"I guess I took it for granted. No. I could tell by the footsteps. His room is close to the upstairs entrance. Hers is almost over my head."

"Good. What time was it?"

"Five after twelve. I looked at my watch."

She was getting into the swing of it, Norah thought. "Then what happened?"

"I didn't hear any more."

"Now Mrs. Wrede, you're not going to ask me to believe that you just turned over and went back to sleep?"

"No, ma'am, I couldn't do that." But the question eased May Wrede's last nagging reservations. "I put on my robe and went to the foot of the stairs. Everything was quiet again, real quiet. I didn't know what to make of that; I didn't know whether I should be relieved or scared. Then I heard her, Miss Christie, yell to him to get out. Not long after that, his door opened and closed, then so did the upstairs vestibule door. I heard the elevator go down, so I knew he had left. And I knew she'd be falling asleep and everything would be all right for the night."

"Mr. Isserman went out like that frequently?"

"Yes, ma'am."

"How frequently? Every night?"

"Two or three times a week."

"On this particular night did you hear him come back?"

The housekeeper shook her head. "I went back to bed and I dropped right off." She looked relieved, as she must have been on the night she spoke of.

But Norah wasn't finished. "Let's talk about the next morning, Mrs. Wrede. You didn't look in on Mrs. Isserman till close to twelve-thirty."

"She often slept late."

"What finally made you decide to go in?"

The witness did not hesitate over this. In unburdening herself she had gained confidence in Norah's sympathy. "I was uneasy because of the fight the night before. I thought Miss

Christie might have taken too many pills. We'd nearly lost her twice before.''

Norah nodded. "So you went in and found her unconscious.''

"Mrs. McCullough and I went in together. Then we called Mr. Isserman at the office.''

"And he, in turn, called the ambulance?''

"Oh no, ma'am, he didn't want the ambulance.'' And now at last, May Wrede no longer sought her own justification but placed full reliance on Norah Mulcahaney, letting all the pent-up anxiety and resentment pour out. "You see, the last time I called 911 on my own responsibility the emergency ambulance came and took Miss Christie to Bellevue, and Mr. Isserman was very angry. He didn't like it that they took her there and he blamed me for all the publicity. So this time I called him first, and he said, 'Don't do anything; she'll be all right.' But he didn't come home to see her. Mrs. McCullough and me, we couldn't leave her like she was. So we called her doctor, Dr. Kuhn, and he made the arrangements to take her to Chazen-Hadley.''

"How did Mr. Isserman find out she was in the hospital?''

"Dr. Kuhn told him.''

Norah considered. "Let's get back to when you entered this room and found Mrs. Isserman. How did you know what was wrong with her?''

"Because we couldn't wake her up and because she looked the same as the other times.''

"Mrs. McCullough was with you on those previous occasions?''

"Yes.''

"And on those other occasions did you look around to see what Mrs. Isserman might have taken to cause the condition so that you could inform the medics?''

"Not the first time. We were too upset and confused. The medics looked and they found the empty glass of Scotch and a half-empty container of the Valium. The second time we knew to look for ourselves. There was the glass and some pills that had spilled. This last time, we didn't bother to look.''

"How about later, when the room was cleaned?''

The housekeeper shook her head. "I didn't think to look, but . . . I'm sure I would have noticed."

"Could Mrs. Isserman have finished the supply and thrown away the empty container?" Norah asked.

"It wasn't like her to bother, especially not if she was . . . drunk." The housekeeper finished when no euphemism suggested itself.

"But she wasn't supposed to have any more Valium," Norah reminded her. "Might she have disposed of the container so nobody would find out?"

"I can't say." May Wrede shrugged it off.

But Norah couldn't. Alcoholics, addicts of all kinds were cunning, conniving, sly. Christina Isserman could well have had a secret niche for her drug. If so, Norah had to find it. What she feared was not the removal of evidence, but that something that hadn't originally been in the apartment might be planted there.

Norah requested a team of four for the toss. She remained on the premises while Brennan got the search order and Arenas made the assignments. It was a routine job and Norah expected four of her own people. Apparently, Jacoby had gone over Ferdi's head and sent two uniforms. She was annoyed, then she realized that the captain was right; she didn't need heavy artillery. Officers Bruce Denny and Audrey Jordan were recently graduated. This was probably the first special duty for each of them. Norah hoped what they lacked in experience they would make up in enthusiasm. Everybody had to start somewhere. Much had been made of the rise in quality of police recruits in the last years. The PC, all the top brass, stressed that the applicants had better educations—many were college graduates—and showed superior desire and dedication.

These two, at least, appeared above average, Norah thought. Both were exemplary in appearance: physically fit, hair in place, uniforms clean and freshly pressed. Denny's shoes were scuffed and could use a shine. He was short and stocky, brown eyes shining with enthusiasm. Jordan was unexceptional. She was thin, medium height, pale complexion. Her hair was dark and curly, reaching just to her shoulders. Pretty, but she could have used some of her partner's spirit.

"Mrs. Isserman was allegedly using Valium. We're looking to find where she kept her supply," Norah explained.

She assigned the areas of the search and the toss began. By late afternoon, every possible hiding place had been examined. Neither Valium nor any other kind of tranquilizer or painkiller had been found, not in any of the bathrooms—including those of the staff and the guest bathroom—not in the kitchen or pantry, not behind the bookstacks in the library, not in any closet or drawer. The two detectives went over the walls and paneling for secret compartments, without result. Maybe Christina Isserman had ingested the Valium before coming home, Norah thought. Unless there had been a stop on the way, that meant she'd carried some pills with her. There was no trace in the evening purse she'd used that night. The only other possibility: the Valium had been put into her drink by someone else, someone at the party who didn't know she'd stopped using it.

It was time to talk to Sarah Hoyt.

The next day Norah set out for Sarah Hoyt Sportswear. It was located on Seventh Avenue in the heart of the garment district. The building was old and shabby, typical of the area. The office was no better or worse than any other, combining a poky showroom and gloomy workrooms. Certainly it was no glamorous front for a rich woman's pastime. Sarah Sexton Hoyt designed women's sports apparel. Her line was colorful; it had flair. What made it sell, though, was its appeal to the realistic needs of the average woman's life. Every item was constructed to fit the average woman's body, not camouflage it. Sarah Hoyt slacks hugged and Sarah Hoyt dresses clung—just right.

If Norah needed further proof of the validity of the Sarah Hoyt operation, she got it crossing the big cluttered workroom. It was the ordinary assemblage: cutters hovered over huge tables, sewers bent at their machines, pressers sweated, and racks of partially finished as well as ready-to-be-shipped garments stood in every available space. Sarah Hoyt's office, a smaller version of the workroom, was dominated by a platform, not much higher than a footstool, on which a bored model stood very still. The three people around her stared intently at the dress she was wearing.

"It's not right."

A slim, dark, nervously charged woman walked around the model. "It's the cut of the skirt. It's got too damn many pleats. Makes her look broad in the beam. What do you think, Sid?"

The man she appealed to was at least fifty, short, corpulent, and in his shirt-sleeves. "I wouldn't want a plain skirt. It wouldn't balance the top. How about we leave the pleats in the front only? A panel."

The woman stopped pacing. A bright smile dispelled the intensity and illumined her face. Yet for all its flash that smile was only in part genuine; the product of long practice, Norah thought.

"You've got it, Sid! That's it. What would I do without you? Go ahead and cut it."

"Don't you want to see a sample?"

"What for? I know it's going to work." With a wave and a slightly less dazzling version of The Smile, she dismissed the model. "Thanks, Molly." An ample-bosomed woman, the third of the trio, who used her natural endowment as a place to stash pins, was also dismissed. "Thanks, Irma." The Smile diminished in brilliance so that by the time she got around to Norah it was just the exposure of a double row of very white teeth. "Are you looking for someone?"

"If you're Mrs. Hoyt, I'm looking for you. I'm Lieutenant Mulcahaney."

"Lieutenant, of course. I apologize. It's been one of those mornings."

"I'm sorry to interrupt."

"No, no, nothing's more important. I'm glad you called. If you hadn't, I would have got in touch with you. Come in, please. Close the door. Sit down." As Norah did these things, Sarah Hoyt gestured to a Pyrex coffeepot and Styrofoam cups laid out on a card table. "Coffee? If you're hungry I can send out . . ."

"Nothing for me, thank you." Naturally hyperactive, or tense because of the circumstances? Norah wondered. Both, probably. She took the chair beside the desk and waited.

"What do you want to know, Lieutenant? Just ask whatever you want." Sarah Hoyt pulled so close their knees were almost touching.

"Why do you think your sister's condition is not due to accidental overdose?"

"Because it's the third time around. She stopped taking Valium after the first incident. My sister's no fool, and she does *not* have a death wish."

"Why do you think her husband wants to kill her?"

"To get her money, of course."

"I understand he's in business for himself and he has good expectations . . ."

"That's right," Sarah Hoyt interrupted. "That's all Walther has ever had—expectations. He thought he'd be president of Sexton Industries, but my father didn't trust him. We come from humble stock. My great-grandfather was a peddler. He went door-to-door selling dry goods to housewives—pins, needles, machine-made lace, stove polish. He worked on the railroad. When he had enough money he invested and made a fortune. Every generation of our family has added to it. Walther comes from the aristocracy. Their fortune came from grants of land, of privilege, and every generation has depleted it. Oh, Dad gave Walther a job; he gave him a chance to learn the business and show what he could do. That was too slow and too much like work for Walther. He's obsessed with the past, with restoring his own family glory. After Dad's death he expected that Christie would name him to the presidency— she's the majority stockholder."

"Excuse me. Did you receive shares in the company when your father died?"

"Oh yes. I sold out in part to Christie and to Frank Veloney, who was president and took over as chairman of the board during Dad's illness. I put some of the money into this business and invested the rest in my husband's depository company."

"So you don't have a say in the decision making at Sexton?"

"No. Christie was always the one who took an interest, and, believe me, when it comes to money, she's no fool. Dad taught her that family is one thing, but money is another. She consulted with the board and they decided Walther's ideas were outmoded. He's not flexible. He's not looking for the general progress of the company, but rather of his own pet projects. When he didn't get the promotion, he resigned." She shrugged. "He hasn't exactly set the world on fire since."

"I suppose it takes time. He started his own company," Norah pointed out. "Where did he get the money to do that?"

"He must have had something from his salary at Sexton—Christie pays all the household expenses. I suppose he also borrowed from European contacts and the banks. I'm sure you can check out his present financial status without any trouble."

"Aside from needing mney, what other reason do you have for suspecting your brother-in-law of attempted murder?"

"I don't understand."

"Do you have any evidence that he did, in fact, doctor your sister's drinks?"

"I didn't see him do it," Sarah Hoyt snapped, forgetting to be genial. "But everything points to it. Walther is greedy, proud, lazy. That company of his, Isserman Shipping, is a joke. Do you know what it's set up to do? Buy ships. Not one, but a fleet. And what does he want a fleet of ships for? To bring back luxury passenger service across the Atlantic. Now I ask you. Talk about reviving the past! Who has time to spend four days when the Concorde can get you there in less than four hours? He thinks he can create a demand and he doesn't care what it costs to do it."

"Isn't it possible your sister continued to take sedatives without your knowing it?" Norah suggested. "She might have overdosed accidentally. Taking into consideration the state of her marriage, she might even have done it on purpose."

"Christie kill herself over Walther?" Sarah flashed a tight, sarcastic version of The Smile. "You don't know my sister. If the marriage wasn't going well and Walther didn't suit her, she'd get rid of him. As for the other, the possibility of an accidental OD—forget it. Christie's no spoiled millionaire's daughter. She's gorgeous and she's got brains. She's much too smart to fall into that kind of trap."

"Unfortunately, smart has nothing to do with it, Mrs. Hoyt," Norah replied. "You won't deny your sister's drinking was out of control."

"What would you call her condition the night of the ball? By your own account, she was removed kicking and screaming."

"That's right, yes, she was weaving. Walther wanted her that way. He slipped stuff into her drink so he could have two hundred witnesses to her instability. He wanted two hundred witnesses to her predisposition to an overdose."

Interesting idea, Norah thought.

"I'm telling you Walther was slipping the Valium into her drinks on a regular basis," Sarah Hoyt insisted, her dark eyes burning. "It was causing hysteria, confusion, and loss of memory. She didn't know what was wrong with her. She complained to me about her condition. My sister was normally well-balanced, capable, intelligent." Sara Hoyt paused, a mist of tears in her eyes. "If only you had known her, Lieutenant. Christie was more than beautiful; she was smart. All my life, I looked up to her. I tried to be like her. She was my ideal. And now to see her reduced to this condition! I'm not going to let him get away with it. I'm not."

"Did your sister consult a doctor?"

"She was already under the doctor's care. Dr. Kuhn. He had put her on the Valium and then took her off. Next, he suggested she go to one of those drug rehabilitation retreats. She was considering it. My sister had everything to live for, Lieutenant." The designer jerked a desk drawer and found a pack of cigarettes. She lit up.

"You're suggesting the two previous times your sister went into coma were failed attempts at murder by her husband. As well as this last time, of course. He would seem at the very least to be inept."

"That's where you're wrong, Lieutenant Mulcahaney," Sarah Hoyt retorted with grim satisfaction, as though at last Norah had reached the point to which she'd been leading her. "They weren't failed attempts; they were practice runs. He was testing the dosage."

"And he failed a third time? That's hard to believe. It's a relatively simple . . ."

"Failed? The wide mouth stretched beyond the practiced Smile into an honest and very bitter grin. "No, no, he hasn't failed. He's got poor Christie just the way he wants her. Dead, he gets her money but loses control of the company. Alive and competent, she might cut him out of the will completely or even divorce him. The way she is—he has it all." She took a deep drag of her cigarette. Sarah Hoyt had made her case.

"Was divorce under consideration?"

"Ask Lucine Northcott," Sarah Hoyt replied. "Walther's mistress."

Norah got up.

"Meantime, I think there should be a guard on the door of my sister's room."

"Why? According to your own theory, it's to Mr. Isserman's advantage to keep his wife alive."

"And in her present condition," Sarah Hoyt pointed out.

"I'll discuss it with Captain Jacoby," Norah said.

But there was no discussion. Norah didn't get back to the squad till late in the afternoon, and Roy Brennan was waiting for her.

"Somebody pulled the plug on Christina Isserman's respirator," he told her.

Norah stopped where she was. Wadman's fear had been justified, she thought "My God!"

"And she survived." Brennan broke into a wide grin. "She's breathing on her own. There's every indication that she'll continue to do so."

Norah had a vision of the bloated blue face, the tightly shut eyes. "I can't believe it."

"Neither can the doctors."

"I'd better get over there."

"Her husband's already there agitating to take her home."

Norah gasped. "He can't do that."

"Why not?" Brennan regarded her quizzically.

"You're right." She sighed. "Dr. Jeremy Kuhn confirmed that Christina Isserman had developed a dependence on Valium. He had taken her off it, but he couldn't say she hadn't continued to use the stuff without his knowledge. The Isserman chauffeur, Paulson, suported Walther Isserman's account of his wife's condition when they brought her home from the Rose Ball," she told Brennan. "I haven't got one piece of evidence that he ever tried to harm her."

"So?"

"So, if he wants to take her home, there's no way anybody can stop him."

CHAPTER FIVE

Walther Isserman would not be dissuaded. The arguments of the assembled doctors that his wife could receive better care in the hospital were easily countered by the very fact of the careless or criminal disconnecting of the life-support machines. It could not be gainsaid. For the moment, Isserman waved off how it had happened—that was for hospital authorities and the police to discover. It had; that was all that mattered to him. He would duplicate the support system and the monitors in his home, install all the necessary equipment in his wife's bedroom. He would supply round-the-clock nursing.

"And nobody is going to be stepping out to go to the bathroom, or make a phone call, or anything else and leave her unattended. I guarantee that. There will be no recurrence of this incident."

The hapless nurse on duty who had indeed stepped into the private bathroom cringed.

"Christina will be a lot safer in her own home, and more comfortable. Being in familiar surroundings will aid her mental state and speed her recovery."

No one pointed out that as she was unconscious she wouldn't know where she was. He had intimidated them all.

Except Sarah Hoyt. She refused to give up. She had accused

Isserman to his face, in the presence of the administrator, assorted doctors, nurses, security guards, Lieutenant Mulcahaney, and Detective Brennan, of being responsible for Christina's condition. "Now he wants to take her home so he can finish the job!" She appealed to Norah. "You can't let him do it!"

Her earlier theory that Walther Isserman wanted only to render his wife incompetent seemed forgotten. There was no trace of The Smile.

"That's slander," Isserman retorted. "I can sue you."

"Go ahead. I'll see you in the chair for murder."

Norah stepped between them. "The patient isn't going anywhere for a while," she told them both. "You can't move her till the equipment is installed in your home," she reminded Isserman. The machines and monitors were sophisticated, expensive, and not available at a moment's notice from a local surgical supply store. Even a rental could not be immediately arranged. It would all take time, and Isserman had no choice but to accept that.

Sarah Hoyt was only partially mollified. "I want a guard. I want a guard placed on this door day and night!"

"So do I. I certainly agree with that," Isserman took it up. "I consider the hospital directly responsible for what happened, criminally negligent in fact. I will hire my own guards."

"Mr. Isserman, calm yourself," Wadman exhorted.

Sarah Hoyt overrode him, challenging Isserman. "You'd like that, wouldn't you? That way you'd have access to Christie anytime. You could be alone with her and do whatever you wanted." She clenched her hands and shook her fists as she fought back tears of frustration. "No way. There's no way I'm going to allow that. I want police protection for my sister. You hear me, Lieutenant? I demand it."

"Whatever is necessary will be done," Norah assured her.

"That's not an answer. I want round-the-clock protection for my sister."

"How do we know you weren't the one who pulled the plug?" Isserman accused in turn. "You claim you walked in here and found Christina unattended. After a couple of

moments you became aware the machines weren't operating.
You ran out into the hall and screamed for help. How do we
know you didn't pull the plug yourself?"

"That's crazy. Why would I run out and call for help?"

"To cover up, of course. At any moment the nurse might
return and find you standing there. You waited until you
thought Christina was beyond saving. You waited as long as
you dared."

"Why? Why should I do such a thing?"

"You're jealous of Christina. You always have been. You
always have been in competition with her. Christina told me
that even when you were children you tried to discredit her to
your father."

They were too well-bred to shout at each other in the
presence of strangers, but though they kept their voices
modulated, the two shook with intensity. Standing on either
side of the stricken woman, they hissed across her with total
disregard. In fact, they had all—hospital staff, Roy, and
herself—Norah thought, behaved as though the patient wasn't
merely unconscious but also not present. No one so much as
glanced at her. Nobody noticed as Christina Isserman's eyelids
flickered.

Norah put an end to the argument. "I ask each of you to
accompany Detective Brennan to the precinct and put what you
have to say into a statement and sign it."

That didn't please either antagonist and, for a moment,
Norah thought they would protest to try to beg off. Then
Isserman shrugged. Not to be outdone, Sarah Hoyt produced a
weak version of The Smile. "I'd be delighted."

They left with Roy and the room was cleared. Norah stayed
behind to speak to the nurse.

"You are Harriet—is your name pronounced 'nell' or
'nestle'?" Norah asked.

"'Nell.'"

Harriet Nesle was a nice-looking black woman in her forties,
tall with a stately bearing. Her complexion was luminous, her
dark eyes large, clear, but troubled. Obviously and understandably, she was upset.

"The questions I'm going to ask, Mrs. Nesle, are intended

to clarify exactly what happened here. I'm not out either to blame you or to exonerate you. What happened could have resulted in tragedy. It didn't. For the moment, let's leave it at that."

"Yes, ma'am—Lieutenant."

Norah took a chair and indicated that Nurse Nesle should sit too. "What time did you come on duty?"

"I came to Mrs. Isserman at three-thirty."

She had a soft voice and an accent Norah recognized: she came from the Islands, probably Jamaica.

"You have another patient?"

"I work regularly on the floor and I take special duty from time to time when they need somebody."

"I see. So what time did you actually report for work today?"

"Seven-thirty."

"In the morning. And you were scheduled to go off at eleven-thirty tonight. That's a long stretch."

"It's easy work," Harriet Nesle defended. "I just make sure her IV is running properly, change the bottle when necessary, rotate her position every two hours, and watch the monitors."

"And for how long have you been maintaining this schedule?"

"Since Mrs. Isserman was admitted."

"That's over a week. You had a day off, I presume."

"Yes, Lieutenant."

Norah shook her head but made no further comment. "According to the visitors' book downstairs, Mr. Isserman visited his wife about four this afternoon. How long did he stay?"

"Fifteen or twenty minutes."

"You remained in the room?"

"No, ma'am. Mr. Isserman told me to go and have coffee or a smoke. He's very considerate."

"And when you returned, things were normal?"

"Absolutely."

"You checked?"

"I would have known, believe me."

"All right." Norah paused for a moment. "Again according

to the visitors' book, Mrs. Hoyt signed in at four-thirty. She must have just missed Mr. Isserman."

"Yes, that's right."

"When she got up here, she claims the room was empty. You were in the bathroom with the door closed."

"But I left the door of the suite open and I alerted the aide across the way, Miss Gallagher, to keep an eye on the patient."

"You'd just had a twenty-minute break," Norah reminded her.

"Yes, that's right." The dark face glistened with sweat. She licked her lips. "I didn't feel so good. I have one of those stomach viruses."

"How long were you in the bathroom?"

"A few minutes. I'm not sure."

"Obviously long enough for someone to come in and pull the plug on the equipment," Norah commented. "You were too preoccupied with your condition to hear anything or to be aware the machines were silent. You didn't know Mrs. Hoyt had entered till she started screaming for help."

Harriet Nesle put her hands to her face and kept them there for a long moment. Then she lowered them and looked straight at Norah. "I shouldn't have come in. I was real sick. I shouldn't have reported for duty at all, much less for two shifts," she admitted. After a pause, she added, "I've got two teenage girls at home and a seventy-five-year-old mother, and there's nobody else to provide for them." She sighed. "I realize that's no excuse."

So the opportunity could not have been anticipated, Norah thought. Isserman could have come back—for whatever reason—found his wife unattended, and the opportunity was too good to pass up. Of course, Sarah Hoyt had been close behind him. The timing favored her.

"Did anyone besides Mr. Isserman and Mrs. Hoyt visit today?"

"Mrs. Wrede. She works for Mrs. Isserman. She comes every day and sits, just sits for an hour or so staring at her. Then there was Mr. Veloney. He brought those flowers." Nurse Nesle indicated a large, formal bouquet. "He's known Mrs.

Isserman since she was a baby and he was a close friend of her father's."

Amazing how well-informed the staff was, Norah thought.

Harriet Nesle got up. "If that's all, Lieutenant, I'll ask to be relieved and go home."

"How do you feel?"

"Okay. I think that last session was the end of it."

She made no appeal. She had dignity, a respect for self, and a sense of duty to others that was rare, Norah thought. "I imagine it will be difficult to find someone to take over for you in the middle of the shift. Perhaps you could stay?"

"I'd like to. Thank you, Lieutenant."

"We'll be putting a police guard on the door, Miss Nesle," Norah told her. "Visitors will be only immediate family, but even so you should keep a close watch over your patient."

"You can count on it, Lieutenant."

Norah took a last, long look. Christina Isserman's face was still bloated and cyanotic, and her eyes were shut. Yet there was a subtle difference. Was it because she was breathing on her own? How long would she continue? Norah knew of cases in which the comatose patient had gone on for years and others in which a crisis had come within hours. Christina Isserman was still hooked to the cardiac monitors. The pattern on the screen was regular, so were the audible beeps; even a nonprofessional would be reassured. Her condition was stable. How long would it remain so?

"Ah . . . Lieutenant?" Harriet Nesle hesitated, made up her mind, yet couldn't quite go the whole way. "A lot of people come in and out of here that don't sign the visitors' book. Maintenance and cleaning people. Volunteers. If you're wearing any kind of smock, nobody asks questions."

"You have someone in particular in mind?"

"She says she's an old friend, that she and Mrs. Isserman grew up together. She looks in—maybe a couple of times a day."

"What's her name?"

"But I didn't see her today. I don't think she came around today at all."

"Who?"

"Mrs. Northcott."

Lucine Northcott was a member of the International Set, Jet Set, Beautiful People—whatever one cared to call it. Yet her name did not automatically appear on letterheads of charity appeals; she did not regularly and automatically attend the major functions of the social season. She was seldom included in the large, highly publicized, promotional society junkets, but she was invited and did attend the select and intimate dinner parties whose guest lists were rarely published. She was lesser royalty; however, as she was attractive, elegant, and well-dressed, she was a familiar public figure nonetheless. Lucine Northcott was rich but not in the Sexton class. She was not big money, but old money. Her family, the Taplins, were aristocrats, blue bloods in the mother country. The younger son had been shipped to the colonies for discipline, but Joshua Taplin didn't learn his lesson; he made a fortune instead. The Taplins were in the forefront of New York society when the Astors and the Vanderbilts were parvenus. Succeeding Taplins did not have the financial acumen of the founder of the American branch. The money Joshua passed on was safely but not imaginatively invested. Lucine Taplin married Marcus Northcott, socially and financially her equal. The marriage was companionable, easy, without high passion. The young wife had no idea there should be more—or that Marcus was looking for it—until he asked for a divorce.

Lucine Northcott's apartment, though prestigiously located on Park Avenue in the Seventies, was small. Those who liked Lucine dubbed it "intimate," others "cramped." Norah though it charming, with a little too much blue and yellow chintz maybe, and too many lace-edged pillows, an ostentatious array of portraits of the great or near-great on the magnificently ornate baby grand, but she admired the country-house effect created by the trellised wallpaper in the hall and accentuated by a bright brass bucket filled with rhododendron leaves on the fireplace hearth. When Norah arrived it was twilight and the terrace lights had been turned on to illuminate a row of cone-shaped yews. In winter, with snow outside and a fire burning inside, the illusion would be complete.

Lucine Northcott didn't keep Norah waiting long. Tall, a tawny, elegant blonde, she strode into the room with the energy of an athlete and the assurance of her class. Norah had had little time for research but she knew Mrs. Northcott was an accomplished horsewoman and a top skier, and that her skills went beyond the proficiency in sports taken for granted in her upbringing. A row of trophies displayed on the shelves on either side of the mantel attested to that, though Lucine Northcott had not turned pro—it would not have been part of the mystique. Her face was long and narrow, the nose straight, the mouth wide, the eyes large. High cheekbones made her look almost gaunt. She was too big to be called pretty; certainly she was not beautiful. But she had style, a style based on confidence of birth and breeding. Her hair was straight, cut mid-length and brushed back. She wore little makeup. Her outfit consisted of tailored black slacks and a white silk shirt. Her only jewelry: large gold hoop earrings.

She held out a hand forthrightly.

"Lieutenant Mulcahaney. I can imagine what this is about. Walther called me just a short time ago. I'm relieved that Christie is all right. In fact, it seems to have been a blessing in disguise. I doubt the doctors would ever have risked taking her off that respirator." She waved Norah to the sofa in front of the fireplace. "Can I get you something? A drink? Coffee?"

"Nothing, thank you. I appreciate your seeing me. I hope I haven't interuupted your evening."

"I have no plans. What can I do for you? What do you want to know?"

"I have to ask about your relationship to Walther Isserman."

The answer was preceded by a raised eyebrow, a hitched shoulder. "We're friends."

"I've heard you're a lot more. Guests who attended the Rose Ball were witnesses to a very loud and vituperous quarrel between the Issermans. They say it was over you."

Lucine Northcott frowned and looked away.

"Both the housekeeper and cook at the Issermans' say that husband and wife quarreled frequently."

"About me?"

"They couldn't specify."

The socialite sighed. "More likely the subject was her drinking."

"Are you saying alcohol was stoking Mrs. Isserman's jealousy when there was, in fact, no basis for it?"

Lucine Northcott bit her lips, tossed back her hair, and looked straight into Norah's eyes. She sighed. "Walther and I are very much in love. We plan to get married."

"I see."

"But that's not what started Christie drinking or got her hooked on tranquilizers. The marriage was in trouble before Walther and I even met. It was in trouble right from the start."

Norah had heard that sort of contention in similar situations, but she was prepared to listen one more time.

"It wasn't a love match, not as you and I understand the term, but it wasn't an arranged marriage either. It fell somewhere in between. The union was intended to benefit both parties. Walther, with his European background, accepted that, was comfortable with it. Christie, wildly infatuated, chose to ignore it. To be fair, an earlier marital interlude hadn't exactly prepared her for reality. Maybe if Theo Sexton had let her first marriage stand, had let her try to face the responsibilities a man and woman living together owe each other, she might have had a better understanding and a better chance of making a go of it."

"Do you mean she was married once before?"

"Actually, twice before. Very few people know about the first marriage; fewer remember. I'll bet Christie herself would be pretty vague about the details," she observed wryly. "She was sixteen. We were all up at Paul Smiths, that's near Lake Placid, for the summer. My family had a place there too, but not as elaborate as the Sextons'. They were the ones with the beach and the float and the tennis courts and the horses. Mr. Sexton was very generous. He gave us all use of the facilities, even the village children and the children of the employees. So Christie fell in love with the groundkeeper's son, and they eloped. Her father was furious, of course, and went after them. He found the two of them at the Justice of the Peace, just as the ceremony was ending. He plucked Christie right out of her young man's arms. The marriage was never consummated."

Lucine Northcott leaned forward and took a long filter-tip cigarette from a silver case on the coffee table and fitted it into an ivory holder.

"Christie was used to having her own way; she teased and cajoled and she got what she wanted. This time she'd just taken and her father didn't like it. He showed his anger, and that frightened her. She worked at getting back into favor. One way was to take an interest in the business. She learned to read a financial statement and even double-entry bookkeeping. But she'd been sexually aroused and she was restless. Theo Sexton knew it. The next time she presented her choice and asked for her father's blessing; he gave it.

"Ruthven Duveen was twenty, a beautiful young man, and one of the Wilmington, Delaware, Duveens—a match for the Sextons both socially and financially. There was nothing Theo Sexton could take exception to. Not then. Not till after the honeymoon.

"Young Duveen turned out to be a playboy. He didn't want to work, not at Sexton nor anywhere else. Why should he? He had as much money as he could ever need with or without Christie's inheritance, so threats to cut her off didn't mean a thing. The two of them had a couple of wild years. If you ask me, that's when Christie first learned to drink. Theo Sexton worked on his daughter; he told her Ruthven was an alcoholic and a womanizer. An alcoholic he certainly became, but I believe he was always faithful to Christie. He loved her—as much as he was capable of loving anyone. The real trouble for Ruthven was that Christie was too close to her father. He couldn't come between them. Two years after the magnificent ceremony, they were divorced." She paused for a long drag on the cigarette.

"So Mr. Sexton selected Walther Isserman as his daughter's next husband," Norah prompted.

"He accepted him. Walther is intelligent, a good businessman, a hard worker; he has all the qualitites the old man was apparently looking for in a son-in-law. He had the capability to take over Sexton. But Theo wasn't ready to let go. What he really wanted was to keep the business *and* Christie. Walther was eager to work and to contribute to the progress and diversification of Sexton Industries, but the old man put him in a dead-end job and kept him there. Walther was frustrated, but he hung on. Then Theo died and the girls inherited the major part of the empire. Sarah sold out to Christie; Walther naturally assumed his troubles were over. But Christie refused to move him into the presidency. J. Parker Felnick got the job and Frank Veloney remained chairman of the board. Naturally, Walther was shaken. He reasoned; he pleaded. How could she love him and not trust him? She answered that she'd known Felnick and Veloney all her life, and her father had trusted them.

"She wasn't interested in Walther's ideas. She didn't want any changes in the business or in the way it was run. She wanted everything to be the same as when Daddy was alive."

Lucine Northcott took another deep drag and released the smoke slowly, thoughtfully.

"Christie indicated that if Walther wasn't happy with the job, he didn't have to work. It wasn't necessary. Now that her father was gone, why bother? Why not give up the job? They could travel, go anywhere, do anything. They could have a wonderful life. In effect, she wanted Walther to be Ruthven Duveen all over again. She wanted to turn him into an amalgam of the two young lovers her father had taken away from her. But Walther didn't want to lead that kind of life."

"That's when he started his own business?"

"Not then, no. He did leave Sexton. He had several job offers; after all, he'd held a good job before he married Christie and he had an excellent background in shipping. He chose to go to Cunard as executive vice-president. Then he was offered the presidency of a small freight line. It went bankrupt, through no fault of Walther's. It was in trouble when he took over."

Lucine Northcott put out the cigarette and laid aside the holder. Restlessly she got up, walked around the pair of sofas where she and Norah had been sitting facing each other to the terrace doors, and stood looking out across Park Avenue. "Walther never told me this, he's too much of a gentleman, but I believe Christie had a hand in his being offered that last job. I think she led the freight company to believe that if they hired

Walther, they would benefit from the Sexton connection and influence, if not an actual influx of Sexton cash. She may have let Walther think so too. Then by withholding that support, she embarrassed and humiliated him and allowed the company to go down to ruin."

And that, Norah thought, marked the end of the prepared statement. Lucine Northcott's account had been a shrewd blend of common knowledge and calculated honesty. Now maybe she would elicit some spontaneous response.

"How long have you and Walther Isserman known each other?"

"Actually, we met at the wedding. I'm an interior designer. While they were on their honeymoon I redid the apartment. I didn't have any close contact with Walther until two years ago, when he went with Cunard. I was on the board; we met at a directors' meeting." A slight smile of reminiscence illumined her narrow face. "We were immediately attracted."

That smile at least was genuine, Norah thought.

"Two years," she repeated thoughtfully. "Walther has asked Christie for a divorce several times and she's put him off."

"What exactly does that mean, Mrs. Northcott?" Norah asked.

"It means she wants to be the one to say when it's over. She wants to be the one to throw him out."

"How long have you been working as a volunteer at Chazen-Hadley?"

It took only a moment for the socialite to adjust to the abrupt change of subject. "About two years."

"As long as you've known Walther Isserman."

Some of the tension eased. "There's no connection, Lieutenant."

"You've been dropping in on Christina Isserman as often as twice a day."

"Yes. I know it seems strange, but we did grow up together. We were friends. I think we'll be friends again . . ."

"Did you visit her today?" Norah asked.

"No. I wasn't on duty today."

Norah had already checked with the director of volunteers and knew that was true. However, as a volunteer Lucine

Northcott had the run of the place pretty much. She could come and go without question. The guard did not remember having seen her today, but that didn't mean she couldn't have slipped by him in a crowd or while his attention was on something else.

"How did you spend your afternoon?"

"I don't have an alibi, Lieutenant Mulcahaney. I went shopping. I didn't buy anything. If I'd known I'd be needing verification, of course, I would have made it a point to go with a friend or make an expensive purchase so the saleswoman would remember me."

Her assurance bordered on arrogance. Bolstered by generations of privilege, it never occurred to these people their word might be doubted, Norah thought, much less challenged—and that applied whether they spoke the truth or lied. "You know Mrs. Hoyt is charging Walther Isserman with attempted murder. She claims he introduced drugs into his wife's drinks, and that he's responsible for her condition. Do you believe he's guilty?"

She had expected instant denial, staunch and fierce support for her lover, but the elegant woman was silent and thoughtful. When she spoke at last her voice was dry, her words chosen carefully. "I don't believe Walther could do that."

"Mrs. Hoyt is also accusing him of pulling the plug on the respirator. Could he do that?"

Again Lucine Northcott pondered. "I don't know what to think about that. If you had seen her before—Christie, I mean—how strong she was! In spite of her drinking and the pills, she was in charge of her destiny. Then to see her as she is now and ask me if I thought Walther could be responsible . . ."

The words echoed Sarah Hoyt's. It was evident that in their group Christina Isserman had been queen. She had elicited admiration, respect—and envy.

"Are you in favor of euthanasia, Mrs. Northcott?"

She sighed. "It depends on so many things. There are instances . . . oh, I don't know. On the other hand, no matter how bleak the situation, and particularly when the patient is young . . . well, there's always hope, isn't there? There has to be, or how can any of us go on?"

Not once during the interview had Lucine Northcott lost composure. The intimation that as a volunteer at Chazen-Hadley she'd also had the opportunity to pull the plug on her rival hadn't even been acknowledged. She was too calm, too poised, Norah thought. She got up.

"I appreciate your cooperation, Mrs. Northcott. I may want to call on you again."

"Of course, Lieutenant. You're welcome at any time."

Nothing fazed her.

Norah rode down in the elevator mulling over the interview, assessing what she'd learned. As she got out at the lobby, the doorman approached her. "Lieutenant Mulcahaney?"

"Yes?"

"Mrs. Northcott just called down. Your office is trying to reach you." He indicated the open door of the package room. "You can use the phone in there."

"Thank you." She entered and dialed. "Mulcahaney."

"Norah." It was Brennan. "We just had a report from Chazen-Hadley. It seems there was an instance about two weeks ago of a patient dying under suspicious circumstances. He disconnected himself from his respirator."

"He killed himself?"

"He shouldn't have been able to. His hands should have been tied."

"Who untied them?"

"That's the question."

"Who supplied the information?"

"We don't know yet. One of the uniforms doing guard duty on Mrs. Isserman called it in. Officer Jordan."

Norah remembered. The thin, dark girl who had participated in the toss of the Isserman apartment. She sighed. "I'm on my way."

CHAPTER SIX

"Where did you get the information?" Norah asked Audrey Jordan. She had taken the rookie from her post in front of the Isserman suite into the enclosed veranda at the end of the corridor that doubled as staff lounge.

"I overheard a couple of the nurses talking."

Norah's jaw set. Gossip, rumor, could be and often was based on truth; it could lead to facts. But she had expected more. The report Jordan had called in had promised more. Norah had had a long day; she'd conducted a series of sensitive interviews, and she was tired. This was her first major case as head of Homicide Fourth Division, but she knew she shouldn't have come running over herself. She'd have to start delegating. But since she was here . . .

"You overheard?"

Audrey Jordan admired Lieutenant Mulcahaney, respected her, and was very much in awe of her. "I'm sorry, Lieutenant. I thought it was important."

"It may very well be, but we need names, dates, specific circumstances."

"The name of the patient is Bertram Arnow," Jordan replied steadily. "He was in Intensive Care and making a good recovery when on the night of May 4 his hands were untied,

enabling him to pull out his endotrachial tube. He died early
the next morning. The nurse on duty was Kate Lavarette. She
came in for a lot of criticism, but she insists she did not untie
the patient's hands and she has no idea who did."

Audrey waited for some comment from the Lieutenant.
When Norah made none, she continued. "Nurse Lavarette was
working on the charts in the adjoining office when she became
aware, by a sixth sense apparently, that something wasn't right.
After discovering what had happened, she immediately paged
a crisis alert. But by the time the emergency team got to work,
it was too late."

"You overheard all this?"

"Once I found out what was up, I made friends with some of
the staff and asked a few questions."

And got answers, Norah thought, the hard set of her jaw
easing. "Care to tell me the name of your 'friends'?"

Audrey Jordan looked uncomfortable. "I'd rather not,
Lieutenant. They talked to me in confidence, you know? The
hospital management isn't anxious for the story to get out, and
they're afraid for their jobs. I mean, buzzing among themselves is one thing, telling a police officer . . ." She shrugged
and looked pleadingly at Norah. "I promised."

"We have to respect that," Norah replied. She was pleased.
"That was good work, Jordan."

The strain on Jordan's face eased; her eyes brightened. For a
moment she became almost animated. "Thank you, Lieutenant."

"So you can go back to your post now. And continue to keep
your ears open."

It was past eleven when Norah left Chazen-Hadley. The halls
were dim and quiet. Always a limbo between life and death,
self-contained, the separation between hospital and outside
world seemed absolute. Stepping out into the street, Norah felt
as though she'd escaped back into normality. No matter that the
pace was hectic—traffic on Central Park West was still heavy
despite the hour, and people fresh from a movie or late dinner
pushed to hail a cruising cab or squeeze onto an already
overcrowded bus—it was a reaffirmation of life. Norah walked

over to her car and got in. Tomorrow would be time enough to talk to Vincent Wadman. Now, she was going home.

She put the key into the ignition, but didn't turn it. Instead, she sat quietly in the darkness of her car. This was, really, the first chance Norah had had to slow down and think. There had been the excitement of her appointment and her party. Then the breakup with Gary. It was only a couple of days ago, Norah realized with a pang, but it seemed forever. And now when she allowed herself to remember, the wound still throbbed. The very next morning she'd been handed the Isserman case. It had been no more than an inquiry into Mrs. Isserman's condition on the complaint of her sister, a gesture to placate a prominent and powerful woman. Norah had pursued it with extra intensity in part to fill the void left by Gary. But things began to happen, and the complexion of the investigation changed.

Was there a connection between the pulling of the plug on Christina's life-support machines and the untying of Bertram Arnow's hands? Were there other similarly suspect deaths at Chazen-Hadley? Was that what the administrator was trying to hide—and what Nurse Nesle had come so close to divulging? Norah was disappointed that none of the staff had approached her about a matter greatly concerning them all. She was accustomed to drawing this kind of confidence.

Was her rank already putting distance between herself and the ordinary witness? More likely, she just had less time to spend on general interrogation. That wasn't her job anymore. She would have to get used to having facts collected by others and passed on to her. She must inspire trust in those who worked for her and then evaluate what they brought in. It was one of the things Joe had tried to teach her—reliance on others.

Norah had reached one conclusion: however Christina Isserman had fallen into coma—by accident, self-destructive drug abuse, or foul play—the pulling of the plug on her respirator was a blatant attempt at murder.

The killer had come out into the open. Having done so, he was bound to try again.

Norah turned the key; the motor started, and she pulled out of the parking lot.

* * *

At midnight, Officers Jordan and Denny were relieved and went off duty. Bruce suggested a beer before going their separate ways, but Audrey wanted to get home. She wanted to get to bed, get a good night's sleep, and be fit and fresh for the next day's work.

The brief interview with Lieutenant Mulcahaney had left her charged up. She felt she had made a real contribution. Now visions of the case being solved because of the information she had uncovered danced in her head. As she strode briskly toward the subway station at Columbus Circle, thoughts of commendation—of maybe even making detective—filled her imagination. Why not? You didn't make detective by length of service or passing an exam. It was a merit promotion. You were appointed by the PC as a result of initiative and performance. Well, she had shown initiative. The lieutenant had as much as said so. Officer Jordan wasn't quite so high that she didn't remember she was still only a rookie of six months— even the lieutenant, her ideal, hadn't been appointed to detective till after two years. Still . . . she indulged her fantasy. What would Mom and Dad say? Maybe she'd give them a call when she got home. By then it would be ten P.M. on the coast.

Donald and Phyllis Jordan were actors. When Audrey was born, touring, the major source of employment for theatrical people, was just about extinct. But the Jordans were musical comedy artists and regulars in the J. J. Shubert stock company. The Shuberts owned theaters across the country that couldn't be left dark. So though they were paid little above scale, the Jordans worked. They toured in *Blossom Time, Student Prince, Rose Marie*, all hits of a past time. They played months of one-night stands, and the proper care of an infant was close to impossible. Audrey was turned over to her doting aunt and uncle. When she was five, Aunt Camilla died of pneumonia and Uncle Oswald followed soon after. Donald and Phyllis Jordan perforce had to take their daughter back.

By this time they found regular employment in regional theater. Even so, there was constant rehearsal by day and performance by night. Audrey was an encumbrance and she knew it. From a happy, outgoing child she became withdrawn and shy. As soon as she began to make friends, gain confidence in her teachers, stabilize—the show closed or the company folded and it was on to the next town. She learned not to form attachments. It was easier. It hurt less.

Television was the salvation of the Jordans, as of many unknown but competent performers. For actors, it was the modern gold rush. The Jordans packed their bags and made the trek west. Gaining acceptance as supporting players, they began to work regularly. Donald was a principal character on a hit prime-time series. Phyllis had a running part on a morning soap. But the stability had come too late. Audrey had become introverted. She kept to herself, rejecting all overtures of friendship.

The Jordans expected Audrey to follow them into the business, but she had no interest in acting. In fact, she moved to New York to be far enough away to make her own career decision. All she wanted was a steady job that did not involve travel. She had a vague notion of social work, maybe with children, and took a course but couldn't get a job. While waiting, she worked as a receptionist. She had no idea of becoming a cop. One day, one of the girls at the office went over to take the exam and teased Audrey into accompanying her.

From the moment she sat down at one of the four hundred portable desks set up on the drill floor of the Seventh Regiment Armory on Park Avenue and Sixty-sixth Street, Audrey Jordan knew she'd found what she was looking for. You could say she'd stumbled onto it; Audrey called it fate. She was going to be a cop. The Jordans thought it beneath her, plebeian. But what would they say when she made detective?

Audrey Jordan reached the subway entrance, went down the stairs and out on the deserted platform. By taking the express and then switching to the local at Borough Hall she could usually get to her apartment in Cobble Hill in about twenty-five minutes. Elated though she was, Audrey was beginning to feel weary.

The car she entered carried half a dozen passengers. They looked up when she came on, and there was a noticeable release of tension at seeing a uniformed police officer. Glancing casually into the car ahead, Audrey noted it was at least half full. A group of teenagers, nine or ten of them, laughed, pushing each other, slapping, swinging from one vertical pole to the next. Innocent high spirits. The passengers, however, kept heads bowed over newspapers, very carefully ignoring the antics. As Audrey watched, the atmosphere changed; she could sense it through the closed glass doors between cars. For whatever reason, at whatever instigation, it turned ugly. The group closed together, solidified, forming a wedge pointing at a young black man who sat along the side of the car, reading. He was intent; under the book he had a note pad—he might be studying. The leader spoke. Over the rattle of the train and with the doors between the cars closed, Audrey had no idea what was said, but the looks on both sides were disturbing. She went up to the door and pounded on it with her nightstick. Nobody so much as looked in her direction. She yanked at the door, but it was stuck.

The leader, older than the rest—probably in his mid-twenties—thin and vicious-looking, dressed in jeans stiff with dirt and a leather jacket filmed in slime, slapped the book so it fell out of the student's hands. As he bent to pick it up, one of the gang kicked him and sent him sprawling on his face. Audrey couldn't hear the laughter, but she could see the grins of derision as the fallen youth was kicked again and again.

"Hey! Stop that!" she yelled through the car doors. Useless, of course. Why didn't the other passengers do something? They were sitting there literally looking the other way. The train slowed. Thank God, Audrey thought, we're pulling into the station. It stopped. She didn't spot any transit police but they had to be around. She couldn't afford to wait. "Send the cops," she yelled over her shoulder as she left the train. She ran out along the platform, and entered the car ahead. She was nearly knocked down by the passengers fighting to get out.

"Tell the conductor," she gasped as she pushed through.

The young black was on his knees with his attackers standing over him in a ring. He held his right arm and grimaced with pain as more kicks were aimed at him from every side.

"Police. Stop it," Audrey ordered.

Nobody heard. At least, nobody paid attention. There must be fifteen of them, more than she'd thought, young men and girls taking part in the assault. Fifteen young punks shrieking with glee in an orgy of cruelty.

"Fight. Fight. Get up and fight," they taunted.

The victim shook his head. "No," he groaned. "No. I don't want to fight."

Audrey Jordan stood at the edge of the circle, uncertain, frightened. She assumed a courage she didn't feel.

"Okay. I'm a police officer. Break it up," Audrey called out. "Let me through."

One girl turned around. A blonde, her hair in tight cornrows, she looked at the policewoman with contempt. "Get lost." With a vicious shove she sent Audrey careening across the aisle just as the subway doors hissed shut.

The train pulled out of the station and the game resumed.

This time the kicks and blows were no longer accompanied by laughter but grunts indicating grim intent to injure. The victim could only cringe, huddle on himself, and try to shield his bloody face as the train gathered speed, hurtling along the tracks. Why hadn't the transit cops got on? Audrey agonized. Why hadn't the conductor held the train in the station? Hadn't any of the passengers advised him? What should she do? What could she do? She was thinking so hard she forgot to be afraid. She pulled her gun.

"I'll shoot the next person that moves," she called out. Loud. They hear her over the roar of the train, the clatter of the wheels, the low grunts and curses of the gang. She got their attention.

"I swear to God, I'll shoot the next person that moves."

They believed her.

Not another word was spoken till the train pulled into Fourteenth Street.

There were four NYPD officers waiting on the platform when the doors opened. As soon as Audrey saw them she began to shake.

CHAPTER SEVEN

Norah paged Dr. Benning, then while waiting strolled down the third-floor corridor to the door of IC Unit A and looked in.

It was a small, ordinary room; four hospital beds crowded it. The machines at the head of each were not particularly impressive; in fact, they appeared primitive and fragile to be performing a life-sustaining function. Instinctively Norah flinched as she scrutinized the patients they served, inert as dummies, and shifted instead to the homely things—cracks in the walls, peeling paint on the ceiling, the air conditioner that wheezed as though ready to quit. She watched the nurses moving between the beds and going in and out of the alcove station. It seemed an unnecessary amount of activity, she thought, almost a subconscious need to reaffirm strength and vigor in the proximity of death.

"Lieutenant Mulcahaney? I'm Clyde Benning."

The resident had come up behind her. Norah turned and smiled. "How are you, Doctor?"

He didn't return the smile. "Mr. Wadman said you'd probably want to talk to me."

"Yes. About Bertram Arnow's death."

"There's nothing I can tell you, Lieutenant. Believe me, if there had been, I wouldn't have waited for you to look me up."

"You're convinced there was no irregularity?"

"I believe . . ." He searched for the precise words. "I believe as far as the staff is concerned, there is no blame."

"And what do you think about Christina Isserman? About the plug being pulled on her respirator?"

"She's not my patient."

"You have no opinion on what happened?"

"None." Emphatically as he said it, he nevertheless avoided Norah's eyes.

Doctors were notorious for supporting each other, for covering even the hint of any negligence, Norah thought. They practiced defensive medicine, always with the idea of protecting themselves and each other against possible malpractice charges. Clyde Benning was only a resident and he was afraid for his job. He would, even more than most, follow the official line.

"This is the unit in which Mr. Arnow was treated, isn't it? I'd like to take a closer look around."

Instant resistance was evident in Benning's look, in the stiffening of his body. Wadman apparently had not briefed him for this; he didn't know what to do. It didn't take him long to make up his mind, however. "I think you should, Lieutenant. I'll come with you."

"I'd appreciate that, Doctor," Norah said. Silently, she applauded.

Dr. Benning held the door. Squaring her shoulders and raising her chin, Norah walked in.

A few steps brought them to the center of the room, where they could get a good look at each of the patients. Norah noted that even unconsciousness could be of varying degrees. She was drawn to a young man near the window who worked his arms and legs restlessly. His hands were bound to the bed railings with wide lengths of gauze. His eyes were blue and wide open; there could be no doubt he was aware of what was happening to him. And he was frightened. Norah couldn't blame him. He was helpless in the ultimate sense. She had never before fully understood what that could mean.

At first he took no notice of Norah. People came and went in that small room that was quiet yet pulsing with sound. They were staff or relatives—no others were admitted. He was astute enough to understand she didn't fit either category. She was someone special. His blue eyes fixed on her and willed her to his side.

He tried to speak, but instead a low gurgle rose up from his throat, harsh and completely unintelligible. Bloody spittle trickled down his chin. He was near thirty, Norah judged, with a square face and regular features. Nice-looking; under other conditions he might even be handsome. His color wasn't all that bad and his body still appeared strong.

"What happened to him?" Norah asked Benning. "He doesn't look like he's been sick for any length of time."

"He hasn't. It was an automobile accident. He was brought in three days ago, apparently stabilized, and then he had an episode. A myopathic defect of the heart muscle, a weakness of the heart muscle. Could have gone unnoticed for years."

"Can't anything be done to make him more comfortable?"

"That breathing tube has been in his throat for only two days, so there's no damage to the membranes yet. He could sustain it for as long as two weeks, but it won't be necessary. We intend to start weaning him off the machine very soon. Maybe even tomorrow."

Norah moved up to the head of the bed where the patient's name was lettered on tape: CLARK HARRISS. "Mr. Harriss, I'm Norah Mulcahaney, I'm a police officer. I know you're in pain, but you're going to make it okay. Just hang in there a little longer."

It didn't calm him. If anything, it seemed to agitate him. Harriss made another attempt to speak and more blood ran from his mouth.

"Don't try to talk." Benning stepped forward. "Be patient for a couple more days. The tube will be out and you'll be back in your own room." He turned and spoke softly to Norah. "I think we should leave him, Lieutenant."

Harriss stopped straining. The muscles of his throat relaxed but his blue eyes remained fixed on Norah, unwavering, fiercely imploring, willing her to stay and listen, to try to understand. She hesitated. Then he blinked once, paused, and blinked a second time.

"Does that mean yes?"

Clark Harriss blinked again—twice. Norah and Benning exchanged glances.

"Is there something you want to tell me? About your accident?"

Yes.

Benning gasped.

"I'll come back," Norah said. "I'll come back when the tube is out and we can talk. I promise." She took his hand and squeezed it. Then, with a last encouraging smile, Norah followed Benning out of the room.

"Is he going to make it?" she asked when they were out in the corridor.

"He's got a very good chance. Being in IC doesn't mean the end. On the contrary, most of the patients do recover. I'll keep an eye on him. You can count on it."

He walked her to the elevator and they rode down to the main floor in silence, each busy with his own thoughts and concerns. At the door of Wadman's office the resident offered his hand. Norah took it.

The administrator rose when she came in. "I hope Dr. Benning gave you what you wanted."

"He did his best for me."

Wadman's eyebrows went up; he hesitated, then sat down again. "A hospital's reputation is a precious thing, Lieutenant. We didn't want to panic our patients or their families. At the same time, we do have a sense of responsibility. We feel very distressed by what happened to Mr. Arnow, but we have determined there was no culpability on the part of any member of our staff. Believe me, Lieutenant, there is no fanatic walking the halls of Chazen-Hadley playing God." He was all blandishment now. "We investigated Mr. Arnow's death thoroughly, and it was an accident."

"You should have reported it."

"We had to find out what the situation warranted."

"Just exactly what have you decided?"

He didn't like the way she put it. Wadman picked up a rubber band from a tray at the center of his desk, stretching and twisting it as he talked. "I don't know if you've ever had a breathing tube down your throat, Lieutenant, or a nose tube running into your stomach for feeding, or even an IV in your arm, but they're not pleasant."

"I've just now had an indication of what it's like," Norah replied.

"Mr. Arnow was hooked up to half a dozen devices. He was conscious and extremely uncomfortable. He was desperate for relief. He wanted that tube out. He'd been on the machines for nearly two weeks. He was an elderly man in a very depressed state. Most such patients are. That's another reason their hands are tied."

"Who untied them?"

Wadman continued to work the rubber band into every kind of cat's cradle. "The hands are untied every time the patient is turned, when he's washed, or certain injections given. Apparently, they were not retied securely enough and he managed to work them loose. He bided his time till the nurse went into the adjoining office. Then he removed the chief source of his harassment."

"What about the alarm?"

"At first the alarm indicated an ordinary accumulation of secretions or momentary high pressure. As soon as she realized it was something more, the RN on duty, Miss Lavarette, went in. She saw what had happened and immediately paged the medical emergency. She did everything she could in the interim. But it was no use. He'd been resuscitated twice before and his system just wouldn't come through a third time."

"I might accept that if it weren't for what happened to Mrs. Isserman," Norah said.

Wadman sighed deeply. His hands stretched the rubber band till it snapped. That seemed to bring him to a decision. He tossed the broken band into the wastebasket, then folded his hands on the desk in front of him. "Seeing the patient in intensive care with all those needles and wires sticking out of him is very distressing for the family."

"Of course," Norah agreed and waited.

Sunshine poured into the office through the arched windows. The room, with its flowered slipcovers, seemed part of the garden outside. Though the morning was full of spring promise, between Norah and the administrator there was darkness and regret. She knew where he was heading, but she could not make it easier for him.

"Mrs. Arnow visited her husband on the night he died. She stayed late, well after visiting hours. She was permitted to do so because of the seriousness of his condition. Each time she saw him could have been the last. She was well-known to the nursing staff and always very cooperative. She never got in the way, so she was frequently left alone with him." He paused. "Though, of course, there were always the other patients."

Who were hardly in any condition to testify, Norah thought bitterly.

"Mrs. Arnow signed out at eleven that night. Mr. Arnow died at a little before three in the morning. It is possible that Mrs. Arnow loosed the knots for him before she left. Then he waited for what he considered the right moment." Vincent Wadman sighed heavily.

"What was Mrs. Arnow's reaction when you told her?" Norah asked. "I assume you did tell her how he died."

"Yes. She took it very well. She didn't try to blame anybody. In fact, she appeared relieved."

Norah understood. Her father, stricken by terminal cancer, had developed pneumonia. It was the direct cause of his death within days. Norah had grieved; the sorrow had been devastating, but she had also thanked God her father had been spared months of pain. "That doesn't mean she was responsible. Did you ask her?"

"She would not have been likely to admit it," Wadman retorted with a tinge of asperity. "Assuming it could be proved, what could she be charged with? What would she be guilty of? All she did was give her husband of forty-two years a choice, the opportunity to make his own decision. I'm not sure that every terminally ill patient shouldn't have that option."

Yet Wadman himself had said physical deterioration brought on mental depression, Norah thought. A patient in such a state could not make sound judgments. The family too was subject to severe emotional stress bound to distort reasoning. But this was not the time for philosophical discussion. "I'd like to talk to Mrs. Arnow. Can you give me her address?"

"Certainly. My secretary will get it for you. May I ask you one question before you go, Lieutenant? How did you hear about Bertram Arnow?"

"You can't stop people talking, Mr. Wadman, particularly about a thing like this. They discuss it among themselves and somebody hears."

He bit his lip. "It doesn't need to go any further, does it? I mean, as I said before, I don't want to frighten the patients."

"I have no intention of allowing the patients to be frightened, Mr. Wadman. I can promise you that. But the matter is not resolved. Mrs. Arnow may or may not have acted to stop her husband's suffering, but what about Christina Isserman?"

"Oh God." Wadman's plump face sagged. He didn't bother to get up to show Norah out.

Vincent Wadman's reconstruction of the events leading to Arnow's death was logical, Norah thought as she drove from the hospital to the address on West End Avenue given to her by his secretary. Considerations of compassion aside, untying Bertram Arnow's hands was the same as placing a lethal weapon in them. Naturally, unless whoever had done it confessed, there would be no way to prove it.

West End Avenue was broad, lined with massive, old, elegant apartment houses. Like every New York neighborhood it had its own distinct character: conservative, reserved; people here had money but didn't flaunt it. For Norah it was achingly familiar. She had grown up a block over on Riverside Drive. Nothing had changed, she thought, except it was harder than ever to find a parking place. She managed finally, but had to walk back three blocks.

"Mrs. Arnow," she announced to the doorman.

He was Hispanic, thin, medium height with short curly hair and a mustache. He gaped at Norah.

Maybe his English wasn't too good. "Is Mrs. Arnow at home?" she articulated slowly.

He swallowed. "No, ma'am."

"When will she be back?"

"Mrs. Arnow died over a week ago."

Norah took a deep breath, then pulled out her shield case and showed it to him.

"The police were already here."

"Who called them?"

"Mr. Frost, the super. Her daughter had been trying to get hold of Mrs. Arnow on the telephone and got worried when she didn't answer. She called Mr. Frost. We hadn't seen her in a couple of days, so he went up and knocked. When there wasn't any answer, he used his key and went in."

"Go on."

"She was in her bed. Peaceful-looking. We thought she just decided she didn't want to live anymore. Mr. Arnow died . . . exactly a week before. They were real close. She missed him. You could tell."

"Had Mrs. Arnow been under a doctor's care?"

"I wouldn't know, ma'am—Officer."

"I'd like to take a look at her place. Can you get me a key?"

"There's nothing up there, Officer. Her daughter cleared out all her stuff."

"Do you have an address for the daughter?"

"Sure. For forwarding mail. Sure."

"May I have it?"

"Oh? Oh! I'm sorry. I'll get it." Flustered, he backed into the vestibule to a small desk. From a drawer he extracted a lined copybook and fumbled through the pages.

CHAPTER EIGHT

Norah decided she would wait to contact Mrs. Arnow's daughter till she had all the available information on both her parents' deaths. As Helen Arnow had lived within the jurisdiction of the Two-Oh, it was no problem to pull the report. Seated in her own office, still a novelty, Norah wondered whether Vincent Wadman knew Helen Arnow was dead. She didn't think he would have hidden it. In fact, he would have made the case against Mrs. Arnow stronger, not out of malice, but simply to clear the hospital. Norah pulled the stack of reports on her desk toward her—other cases, other problems. She had barely started to go through the pile when Brennan knocked and walked in.

"I've got the information, Norah."

"Oh, good."

"According to the autopsy report, Helen Arnow died of an overdose of Librium. There was no question of an accident; the overdose was massive and the prescription bottle beside the bed—empty."

Just as the Valium bottle should have been beside Christina Isserman's bed, Norah thought. Was Mrs. Arnow's suicide an admission of responsibility in her husband's death? Wadman would say it was, but it didn't have to be. Norah could empathize with the woman's loneliness; she'd had a taste of it after Joe died. But her work had saved Norah. Helen Arnow hadn't been so fortunate.

"Did anyone talk to Mrs. Arnow's doctor?"

"The detectives gave him a call to check on the prescription. It was geniune. She'd asked for something to calm her during her husband's illness. Both of them had been his patients for a lifetime. He saw no reason not to give her what she wanted."

"Who carried the case?"

"Wyler."

Simon Wyler, detective first grade, a recent transfer from Manhattan South. Norah knew him, though not as well as most of the others in her command.

"It was open and shut, Norah," Brennan said, defending the absent detective.

"I'm not questioning it. I'd just like to see the report."

Older than Norah, Roy Brennan had at one time been her superior. Now she was his, but they were friends now as then. Yet he was obviously uncomfortable.

"What's the problem?"

Brennan pointed to the stack of papers in front of her. "It's in there."

"Oh, boy!"

"There was no reason for Wyler to call it to your attention."

"I know." She frowned. That she hadn't got to the report wouldn't have mattered except for the link to the Isserman case. The *possible* link. She had learned something: keep current; don't favor one case to the neglect of the rest. The job was not only a matter of greater responsibility but of different priorities, and she had just learned one of them. In the squad room the filing of reports was regarded as a tedious formality, bureaucratic red tape. Norah now perceived it to be a necessary means of keeping records, and more—a means of coordinating separate events.

Suppose she had read Wyler's report? Would she have given it a second look? In all honesty, the answer was no. Without the knowledge of Arnow's mysterious death, why would she have concerned herself over an elderly widow's lonely suicide? She needed to know more about Helen Arnow's relationship with her husband, her attitude toward his sickness, her philosophy regarding artificial life support.

"Tell the duty sergeant I want to see Audrey Jordan before she goes off duty tonight, will you, Roy?"

"Sure. Anything else?"

"Yes. Thanks."

"For what?" Their eyes met. It was enough.

Norah hadn't been working fifteen minutes when the interoffice phone rang. It was Roy.

"About Jordan. She stopped an assault on the subway last night. Collared fifteen suspects single-handed."

"No!"

"That's right." Brennan chuckled. "Jordan was riding home on the A train when she observed a gang of teenagers harassing a youth in the next car. They started beating up on him. It got vicious. At the first stop, she ran out along the platform and got on with them. She herded the bunch together and held them at gunpoint till four officers met them at Fourteenth Street."

"Good for her."

"She's still at arraignment. You want somebody else?"

Norah considerd. Jordan had established herself at Chazen-Hadley. The staff would talk to her. "No, thanks. It can wait."

Justin Hoyt drummed his fingertips nervously on the polished mahogany of the bar counter. He was angry at being kept waiting and at the same time dreaded the coming interview. Raffanti had some nerve to make him cool his heels like this! Who did he think he was? What the hell, his business was founded on losers, right? Without losers he couldn't be the winner. And losers needed credit.

The bartender reached for his empty glass. "The same, Mr. Hoyt?"

Justin started to nod, then changed his mind. The drinks were on the house, so was the food, the room, transportation— and more, if he wanted it—all complimentary, part of the bait to get the high rollers in. Now that he had gambled his money away, the ploy was to humiliate him by making him wait and getting him muddled with liquor. Justin Hoyt's head was absolutely clear, but he'd had three Scotches already and more would be risky. He sensed a presence at his shoulder.

"Mr. Hoyt?"

It was Sal Fontana, one of Mario's flunkies—young, good-looking. "It's about time," Hoyt snarled, and got off the stool.

Fontana merely smiled. He knew when, and when not, to take offense. "This way, sir."

Hoyt knew the way only too well, but of course he accepted the escort. What choice did he have? The two men threaded their way through the principal gaming room of the Alhambra, one of San Juan's newest and grandest casino-hotels. The decor was standard: crystal chandeliers, plush carpeting, mirrors, and gilt. The staff was elegant in tuxedo and evening dress. The customers' attire varied; their intensity did not, though it took different forms. Hoyt was taller than the man he followed, and he carried himself so he was literally head and shoulders above most of the players hunched over the tables. By his manner he indicated he was above them in every way. It was a façade. Underneath the haughtiness, Justin Hoyt III was nervously rerehearsing his pitch.

As soon as they entered the office, Mario Raffanti got up and came around the desk, hand outstretched. "What can I get you, Justin?"

Hoyt wasn't prepared for cordiality. It threw him off and made him cranky. "I don't want a drink."

"Coffee maybe? A Coke?"

"Nothing."

"Suit yourself," Raffanti replied cheerfully. Of the three men, he was the least prepossessing. Scrawny, ears sticking out and too big for his head, he looked younger than thirty-five. But he had power and he understood its use. "You wanted to see me, Justin," he stated, making it clear who was the suppliant. "What can I do for you?"

"My credit has been stopped."

"It has? Salvatore, is that right? Justin's credit has been stopped?"

"Oh hell, don't play games with me, Mario. You know it has. You gave the order."

"In fact, I didn't, Justin. When you pass the limit, it's automatic."

"Well, I want it extended."

"You know the terms."

Justin Hoyt took a deep breath. His long tapering fingers felt for the button of his jacket, loosed it, then reached inside to the vest pocket. He brought out a small tissue-wrapped item and placed it on the desk before Raffanti. "I want another fifty. This is worth a lot more."

Hoyt towered over him, but Raffanti wasn't bothered. He neither jogged nor worked out; he wasn't interested in the current rage for physical fitness. He could buy muscle—and did. With almost finicking care he picked up the little bundle and peeled the tissue from it to reveal a ring. He held it up to the light. The central stone, an emerald, was at least twelve carats, maybe fifteen. The circling diamonds were a quarter carat each, full-cut. He didn't need a jeweler's loop to estimate its value. "I won't ask where you got this."

"It's none of your business."

"In fact, it is, but never mind. I could keep it on account of what you already owe."

"No!" Hoyt cried out. "You can't. It's not due."

"Right. Right." Raffanti lifted a bony shoulder and dropped it. "Anyhow, I don't want this. I'm not interested in jewelry." He returned the ring to its paper and pushed it back toward Hoyt.

"I'm not selling. I'm offering it as additional security."

"And I'm turning it down."

"You can't do that!"

"We're not children anymore, Justin. You're playing on my turf now. I can do whatever I want. I don't even have to allow you in here."

"Allow! I'll go somewhere else. Across the street."

"Suit yourself."

Hoyt gasped. Though they had conducted their business up to now with a certain warmth, even friendliness, neither one had mentioned the past. Hoyt had gulled himself with the thought that he was doing Raffanti a favor by playing at the Alhambra. Apparently he was wrong. It was hard to stand in front of this ornate desk in this vulgar room and plead with a man who had been the son of the head gardener of his father-in-law's estate. It had been Theo Sexton's fantasy that his children and their friends should play with the village children and those of the employees as equals. They hadn't. Children are extremely sensitive to status and fall easily into a caste system. Justin and Mario had played together by Sexton's decree, but Justin had been one of the privileged and he had taken full advantage of it. It was humiliating to have to step down, to take orders instead of giving them, but he was already into the syndicate for a couple of hundred thousand. He could feel his color rise, and that added anger and frustration. Payment was due the first of the month, a short two weeks away. He had no means of raising the cash except by winning it back. It was his only chance. His luck would change. It was bound to. He was due. But he needed a stake.

"Give me a break, Mario. Please."

"If you want to play somewhere else, that's your privilege." Raffanti shrugged.

"For God's sake," Hoyt began in exasperation, then sighed. He was an obsessive gambler. He craved the excitement—heart pumping, blood surging, the thrill of the risk. Winning was the high. Blackjack was his favorite, but he played the wheel, or the horses, or put a bet on any sport. Outside his illness, Justin Hoyt was a shrewd and successful businessman, but the illness was consuming him. "Okay, setting the past aside and as one businessman to another—what do you want?"

"Salvatore?" Raffanti looked to his aide. In silent response Sal walked to an oil reproduction of a Venus by Titian, sliding it to one side to reveal a safe. He twirled the dial and opened the door. Taking out several packets of bills, he closed the safe, and brought the cash over to his boss.

"Sit down, Justin, relax."

Hoyt did as he was told and another look from Raffanti sent Sal Fontana to the opposite side of the room. Again both principals waited in silence while he mixed two highballs and brought them back.

"I am not unfeeling," Raffanti said when each man had his own drink in hand. "I sympathize with your situation."

Hoyt's eyes were fixed on the packets of money. "What do you want?"

"What have you got to offer?"

Hoyt's hand hovered for a moment over the cash. Then he picked up the emerald ring, crushed the tissue around it, and stuffed the crumpled ball deep into his pocket. "You already have everything I own."

"I'm not interested in your shares in Sarah's sportswear business."

"Does that mean you're giving them back?"

"I can't give them back. You can't reasonably expect that. But I'll trade them."

Hoyt scowled.

"I'll trade the shares in Sarah Hoyt Sportswear that you put up as security for an equal number of shares in Alliance Depository. And I'll throw in the extra fifty you want so you can keep playing." Raffanti leaned forward and nudged the bills slightly toward the gambler.

Hoyt had difficulty tearing away his eyes, but he looked up. "That number of shares would give you control of my company."

"I would be a very silent partner."

Hoyt's hazel eyes bored into Raffanti's dark ones. "You want to use it as a laundry, right? You want to use my company to launder your dirty money. It's made to order for you."

Raffanti didn't respond immediately except for a slight narrowing of his eyes. When he did speak it was almost genially. "My girlfriend is studying fashion design. She has some very good ideas and she's dying to get a chance to try them out. Once I officially own the shares in Sarah's company, maybe I can convince her to give Linda a job."

Justin Hoyt groaned.

"On the other hand, Sarah doesn't ever have to know you put up shares in her business to cover your gambling losses." Raffanti pushed the money all the way to the very edge of the desk. "Your luck could change tonight."

Sarah Hoyt signed the visitors' book at Chazen-Hadley on Saturday afternoon. The clock behind the receptionist's desk marked the time as five minutes after four, and she wrote that in. Upstairs, two uniformed officers, neither of whom she'd seen before, stood at the door of her sister's suite. She had to produce identification before being allowed to enter. The afternoon was gloomy, and with the shades drawn the room was shadowy. Harriet Nesle sat beside the bed and looked up from her knitting as Sarah Hoyt entered.

"How are you, Mrs. Nesle? How's our patient today?"

"Hello, Mrs. Hoyt. She's resting more comfortably."

"Good. Good. At least she doesn't have that awful tube down her throat anymore." Sarah went over and took her sister's hand. "Her skin doesn't feel so clammy, either."

Harriet Nesle merely smiled. Instructed on no account to leave the room, she pulled her chair to a far corner to give the visitor a measure of privacy.

Sarah leaned down and kissed her sister's cheek. "You look so much better, Christie darling," she murmured. "Your skin and color are improved, almost normal. Come back to us, darling. Wake up and come back to us," she whispered directly into the patient's ear. For a while she went on talking soothingly, encouragingly. Then she straightened. "I hope some of it got through," she told the nurse. "I think if somehow one can reach the subconscious, that's a big part of the battle." She slipped a twenty into Mrs. Nesle's hand.

They all thought that, and it wasn't up to her to discourage them, the nurse mused, especially not Mrs. Hoyt, who was such a nice woman. "She'll be going home in a couple of days," she remarked.

"Oh? Who said so?"

"Mr. Isserman. He's got all the equipment installed for her."

"Really? Well, we'll see about that."

"Can't you at least try?" Sarah Hoyt insisted. "Can't you get an injunction or a stay or whatever to stop him from taking Christie out of the hospital? I mean, if the judge turns you down, then—well, at least we will have tried. But he won't. Not if you go to the right judge. You must know someone who will do this for us."

John Parker Felnick stood within the embrasure of the old-fashioned bay window of his study overlooking the Hudson, his mouth a tight line of displeasure. "We might have had a better chance if you hadn't gone to the police and accused Walther of murder." He spoke so low she had to lean forward and strain to hear. It was one of his ploys.

A tall, massive man with a craggy face and a full head of white hair, Felnick stood straight without support of any kind, belying his eighty-eight years. He'd had a varied and distinguished career alternating between the public and private sectors. A daredevil pilot in World War I, he'd been disciplined enough as an officer to reach the rank of colonel. He'd served under three presidents, as a member of the national security staff headed by Henry Kissinger, on the White House staff during the Johnson administration, and finally as Under Secretary of Labor for Gerald Ford. In the world of private business he'd headed National Steel, been on the board of directors of Grumman and Lockheed, and currently he was president of Sexton Industries. He carried himself with the dignity of his current status and never forgot he was one of those men who had shaped the nation's destiny. He was accustomed to being attended with respect, and his opinions were never challenged. However, he was inclined to be indulgent to the daughter of his old friend and associate, Theo Sexton.

"I wish you had consulted me before making the charge," he said, tempering his displeasure. "I know you did it out of love and concern for Christie, but it was a mistake. You see, the police have not been able to find definitive evidence of any wrongdoing, neither on the part of Walther nor of anyone in the household. In fact, the disconnection of the respirator suggests she is more at risk in the hospital.

"I talked to Chief of Detectives Louis Deland," Felnick continued. "He assures me he has one of his top people on the case—a Lieutenant Mulcahaney. The lieutenant has long experience in homicide investigation. She's one of the best."

"I met Lieutenant Mulcahaney. I wasn't impressed," Sarah Hoyt retorted sullenly. "I know Walther is guilty. All he had to do was put some Valium into Christie's drinks. And I know he's the one who pulled the plug on her. Once he gets her home, he'll kill her. There'll be nothing to stop him."

"The lieutenant is working under the direct supervision of Inspector James Felix."

"I never heard of him either. I don't know who he is. He hasn't bothered to come around and make himself known."

Felnick's eyes flashed, and Sarah knew she had gone too far. He had used his personal prestige to enlist top police brass; by denigrating them, she impugned his influence.

"I'm sorry, Uncle John. I'm just so upset." He was not her uncle. It was a courtesy title the girls had extended only to the very closest of their father's associates. "Please, Uncle John, try to think of something. There must be something you can do to help poor Christie. We can't abandon her."

His stern face softened. "Of course, we're not going to abandon her. How is the poor child?"

"She's off the respirator, as you know. The doctors say there doesn't appear to be brain damage. They're cautious in committing themselves, but I know her brain is all right. Sometimes I could swear she sees me and knows me."

"Has she spoken?"

"Oh no, but she's definitely improving. I was just there. I talked to her and I believe I reached her."

"Well." Felnick walked over and sat in the leather armchair behind his desk. "Probably our best chance would be to talk to her doctor."

Sarah was disappointed. "Dr. Kuhn has already told Walther Christie can be just as well-cared-for at home as in the hospital."

Felnick was not in the least put off. "That was several days ago, when she proved stable even though not on the respirator, wasn't it? And before she began to show this very marked improvement?"

Sarah Hoyt hesitated. "I don't know how noticeable the improvement actually is, or whether it would show up in tests. I think you would have to know her and then sit with her and watch her for a very long time to have a basis for comparison."

"He's her physician, isn't he? He should know her and take the time to observe any changes. Then, in light of her recent improvement, he must revise his opinion. He will surely decide that she should remain in the hospital where she can be monitored and her treatment adjusted as needed.''

"Uncle John, you're wonderful!" Sarah's pixie face glowed; she looked like the little girl he remembered and took pleasure in indulging. Then her face clouded again. "Suppose Walther refuses to listen to Dr. Kuhn?"

"Then I believe I can find a compassionate judge who will act on a medical recommendation.''

Norah was awakened by the ringing of her telephone. It was two-thirty A.M. Now that she was a lieutenant, she didn't get these middle-of-the-night calls often, or wasn't supposed to, she thought. She wasn't judging by her own very brief experience, but by the years Joe had served as a lieutenant, and on her own reluctance as a mere sergeant to roust out "the lieut'" except under dire circumstances. So she reached for the bedside phone expecting to hear Brennan or Arenas.

"Lieutenant Mulcahaney?"

It wasn't either. It wasn't anyone she recognized.

"This is Clyde Benning. At Chazen-Hadley. I'm sorry to disturb you, but something terrible has happened. Could you come right over?"

CHAPTER NINE

Norah arrived at Chazen-Hadley to find both Dr. Benning and Administrator Wadman waiting. Wadman was pale and agitated, Benning withdrawn and sullen.

"I'm so sorry to get you out at this hour, Lieutenant." Wadman tried to appear calm. "We called to stop you, but you were already gone."

"Oh? Well, it's not the first time I've been rousted from my bed, nor the first time for you either, I'm sure. It goes with the territory." Norah smiled, but the remark fell flat. "So. As long as I'm here, you might as well tell me about it. What's the problem?"

"No problem." Wadman was quick to reassure her. "Everything's going to be all right. Dr. Benning merely overreacted."

"About what?" When Wadman didn't answer, Norah turned to the resident. "Why did you call me, Doctor? You must have had good reason." Reticent by professional habit, Wadman and Benning had closed ranks and she wasn't going to stand for it. "I will not tolerate a conspiracy of silence," Norah said with a depth of emotion she hadn't suspected within herself. "Presumably both of you are in the business of saving lives. If one more person dies or is put at risk in this hospital because of your code of self-preservation and self-interest, I'll make sure you're both charged with obstruction of justice, criminal negligence, accessory after the fact, and anything else I can think of." Having said that, Norah deliberately turned her back on the administrator. "Dr. Benning, you called me at two-thirty this morning. I want to know why."

Clyde Benning raised his eyes to look into Norah's. The strain on the haggard face eased just a little. "Come upstairs," he said.

Wadman started to object. A hard stare from Norah reduced him to silence. He followed Norah and Benning to the elevator and the three rode up to the third floor and IC Unit A.

Norah had intended to come back and visit Clark Harriss, but she had not expected to find him like this! She hardly recognized him. He was connected to the same battery of machines; the same number of tubes and wires protruded from his tortured body, but now he was bloated, his skin a terrible blue. Harriss didn't respond when she spoke to him or touched him. She could have cried.

"What happened?" Norah asked Benning.

The resident was badly shaken. "He tried to extubate himself."

"He tried to pull out his breathing tube," Wadman explained, still pale and distressed, and still trying to hide it.

"How could he?" Norah demanded. "Weren't his hands tied?"

Neither man answered.

Dawn was just breaking and the thin gray rays mixed with the artificial light, making the scene more bleak, more discouraging. There was none of the forced bustling cheeriness so noticeable on her first visit to the unit. The two RNs on duty stayed out of the way as much as possible. Norah sensed neither would seek to excuse what had happened as an accident. They were scared; it showed as they diligently tended to the three remaining patients while anxiously observing Norah and the administrator. Three, Norah thought, including Harriss. She noted the empty space where the fourth bed had been.

"He's been returned to the floor," the nurse tending the patient in the bed beside the empty space explained.

"Ah," Norah sighed. Another night and Clark Harriss also might have been moved back to regular quarters. Now . . . ? She looked to Benning.

His color was still bad, his face sunken, his pale eyes haunted, but he was ready to deal with the situation or at least talk about it. It was, after all, why he had roused Norah and brought her down here. "It's a nightmare," Benning began with a groan, then took himself in hand. "It's like Mr. Arnow all over again," he managed more calmly. "I should have reported his death right away; I know that now. I was his physician. It was my duty. My obligation."

Wadman groaned but the young resident ignored him.

"I don't know how Mr. Harriss's hands came untied any more than I know how Mr. Arnow's did," Benning went on. "I can't really say about Mr. Arnow. Maybe that was an accident. But this was no accident. Harriss didn't want to die."

"That's an assumption you have no right to make, Doctor," Wadman warned in a halfhearted attempt to stop him.

"I was on duty this afternoon." The resident faced the administrator squarely. "I saw the patient. Mr. Harriss was disturbed, excited. He tried to communicate with me. It was obvious he wanted to tell me something. I discouraged it. I put him off. I told him tomorrow the tube would be out and he could talk as much as he wanted to. Then, God help me, I ordered sedation. He was frightened and I rendered him completely vulnerable."

Norah sympathized with the resident, but her heart ached for the patient. "What happened?"

Benning sighed. "Somehow his hands came loose from their bonds and apparently he tried to pull out the endotrachial tube. Before he could do more than dislodge it he went into cardiac arrest. The monitors sounded the alarm; the team responded. They worked on him and were able to save him."

"Is he going to make it?"

"He's in very serious condition. The first time he was resuscitated he came out with strong vital signs and, as far as we could tell, no brain damage. Now, it's another story."

Norah looked at Clark Harriss, or rather at the inert, unconscious form that had been Clark Harriss. *Brain damage,* those were the critical words. "But he has a shot?" she insisted.

"We're doing everything we can."

The standard reply. But Clark Harriss had been on the way to recovery. He had known it. Norah herself had told him so and Benning had assured him of it. She agreed with the resident that Harriss had not done this to himself. Someone else was responsible. Who? How could anyone do such a thing? she agonized. If the man had been without hope of recovery and in unbearable pain, then maybe she could not agree but understand. Norah walked around to the back of the bed to inspect the electrial connection. Four days ago Harriss had followed her every movement with his eyes. On this gray dawn his eyes remained closed. The electric line was heavy-duty and so was the plug. There was no special lock, but jiggling it, Norah discovered it was tightly wedged in the socket, secure but not immovable. Wouldn't it have been easier to pull the plug rather than loose the patient's hands?

Nurse Charlotte Hearn, her name on the identification card pinned to the pocket of her uniform, was short, dark, and curious. She strained to hear what Norah, Benning, and Wadman had been saying. Norah turned on her abruptly. "Can you explain how the patient's hands came loose?"

"No, Lieutenant." She was not in the least disconcerted. "The last time I looked, they were secure."

"When was that?"

"When I came on duty at eleven-thirty P.M."

"Any you, Miss Rivera?" A buxom blonde with very beautiful light green eyes, Nurse Rivera stood as far apart as she could. "When was the last time you noted the patient's hands?"

"I did not check the patient's hands. There was no reason to do so."

A safe answer, Norah thought, and possibly a true one. "And where were you when the alarm sounded?"

She answered that more easily. "At the station." She pointed toward the open alcove.

"Miss Hearn?"

"I was with her."

"How long?"

"We were in and out, back and forth, during the whole shift, Lieutenant." Hearn responded with asperity, but nevertheless Norah read the anxiety underneath. "We were not inattentive to the patients; we were not lost in reports. No one could have walked in through the outer door of the unit without our knowing."

"Then how did it happen?" Norah looked from one to the other and neither could offer an answer. "Unless . . ." Norah frowned. "Did either one of you leave the unit at any time?"

The two searched each other's eyes to discover a mutual defense. "We each took our usual break," Nurse Hearn admitted. She was on the verge of saying something more, then changed her mind.

She looked anything but excited now, Norah thought. In fact, like her friend, she looked as though she wanted to be somewhere else, anywhere else.

Marta Rivera took a deep breath, threw a thin but encouraging smile at Hearn. "The alarm sounded only a minute or so after Charlotte came back from her break. So whatever happened, it happened while I was here alone." Her lovely large green eyes filled. "It's my responsibility."

"It could have happened anytime," Nurse Hearn came quickly to the defense. "Look, look at the way the beds are lined up—three on the one wall and Mr. Harriss's bed off to one side on the other. Separate. Look at the way the outer door opens, partially screening his side of the room from the station. Someone could have slipped in anytime, untied his hands, and slipped out again without being noticed."

She was right, Norah thought. The position of the bed was strategic. She had noticed it, but not thought out the implications. Had the position of the bed dictated the choice of victim? The next step in that particular line of reasoning was obviously terrifying Vincent Wadman.

"I'll need a list of every person in this hospital who was present from midnight till now. That includes patients," Norah told him.

"Patients?" Wadman recoiled.

"Patients," Norah repeated. "Maintenance people, doctors,

nurses, interns, dietitians, therapists, volunteers: we need to
establish alibis and we can't afford to miss one. I'll get some of
my people over here to conduct interrogations. We'll keep as
low-key as we can."

Wadman swallowed hard. "Do what you have to do,
Lieutenant. I want this cleared up."

Their eyes met this time. Finally, Norah thought, Vincent
Wadman would not hold anything back.

"I'll need to make a few calls."

"Use my office."

Norah mulled over the strategic situation. Should she attempt
to secure the building? If the perpetrator was one of the staff,
he would not be likely to attract attention to himself by leaving
before the end of the shift. If he had come from the outside he
would be long gone now, out the same way he had come in.
The primary objective was to interrogate everyone legitimately
in the hospital before the morning crew arrived. In the
confusion of the changeover, someone could be overlooked.

Before doing anything else, Norah called in to register the
complaint, then contacted her team. Detectives no longer
worked the graveyard shift; that had been eliminated at the
very start of the budget cutbacks. At this hour there were a
couple of intermediate rank officers on duty in the squad
room—detective inspectors who did the work of a detective at
a salary somewhere above a patrolman's and below that of a
detective third grade. Probably, they were out on calls. Norah
wanted her own people and she contacted them at home. First
Brennan, then Ferdi.

On paper, Norah had twenty men available to her. In fact,
two of them were on loan to the One-Nine investigating a big
jewelry heist and homicide at the Hotel Pierre. Two others were
working at the One-Seven on a massive canvass for a suspected
arsonist. A fifth would be tied up all day in court.

By six-thirty A.M., there were thirteen detectives conducting
interrogations at Chazen-Hadley. She'd left two men on day
duty to cover the chart, Norah informed Captain Jacoby. She
would release additional men for regular duty as they became
available.

"I don't see the urgency," Jacoby grumbled over the phone.

"It's the third incident, Captain."

"How do you get three, Lieutenant?"

"Well, Mrs. Isserman, of course, then Bertram Arnow, the patient who was in IC on the respirator and whose hands were untied. And then—"

"But that was . . . a week at least before Mrs. Isserman was even admitted."

"Four days, sir," Norah corrected. "And now there's another patient in critical condition whose hands were left untied just like Arnow's."

There was a long silence.

"Inspector Felix called me at home yesterday. He says Chief Deland is very interested in our progress on the Isserman case. He wants to be kept informed."

"Should I send Inspector Felix a copy of my report?"

"You report to me, Mulcahaney, and nobody else. Understood?"

"I was just trying to save you trouble, Captain."

It was almost two years since Manny Jacoby had been appointed captain and assigned command of the Twentieth Precinct. He was ambitious, a hard worker; on the basis of time and effort, ready to match himself against anybody. Politics, though, was something else. Jacoby was well aware of Norah's long friendship with Jim Felix and of how closely her husband had worked with the inspector. He respected Norah, came close to liking her, as much as he could anyone who worked for him. He believed she would not take advantage of that long-standing association, not deliberately, but at the same time he didn't want her to have any excuse to go over his head directly to the inspector.

"Don't worry about troubling me, Lieutenant. Now this first case, Arnow—he committed suicide, right? He pulled the plug on himself?"

"That's what it amounts to, yes. On the other hand—"

"Okay." Jacoby cut her off. "But Mrs. Isserman was unconscious. She couldn't have pulled the plug on herself. No way. Somebody did it to her. Right?" He waited for the admission.

"Yes, sir."

"This man, Harriss, tonight—he could have dislodged the breathing tube himself?"

"Both his doctor and the administrator, Vincent Wadman, are very concerned. They're afraid a crazy is going around untying the patients' hands, maybe even pulling out the tubes and using the loosed hands to suggest suicide."

"So how come he didn't tell you about Arnow in the first place?"

"You know the answer to that, Captain. He was trying to protect the hospital."

Jacoby fell into another of his silences, finally breaking it with a lugubrious sigh. "The way I see it, Wadman has a problem: somebody is walking around giving his patients a choice. Whoever pulled the plug on Mrs. Isserman did not give her a choice. That, Lieutenant, is *our* problem." He grunted. "I suppose as long as you've started the interrogations you might as well finish."

It was as close to admitting there might be a link as he was likely to come, Norah thought.

"Next time I'd appreciate your informing me before you call out the entire squad." Jacoby hung up, cutting off further discussion.

Norah sat for a long moment. She hadn't intended to turn to Jim Felix, not at this point anyway, but if she ever should need to, on this or any other case, Manny Jacoby had clearly warned he would consider it an act of insubordination.

DEATH STALKS CORRIDORS OF ELITE PRIVATE HOSPITAL

That was the tenor of the lead bulletins on both radio and television news programs that Monday morning. Few details had been released, so there was plenty of speculation. Walther Isserman, up early for an unusual ten o'clock appointment, heard the news as he was shaving. He didn't waste any time getting on the phone to his paragon of a secretary.

"Get hold of Dr. Kuhn and have him meet me at the hospital," he ordered. He didn't have to tell Miss Schubart to cancel the appointment; he paid her for the initiative to do things like that on her own. He ordered the car, gulped down a single cup of black coffee, and left.

"I want her out of here and I want her out now."

Walther Isserman kept his voice low but icy. He was in the administrator's office, but he behaved as though it were his own. His manner to Dr. Jeremy Kuhn was so civil as to be insulting. "What is the problem, Doctor? You've already given permission for Christina to come home tomorrow. Her room is ready today. All the equipment you requested has been installed. What difference does one day make?"

Jeremy Kuhn was a small dark man, mild-mannered and given to making gentle jokes to put his patients at ease. At this moment he was in need of easement himself. "Ah . . . she's getting better."

"Is she?" Walther stared. "You didn't tell me that. Well, it's certainly good news. All the more reason to take her home as soon as possible. At home her improvement should accelerate."

"I haven't had a chance to assess the change."

"Why not?"

"We'll have to make tests."

"I saw you Friday, Doctor. You didn't mention anything about tests."

"I wasn't sure then."

"But you are now?"

"Yes."

"You haven't seen Christina since Friday, Doctor. Don't bother to deny it. I happen to know that you and Mrs. Kuhn were in Southampton all weekend getting your house ready for summer. This morning when your service relayed my call you hadn't visited my wife yet: you were still in your apartment. So. What is going on?"

Caught between two factions, the doctor stiffened; he decided his interest was to retain his professional integrity. "My only concern is the health and welfare of my patient. To best serve her needs, my advice is that she should remain here for the next few days. Of course, I can't force you to take it."

"That is correct." Pointedly, Isserman turned his back on the physician. "Well, Mr. Wadman?"

The administrator shrugged. "If you wish to take Mrs. Isserman home today, you have that right."

"Thank you." Isserman made him a slight and ironic bow. "I intend to do just that." He wheeled on Kuhn. "I'm not through with you, Doctor. I intend to find out what you're up to. Meanwhile, you can consider yourself off the case."

The preliminary interrogations by the detectives of the Fourth Homicide Zone proceeded with professional efficiency. Reports would be written and the information contained in them fed into the department's computer. It would spew out inconsistencies or coincidences. Meanwhile, Norah would take copies of the reports home to study. The computer was a marvel, but it didn't have hunches. Norah was a strong believer in instinct—her own. While she and the computer worked, the detectives would move on to a background search of the home and private life of those interviewed. It was tedious and time-consuming, but Norah knew of no way around it.

"I'm sorry," she apologized to the intern she was currently talking to and who was as tired as she was. "You did say that you were assigned to Geriatrics and that you didn't leave the floor the entire night? Did any one of the staff have occasion to leave the floor?"

"We all took our normal breaks."

"Let me just confirm the time on that," she began, and was interrupted by a tap at the door.

Brennan looked in. "Lieutenant, there's some kind of problem upstairs with Mrs. Isserman."

Ferdi Arenas met them as they stepped out of the elevator at the third floor. He didn't need to explain. Officers Denny and Jordan stood shoulder-to-shoulder in front of Christina Isserman's suite facing Walther Isserman, Wadman, a pair of ambulance orderlies with an assembled gurney between them, and assorted nurses and aides as spectators. The two officers were obviously uncomfortable but holding their ground. When they saw Norah with Brennan and Arenas they were also quite obviously relieved.

"What's the problem?" Norah asked.

"I can't get my wife out of this damned hospital," Isserman answered, white-faced with rage. "It's about time someone in authority arrived. Your people refuse to allow me to take my wife home, Lieutenant."

"Now? You want to take her home now? We were told you would be moving Mrs. Isserman tomorrow."

"You think I'd leave her in this place another night? After what happened here? Not another hour, Lieutenant."

Norah hesitated. "You did inform the precinct of your change of plans? You did notify someone"—she nearly added "in authority,"—"that you intended to take your wife out today?"

"As a matter of fact, no."

Relieved, Norah suppressed a sigh. "Then you can't expect Officers Denny and Jordan to know about it. They respond to offical order, Mr. Isserman. They are stationed here to protect your wife and that is what they are doing."

"They are here to keep unauthorizeds persons from entering her room."

"The purpose is to protect Mrs. Isserman."

For the first time, Isserman was uncertain. His face was drawn and tense. He rose on tiptoe and came down, up and down a couple of times, thinking. "I don't want to argue about this, Lieutenant. I just want my wife out of here."

Norah took a deep breath, held it, and slowly released it. She glanced at Roy; he raised an eyebrow. She looked to Ferdi; all he could do was shrug. "Is it medically safe for Mrs. Isserman to go home today?" Norah asked Wadman. "Has the doctor been consulted?"

Wadman sighed. He was nearing the end of his patience. He wanted an end to the ruckus; he wanted an end to the confrontations, publicity, all the disruptions Christina Isserman's presence had nurtured. "Dr. Kuhn does not prohibit her leaving."

Still Norah hesitated. She was convinced the overdose that had put Christina Isserman in the hospital was not an accident. Someone had tried to kill her then and was still trying. She didn't trust Walther, but she had no hard evidence on which to charge him. She had to either charge him and take him into custody, or let him do what he wanted. She could call Jacoby, she thought. He'd wanted to be kept informed, but he wouldn't appreciate this kind of dilemma being dumped into his lap. Besides, it wasn't his problem; it was hers.

"Well, how about it, Lieutenant?" Isserman had regained his composure. "Are you going to order your people to stand aside and let the orderlies go in and get my wife, or do I have to call Chief Deland?"

Norah stiffened. She'd stood up to threats of that kind before. Most of them were bluff. Usually, even should such a complaint reach the Chief, Norah would be confident of Deland's support. But she had never been confronted with arrogance based on money and privilege. Who Walther Isserman was, who his wife was, shouldn't make any difference. It wouldn't, she assured herself; nevertheless Norah's blood heated. It was her own fault, she thought. She had hesitated too long and let him put her in a no-win situation. If she removed the guards and let Isserman go in and get his wife, she would seem to be giving in to his threat. If she didn't, she would be deemed unable to make an independent decision. Norah was in an agony of uncertainty—knowing that not only Isserman and the hospital personnel, but her own people, Roy and Ferdi and, of course, the two uniforms, were watching her. Her face burned, and she knew they were aware of that too. Suddenly, Norah realized she was looking at the problem too subjectively, as it affected her. She should only be considering the patient, the threatened victim on whose life a murder attempt had certainly been made as she lay helpless inside that room. Now, with the possibility that a fanatic had the run of Chazen-Hadley, what choice did she really have?

Norah squared her shoulders and raised her chin. "Take your wife home, Mr. Isserman."

Norah thought she detected approval and relief in the eyes of both Brennan and Arenas. In Isserman's there was definitely triumph.

"And when you get her there, take good care of her," Norah warned. "Be sure you take good care of her."

                              * * *

Brennan and Arenas returned to the precinct. Norah hadn't had breakfast and it was already time for lunch. "How about something to eat?" she suggested to Denny and Jordan.

"I'm supposed to take my wife to the doctor just as soon as I get off, Lieutenant," Bruce Denny apologized.

"Nothing serious, I hope?"

He beamed. "She's pregnant."

Norah smiled back. "That's very serious and very wonderful. Congratulations."

"Thanks, Lieutenant."

"How about you, Officer Jordan? Come on, I want some company."

They were late for breakfast and early for lunch; the hospital cafeteria was nearly empty. They chose a table beside a corner window overlooking the grounds of the Museum of Natural History on one side and the newly green Central Park on the other. All of a sudden Norah was ravenous. She took scrambled eggs and bacon from a hot table, plenty of rolls and butter, and coffee. Audrey Jordan contented herself with a small salad. It wasn't till they finished eating and were relaxing over coffee that Norah made an attempt to draw the young officer out.

"Well, that hit the spot." She leaned back, sighing with satisfaction.

"I enjoyed it. Thanks, Lieutenant."

She was very pretty, Norah thought. Her dark eyes were large, intense, and evasive. "You're welcome. Please call me Norah. I'll call you Audrey, if that's all right?"

The girl nodded but still didn't meet Norah's look. Shy under scrutiny? Too shy.

"How do you like being a cop? Is it what you expected?"

"I like it, but I don't know if it's for me."

"Oh?" It wasn't the answer Norah had anticipated. "You seem to be doing very well."

"Thank you, Lieutenant—Norah. But I don't think so."

Norah looked at her even harder. She'd seen Audrey Jordan on two previous occasions. There was a subtle change since the last time. She was certainly paler, even thinner, but it was her attitude that was disturbing. "Are you feeling all right?"

The girl nodded. Norah had observed her carefully those other times, and she'd been respectful but not reticent. On the contrary, she'd asked questions. She'd been direct and taken initiative. "What's happened?" Norah asked. "Want to talk about it?"

"No, ma'am." Then, sensing she had been too abrupt, Audrey Jordan tried to make up for it. "I'm sorry, Lieutenant Mulcahaney, I appreciate your interest, but there's nothing to talk about."

"All right." Collecting her things, Norah got ready to leave. At first, she'd been put off by the automatic rejection, then she realized it might be an indication that Audrey's problem was deeper than she'd originally supposed. "If you change your mind, give me a call." On a impulse, she reached into her handbag for her notebook and tore out a back page. "Call me at home," she said, and wrote down the number.

Biting her lip and scowling to keep back tears, the girl took it.

"I almost didn't report for duty today," she blurted.

"Why not?"

"I was scared."

"Of what?"

"I don't know if you heard, but on Wednesday night I interrupted an assault on the subway."

Norah smiled broadly. "I heard. You broke it up. You held fifteen hoodlums at gunpoint till the train pulled into a station where reinforcements were waiting."

"I was scared. The gun was shaking in my hand. If those cops hadn't been there, I don't know what I would have done. I would have let the gang get away, probably."

"But they were and you didn't. You collared fifteen young thugs. You're going to get a commendation. Did you know that?"

"No. And I don't want it." But a slight color suffused her thin face and the tears no longer threatened. She thought of her mother and father. They would be proud. Audrey shook her head and raised her eyes to Norah at last. "I don't deserve it. I said I'd shoot if anybody moved, but I don't think I would have. I don't know."

"None of us knows in advance what we'd do or how we'd behave in such a situation," Norah soothed. "You did what you had to do. You handled it."

"I'll tell you what bothers me, Lieutenant. The lack of cooperation from the passengers. When the train stopped they couldn't get out fast enough. That's okay. I can understand that, but somebody should have told the conductor to hold the train or called the cops."

"Somebody must have," Norah replied mildly. "How else did four NYPD officers happen to be waiting at Fourteenth Street? What you're experiencing is a natural reaction," she assured the girl. "You've got to stop brooding. Think of the victim. He's in the hospital, sure, but if you hadn't been riding in the next car, he might be in the morgue."

It eased her a little. "I couldn't do it again."

"You won't know that till the occasion arises."

"I don't ever want to find out."

Norah's jaw tightened; then, slinging her handbag over her shoulder, she got up. "I'll give you a ride back to the station."

CHAPTER TEN

By three P.M. the detectives of the Fourth Zone began to return to the squad. No clues had been turned, no piece of evidence, no contradiction in the statements to point to any irregularity, much less to a possible suspect. They had nothing. Seventy-nine persons on duty during the hours between midnight and eight A.M. had been where they were supposed to be, doing what they were employed to do. The patients had been in their beds, safe—all but one. All exits to the building, front and rear, had been locked, and a security guard on duty. The Emergency Room had had a relatively quiet night—Chazen-Hadley was never very hectic—with all admissions and relevant personnel accounted for. So the detailed search into backgrounds was the last chance to turn any kind of lead. Norah was determined it should be exhaustive. Clark Harriss had been a sick man, but on the road to recovery. His mind was clear. He knew he was getting better and there was no motive for him to yank out his own breathing tube. Norah refused to believe he'd done it.

Harriss had wanted to talk, and somebody had stopped him.

She began to pencil in assignments. In a homicide the track could be quickly obliterated. The longer it took to identify a suspect, the slimmer the chances of ever catching him became.

So she intended to use every man at her disposal and argue with Captain Jacoby later. Norah rested her elbows on the desk and cupped her chin in her hands. Was she moving too fast? As far as she knew now, there was no motive for untying Arnow's hands other than compassion. Certainly there were all kinds of motives for wanting Christina Isserman dead, and plenty of suspects to choose from. But why would someone want Harriss dead? The three incidents must be separated once and for all, or unquestionably linked.

So far, Norah had only the barest information about Clark Harriss. She knew only what she'd seen—that he was young, good-looking, determined, and that he'd been in an automobile accident. But who was he? What did he do for a living? Did he have a wife, girlfriend, family, friends? Who cared about Clark Harriss? Who didn't? He had turned to her for help and she had taken his hand in hers and promised to give it. This was not one of the jobs she could delegate.

Norah picked up the phone. Vincent Wadman wasn't in. On a hunch she asked to be put through to Intensive Care. She had to identify herself in order to get through, and again when the duty nurse answered.

"I'm sorry, Lieutenant Mulcahaney. Mr. Harriss died at one-thirty this afternoon."

"Oh, my God." Norah swallowed. She shook slightly with the cold of shock. "What was the cause?"

"Cardiac arrest. His heart failed. We tried to resuscitate. He didn't respond."

Norah's own heart skipped a couple of beats. "This happened while he was on the machine?"

"Yes, ma'am."

"Thank you." Slowly, Norah put the receiver down.

Clark Harriss had been brought in by emergency ambulance on the night of Tuesday the fifteenth. The day before the plug was pulled on Christina Isserman's respirator. The call to 911 was on record. The caller had been a woman, a friend. She came with him in the ambulance. While he was being treated, she provided the necessary information to Admissions and gave herself as the one to be notified in case of further emergency. Her address was the same as his. Norah asked if she had been notified and was told the hospital had not been able to reach Beatrice Fry as yet. She told them not to worry, she would do it herself.

It was an old-fashioned, Gothic-style building, only a little less ornate and a lot less gloomy than its neighbor, The Dakota. The apartment, Norah discovered, was owned by Beatrice Fry. When the doorman rang on the house phone, she answered. Maybe she worked at home. If so, then why hadn't she been home earlier when the hospital called? Norah set the question aside and rang the doorbell. The door was flung open almost immediately.

"You should have called first!" she admonished. "I was on my way out to meet a client. Never mind. My associate can do it."

Beatrice Fry was around twenty-five, short, overweight but not fat. She had a bland face, heart-shaped with a small nose and bright green eyes that protruded slightly. Her hair, worn loose to her shoulders, was without particular style, drab brown till she pulled the door wider and the light from the window cast a reddish aura around her head.

"Well, come in, Officer. I'm glad you're here, finally. I was just about ready to give up. I'd decided nobody was ever going to show."

"I don't know who you're expecting, but it's not me," Norah told her.

"Aren't you the police? The doorman said . . ."

"That's right." Norah produced her shield case.

Beatrice Fry squinted. "I don't have my contacts in," she apologized. "Lieutenant Mulcahaney? I didn't expect a lieutenant. Come in, please."

The big, high-ceilinged room overlooking the park was bright. Light poured on white walls, ornate molding, on a bare parquet floor, and seemed to spotlight the fireplace and its elaborately carved mantel. In contrast the furniture was stark. Functional. The few knickknacks were displayed on a small brass baker's rack. They left plenty of empty space on the shelves as well as in the room. There was no conflict between the opposing styles; rather, one served to accentuate the other. Beatrice Fry, dressed in a classic no-color linen skirt, bulky fisherman's sweater, and trendy laced ankle boots of aquamarine leather, was herself a dichotomy.

"You were expecting the police?"

"For three days now. The robbery happened Friday night. Well, call it Saturday morning. I came home from a movie after midnight and discovered my place had been broken into. I called 911. They said they'd send somebody around, but nobody came. I mean, no detectives."

"Would you mind reviewing the particulars for me?"

"Of course not. I've been wanting to talk to somebody. I mean, besides over the telephone."

"I'm sorry. Sometimes there just aren't enough officers to go around."

"They lost interest when they heard I didn't lose any real valuable jewelery or artworks or a lot of cash. I take it you people don't move for anything under five figures."

In essence the charge was true, though the figure varied. Or if there was violence involved. "I'm here now, Miss Fry," Norah placated. "Why don't you tell me about it."

The redhead heaved a sigh. The skirt had big pockets. She fumbled through the folds and brought out a battered pack of filter-tip Marlboros. She lit up, inhaled, then exhaled quickly, as though she didn't really enjoy the effect. "Like I said, I came home Friday a little after midnight. I was alone. The doorman had gone off duty, so I let myself in downstairs with my key. The second I got off the elevator on this floor I saw my apartment door was open. Well, it couldn't be Clark, that's my boyfriend . . ." She hesitated. "He lives here." She tried to toss it off casually but succeeded only in saying it loudly, defiantly. "It couldn't have been him, of course, because he's in the hospital. In fact, that's why I was out so late on my own. I'd been visiting Clark. The doctors were very optimistic. They'd said he'd be coming home soon. I was on a real high and I wanted to celebrate. There's not much a single girl can do on her own, so I went to a movie."

She had in that one sentence characterized herself, Norah thought, but made no comment. She had come to tell Beatrice Fry that her boyfriend was dead and suddenly the job became a lot tougher.

"I stood in the hall for a couple of minutes not knowing what to do," the girl continued. "I kept staring at the open door. I couldn't believe it had actually happened to me. I mean, the building has good security. I have the best locks." She indicated three separate devices, including a metal bar. "Actually, how they got in—they knocked out the bottom panel of the door and crawled through. Simple. So how come nobody heard them? I never found that out. When they were finished all they had to do was unlock the door from inside and walk out—with the loot."

She took another nervous drag on the cigarette, stared at it with distaste, and snubbed it out. She substituted movement to cover her agitation, instinctively acting out what she had done that night as she talked.

"It was a shambles in here. They turned over chairs, slit cushions. They destroyed my collection of glass animals." She pointed to the nearly empty baker's rack. "My father started me with a hollow glass deer when I was twelve—the kind with the tinted water inside? It wasn't worth anything in money. They swept the shelf clear; everything shattered, every single piece." Her pudgy face was pinched. "They didn't have to do that."

No, they didn't, Norah thought. It could have been anger at not finding anything of real value.

"It was worse in the bedroom," Beatrice Fry said. "They went through all my things. They scattered my underwear . . . piece by piece . . ." She flushed. "They . . . handled it. I felt violated."

"Most people do."

"After I got over the first shock, I called 911. Then it occurred to me that without a doorman anybody could buzz and claim to be the police, and I wouldn't know whether to let them in or not. So I went down to the lobby to wait. When they came, over half an hour later, the officers didn't even get out of the car."

That shocked Norah, but she said nothing.

"They told me it was a matter for the detectives and somebody would be around in the morning. I explained that my door was broken and I was afraid to stay in the apartment alone. Finally, they agreed to wait till I called and got somebody to come over and fix it."

Again, Norah didn't offer a defense. Technically, the officers had answered the complaint. They should have got out and examined the scene. They should also have shown some compassion. "Did you take their names?" she asked, and Beatrice Fry promptly opened a desk drawer and handed Norah a slip already prepared. "I'll look into it, Miss Fry." Now was the time to tell her about Harriss.

"I just don't know why they picked on me." The girl's compulsive volubility was an indication of her loneliness. "We don't keep large amounts of cash in the house. We don't have anything really valuable. I don't get it. Why us?"

Exactly what she'd been thinking herself, Norah mused. Usually the answer was because the job looked easy. *Usually.* Norah broke out into goose bumps.

"What exactly did they get?"

"I had a beautiful pearl necklace, eighteen inches long, fine cultured pearls, from my mother. They took that. Then there was a small diamond, half a carat but perfect; that was my mother's engagement ring. Those pieces were all I had left of her. Except this apartment, of course." The tears welled and flowed as Beatrice Fry gave in to an assortment of regrets. After a while, she pulled out a handkerchief from one of the capacious pockets and wiped her face. "I'm sorry. I've been doing a lot of crying lately and I don't know why." She offered an apologetic smile. "They took most of Clark's computer stuff out of his office. It was secondhand, but I suppose they can get a good amount for it. That was a stroke of luck for them. I mean, they couldn't have known he had it, could they? I mean, how could they? Then they went through his files. I tell you, they did a real number there. I couldn't even begin to sort everything out. Clark will have to do that when he comes home."

Now, Norah thought, now. She had to tell her. She couldn't wait another moment. "He works out of the house?"

"He has a regular job at Fuller, Yankiver, Selden, but he also has private clients and does their work from home. Clark's an accountant. Top drawer. He's got some really big clients."

"These private clients, would it have been their files that were broken into?"

"I don't know. I told you, I couldn't sort out the papers."

"But he does keep the files of these private clients here rather than in his regular office?"

"I assume so. He never said and I never asked. We don't pry into each other's business."

"Is it possible the break-in was specifically to get documents or confidential papers that Clark kept here?"

"I never thought of that. Sure. It makes sense. Clark never mentioned names, but he did talk about how prominent some of his clients are and how they cheat on their taxes—well, not cheat but misrepresent. He has a strong ethical sense and he doesn't like it. Also, I think he worries about his own culpability. He wants their business, but on the other hand, he doesn't like what he's required to do for them."

"Could that be why these people weren't handled directly through Fuller, Yankiver, Selden?" Norah suggested.

"Maybe . . ."

"Do you mind if I take a look at his office?"

In the days when the apartment had belonged to Beatrice Fry's mother the office had presumably been a second bedroom. Now it was strictly a working space. No studio couch, no plants, pictures, or fancy lamps to make a pretense of anything else. It was tidy, however, swept and dusted.

"I couldn't stand the mess. I stacked everything and stuffed it wherever I could find space," Beatrice Fry explained.

"I don't blame you." Norah went over to the nearest file cabinet and pulled out the top drawer. She riffled through the folders. Each was labeled, but the names meant nothing to her. "Would you mind if I sent someone over to take an inventory?"

There was a long silence, and when Norah looked up she

saw the girl's green eyes fixed on her. "Why don't you ask Clark?"

Norah took a deep breath.

"You didn't come here to investigate the robbery, did you? They don't send lieutenants on jobs like this. I knew that right from the start. It's about Clark, isn't it?"

"Yes. I'm sorry, Miss Fry. Clark Harriss died this afternoon."

"Dead? Clark is dead?"

"I'm sorry."

"What happened? He was doing so well. All the doctors said so. They said he was going to be all right. They promised me! What happened? Why are you here?"

She wasn't handling this well at all, Norah thought. "Beatrice, there's some uncertainty about the way Clark died."

"What does that mean—uncertainty? What? Just tell me straight out. Oh my God, please, just tell me." She pulled herself up straight. Despite the bulky sweater and ridiculous bright blue boots, sorrow dignified her. "I want to know how Clark died."

"His breathing tube was pulled out. The emergency team was called and was able to resuscitate him. But the damage had been too great. Twelve hours later he had a heart attack, and this time they couldn't do anything for him."

She said nothing. The tears did not come; they had already been used up. "He had his whole life ahead of him. We had our whole lives . . ." She broke off. "What do you mean, the tube was pulled out?"

"Exactly that."

She swayed. Norah put an arm around the girl and led her over to a chair.

"Why would anyone do such a thing?"

"I was hoping you could tell me."

"Me? No. I would if I could, believe me, but I don't know anything."

"Think. You may surprise yourself."

"I doubt it. The way it was with me and Clark . . . if

anybody had ever told me a man like him—handsome, smart, with a big job—would want me . . . Naturally, I dreamed about somebody like him, what girl doesn't, but I never thought it would be more than a dream. I was brought up old-fashioned. I can't help the way I am. My dad died when I was five and my mom dedicated herself to me. She drilled it into me what decent girls don't do. But when she was gone, I was so alone in this big apartment, night after night. I started to go to the singles bars. I was ashamed. I knew what my mother would have said, but I went. And I met Clark. Well, all the training, all the strictures, tenets, went out the window. I was just so grateful to have him. I wasn't going to make any demands on him or be possessive or suspicious. But I couldn't help that, either. Oh God, I tried hard not to show how I felt about him, to hide my jealousy.

"He used to get phone calls. From clients, he said. We'd be sitting home listening to Brahms, or Dvořák, Debussy—we're both into chamber music. Sometimes we'd watch the ball game. He's . . . he was . . . a Mets fan. I got to be one myself. Anyway, the phone would ring and he'd go. No matter what the time. Well, I kept quiet. All those other times, I kept quiet, my feelings bottled up. That night I couldn't. It was once too often. I couldn't go on like we were. I loved him too much. I didn't dare say it, of course.

"What I said was that he could go anywhere, anytime, but give me credit for some intelligence. How many times does an accountant get called out in the middle of the night? If he was seeing another woman, that was bad enough, but I couldn't stand his lying about it. We had a real bad fight. He said if I didn't trust him, there was no point in going on. Those were the words I'd been afraid to hear from the very first day, but I couldn't hold back. I told him unless we were honest with each other, we had nothing to keep us together. He cut me off. He said he didn't have any more time to argue, and we'd talk about it in the morning. I told him if he walked out there'd be nothing to talk about, and he shouldn't bother to come back."

She had shrunk inside her clothes and the blue boots were pathetic symbols of an ethic she had never really been comfortable with. "He hadn't been gone long, in fact, there was just barely time for him to have gone down in the elevator when I heard a terrible screeching of brakes in the street. Normally, I wouldn't have paid attention. I mean, it happens all the time, right? But something told me; a hot flash went through me. I ran over to the window and looked down. Clark was lying hunched on his side in the middle of the street. About a block down, a black car was speeding away.

"When the ambulance I rode with him and stayed in the waiting room till they told me he was out of danger. When I got home I took a couple of Miltowns and went to bed. It didn't occur to me till the next morning that Clark's girlfriend would probably have called back to find out why he hadn't showed. I checked his answering machine. I didn't like doing it, but I had to. There was no message from any woman."

She sat down, spent.

"There was no message from any client either."

The lights glowed softly in Christina Isserman's bedroom, creating a sense of warmth and intimacy amid the opulence. To the untrained eye, the French provincial furnishings might seem like any that could be found in a good department store, but the connoisseur would instantly recognize these as authentic. Even the coverings, rose silk faded to silver-gray, were either original or a meticulous recreation. The carpet was a large specially loomed Aubusson. The hospital equipment, including the respirator and cardiac monitor, was installed and stood to one side of the canopied bed, nearly lost amid the splendor. Christina was not connected; it was there in case of emergency only. She was not only breathing on her own, but her vital signs were normal and stable. When her husband looked in on her the evening of her return, she was out of bed and propped up in a large Jerry chair. This was an upholstered armchair covered in Naugahyde and set on small rubber wheels. It differed from the familiar canvas wheelchair in that the patient was better supported but could not operate it himself. Pillows supported her flaccid arms, a handmade afghan covered her stick legs, her head lolled to one side like a broken doll's. There was a special hydraulic lift, but since Christina was so wasted the nurse hadn't needed it to get her out of bed. She still used an IV, and the stomach-feeding tube was taped to the tip of her nose.

Walther stood silently in front of his wife for a long time. The shining glory of her blond hair was now so lackluster it seemed almost gray. Her skin was the color of putty. Her lips, bloodless. A vigorous, assertive woman, five foot seven, one hundred and thirty-five pounds, she had become shrunken, emaciated, a pathetic ninety-one. Christina was thirty-two years old; she looked sixty. Her large eyes, so flashing and demanding, were closed. Passion he had seen in those eyes, never love. But then what had she seen in his? he asked himself. And on a sudden impulse, spurred by regret, Walther bent down and kissed the raddled cheek. It was only a fleeting touch—his warm lips on her chill flesh—but the icy current passed straight through him. Once he had cared for Christie, he had believed they could make a life together, adapt to each other's needs and desires. Wishful thinking? Certainly. Each had wanted to bring the other around, each maneuvered for ascendancy; the result had been complete alienation. In the end Christina had cared more for her father and the money than for him. It was her obstinacy that had destroyed her. Walther thought back to the protracted drinking bouts and the earlier episodes of overdose, the days of coma. He had not imagined her condition could be worse than it had been then. Seeing her as she was, he had to grieve. How could anybody not grieve for her?

As he continued to study his unconscious wife, Walther Isserman thought he saw a slight quiver at the corner of her mouth, almost as though she were wincing. A grimace of pain? Or the start of a smile? Or course, it was neither. A nerve spasm? Even that was unlikely. It was only his imagination, a trick of light, a shifting of shadows. Quickly he turned and walked out into the corridor, shutting the door softly behind him.

He couldn't so easily shut Christie out of his mind.

As he sat across the dinner table from Lucine, his wife's

image came between them. He couldn't dispel it, not even afterward when they were in bed. Christina was with him as she had never been, not even in their courtship nor in the early days of their marriage when they were both trying to make a success of it. It frustrated his lovemaking and he was annoyed at Lucine's attempt to be understanding.

"I'd prefer it if you didn't make excuses for me, darling."

"Sorry, darling."

Abruptly, Walther swung his thin, strong legs over the side of the bed and stood up. "Want a drink?"

"All right," Lucine Northcott replied as her eyes roamed over him, caressing. He was tall and fit—stomach flat, shoulders broad; maybe a bit too bony, but otherwise he was perfect. He was everything Lucine had ever imagined a man could be; they matched in background and ethic; and oh God, how they matched sexually! Her first marriage had satisfied her because she didn't know any better. She'd been shocked and hurt when Marcus walked out. But she no longer agonized over the cause—whether the fault had been hers or his. Since she'd found Walther, it didn't matter. In fact, she thought as she watched Walther put on robe and slippers, she should thank Marcus.

Lucine hadn't expected ever to fall in love again, ever to make a commitment, certainly not to another woman's husband. And she had resisted. As soon as she realized she was beginning to care about Christina's second husband, that her pulse raced when he entered a room, that she flushed if he so much as glanced in her direction, she'd tried to avoid him. They moved in the same limited social world, so she studied the guest lists before accepting an invitation. When the affair was to be so select as to be dubbed intimate, she asked the hostess who else was coming. Her friends put the opposite interpretation on her questions. The gossip began before there was any basis for it. Walther was aware and became intrigued. He started looking for her, seeking her out. A lesser aristocrat himself, he recognized in her at least an equal. He respected her breeding and admired her elegance, as she did his. When love superseded, neither one could say.

Lucine lay in the bed, tawny hair spread out on the pillow, and called out softly. "Walther . . ."

"What?"

"She's perfectly safe. Well-attended. You know all that."

"I shouldn't have left her. Not the first night."

"First night, or second, or third, what difference does it make? She doesn't know. It can't matter to her."

Christina's image grew more vivid in his mind. He saw again that twitch at the corner of her mouth. A nervous spasm? Even that could be encouraging. "You haven't seen her propped up in that chair like a mummy. It's horrible."

It had been a mistake to urge him to come over tonight, Lucine thought. Maybe she shouldn't have gone along with him in his battle to bring Christina home. At the time, it had seemed the best thing. "I'm sorry, darling. It must be terrible for you."

"It is. It is. You have no idea. It's beyond anything I could have imagined." He was at the drinks tray, bottle in hand, but he paused. "Everybody thinks I was the one who pulled the plug on the respirator. Do you think so?"

"Darling, of course not. I know you would never do such a thing."

He nodded and poured their usual careful measure.

"Walther," Lucine called softly from the bed, willing him to turn and meet her look. "You know I didn't."

"Of course."

They held the look for several moments, then broke away at almost the same moment, neither completely satisfied.

"To tell you the truth, I don't think Sarah was the one either," Walther admitted in a more normal, matter-of-fact way. "She's jealous of Christina, but she wouldn't go that far. What's going on at Chazen-Hadley? You're there every day; you must know."

"I wasn't there that day."

"What are they saying?"

"They don't talk in front of me."

"They're blaming me, aren't they?"

"No. Actually, they're more concerned with the two patients

who pulled out their own tubes. They think there's some kind of fanatic loose."

"God!" He came over and handed her the drink. "I'm glad I got her out of there."

"Exactly. You got her out and now you know she's safe, so stop worrying. Christie's strong. We know that. She's breathing on her own, and eventually she'll come out of the coma as she has before." He wasn't listening. "Darling? Do you want to go home?"

"Would you mind?"

"Of course I mind, but I understand."

He came over and sat on the side of the bed and, putting his drink aside, raised her, naked, into his embrace. He nuzzled between her bare breasts. "You're beautiful and wonderful and the most understanding woman I've even known." The kisses moved up from her breasts to her mouth and lingered there. Then he broke free, dressing quickly.

His eagerness to get away was obvious, but she didn't comment.

When he was ready, Walther Isserman returned to the bed, kissed her again, almost chastely. She didn't make the mistake of trying to intensify or prolong the moment.

"I'll call you," he said.

"When?" She couldn't help that. It slipped out.

"As soon as I can. The way things are now, with Christina's condition . . . it wouldn't look good for us to be seen together. We have to be sensible."

"Why? What are people going to say that they haven't already said?"

"They haven't called me a murderer yet, not right out anyway. I'm going to make damn sure they don't have the chance."

Walther took the house elevator directly to the second floor of the duplex. Once he unlocked the entry door, his urgency eased. Reluctance took its place. He walked slowly down the wide gallery where a part of Theo Sexton's eclectic collection of paintings from the old mansion hung: Turner, Cassatt, van

Gogh, Wyeth. As he neared his wife's door, Isserman hesitated. The night nurse was with her, of course, had undoubtedly put her to bed by now. Christie was all right. There was no need to go in. No need to force himself to look at her again. He headed back to his own room.

But he was restless. For one thing, he wasn't accustomed to retiring so early and kept thinking of Christina on the other side of the connecting door. He tried to read the paper, but he had no interest in other people's troubles. At last he tossed it aside, arranged the pillows, and switched off the light.

The next thing Walther Isserman knew he was wide awake and staring into the darkness.

Obviously, he had fallen asleep and slept hard, the sleep of exhaustion. He thought that he had slept hours and that it must be close to morning. The illuminated dial of the bedside clock showed only one-thirty. What had awakened him? The street outside was silent. So was the house. Walther listened intently.

Nothing.

He closed his eyes tightly, determined to get back to sleep, but despite himself he continued to listen.

Then he heard it. A sigh. Elusive, but unmistakable. Then a whisper.

"Walther . . . What have you done to me, Walther?"

His eyes flew open. He was alone. For the second time that night, Walther Isserman got out of a bed and reached for his robe. Putting it on, he headed for the connecting door. Quietly, but quickly, he pulled it open.

Only the night-light shone in his wife's room. It illumined her face. Her hands were folded across her chest rising and falling as she breathed normally.

The nurse started up from a light doze. "Is anything the matter?" she whispered. "Mr. Isserman?" She got up from her chair and went over to him. "What's happened?"

"Nothing. Nothing," he assured her, continuing to stare down at his wife's unmoving form. "I thought I heard a noise," he told the nurse. "I must have been dreaming."

Walther Isserman spent the rest of the night wide-eyed, waiting for dawn. He quelled his impatience to get up till seven-thirty, then forced himself to take the time to shower, shave, and dress. He wanted the visit to appear normal, absolutely. He intended to betray no hint of his anxiety, but he trembled as he approached his wife's bed again.

Christina looked the same; if anything, her color was worse—clayish, but that could be the natural light of the gray morning. She lay in the now familiar half-crouch on her left side, mouth slack, eyes closed—unconscious. Yet he couldn't help feeling she was aware of his presence. He drew closer; he leaned down, bent close. Nothing. No indication of awareness. Straightening, he turned away satisfied that there was no change, that indeed he had been dreaming last night. On his way out he felt the cold tingling of the spine that warns one is being watched. He whirled around.

What was he trying to do—catch her out? He must be crazy, Walther Isserman thought, his breath coming heavily, the surge of blood heating his cheeks. Yet he went back and examined Christina once more for traces of sentience. Then he moved away to test her once more. This time when he spun around, he thought he detected a flickering of her eyelids. They were not as tightly shut as they had been. Could she be slyly observing him through the narrow slits? No, that was paranoid. He was becoming paranoid. He needed to get out of here, go to work, at least get out and get some fresh air into his lungs and clear his head. But he didn't leave the apartment the entire day.

That night Walther had an early dinner served in the first-floor study and followed it with several drinks. He put one of the endless number of news programs on the television and fell asleep in front of the set. He woke at eleven and stumbled up the stairs to his room, where he stripped off his clothes, left them in a pile on the floor, and, naked, lurched into bed. Drifting toward sleep and oblivion, the bed heaving under him, the room spinning, he heard his name.

"Walther?"

He was afraid to open his eyes, afraid of what he would see.

"Walther? What have you done to me, Walther?"

The words were hardly more than a moan in the dark, yet he had no doubt of what was said or who had spoken. He tried to answer, but his vocal chords froze. After several attempts, he managed to grunt. "Christina?"

A click, then the sound of a door closing softly, his door to the hall. He opened his eyes then and sprang out of bed, running to fling it open. The dimly lit gallery was empty.

He stood there naked, drenched with sweat. A nightmare. The whole damned thing was a nightmare. He'd had too much to drink. Just the same, he crept along the hall to the other bedroom and silently edged the door open. Christina was in bed, lying peacefully on her back, eyes closed, breathing in the regular, somewhat shallow rhythm he was beginning to recognize. Just like last night. Relieved, Walther looked to the night nurse. She was slumped in her chair, eyes closed, mouth open, snoring.

His impulse was to go over and wake her. Reprimand her. She wasn't being paid to sleep on the job! She was supposed to keep an eye on Christina. But he didn't even call out. His wife might be improving, even returning to consciousness, but there was no way she could get out of her bed and walk down the corridor to his room.

He had to be close to the edge to even consider it.

He didn't realize he was shivering till his teeth started to chatter.

One thing he knew with certainty—he wasn't going to sleep again and risk another dream. He did go back to his room to put on a pair of pajamas, then returned and pulled up a chair to the side of his wife's bed. Her color was better, he thought. Somehow, her whole aspect seemed improved. More normal.

He sat beside her for the rest of the night.

When he awoke the next morning, her eyes were wide open. She was staring at him.

Lucine Northcott waited two days for Walther to telephone. He didn't. At noon of the third day, she called his office and was told he wouldn't be in. Miss Schubart had no idea when to expect him. Lucine considered calling him at home, then decided to give him a little more time to call her first. By six o'clock that night she put pride and policy aside and dialed.

The housekeeper answered and said she'd get him. It took a long while. When the phone was picked up again, it wasn't Walther but May Wrede.

"I'm sorry, Mrs. Northcott, I was in error. Mr. Isserman is not at home."

CHAPTER ELEVEN

Norah assigned Gus Schmidt to examine the records Clark Harriss had kept on his private clients. Arenas was sent to the firm of Fuller, Yankiver, Selden, where Harriss had been employed. Ferdi was getting all the assistance he needed from the staff there; Gus had nobody. Not that he was complaining or asking for help. Gus was thorough, patient—plodding. Norah was the impatient one.

She called down to the duty sergeant. "I need to borrow one of your people. Jordan. Can you spare her?"

"She's all yours, Lieutenant."

"Thanks. Tell her to report to Detective Schmidt."

Norah sat back and thought about Audrey Jordan for a moment. A different kind of assignment might help get her over her shock, show her another side of police work. She stared at the wall, water-stained, grimy, cracked. She should get it painted. What a hope! You couldn't get maintenance to change a light bulb without a requisition in triplicate. She could put up photographs to cover the worst places, as her predecessors had done. The few pictures Norah had brought in and propped on the desk kept getting shoved to one side or knocked over. They, and others along with them, should be hung properly. They should be on view for herself and for everybody who came into the office. Her office. She had been inhabiting it as though it were borrowed, temporary. It was time to make it her own.

Unfortunately, that would take more than a hammer and a few nails. What she needed, Norah thought, was to get a firm grip on this case that wasn't a case. She knew she had been hand-picked by Jim Felix for the assignment. She wasn't producing. He hadn't said a word. He would never pressure her. The pressure came from within herself. She was not satisfied with her performance. For the first time in her career, Norah was giving orders, not taking them. She couldn't pass on the responsiblity; it was hers. Once and for all, she had either to separate the three cases or find the link.

Start at the beginning. Start with Arnow. Had his hands worked loose? Having examined patient after patient, Norah judged the knots were too secure and the patients, semiconscious at best, were too feeble and uncoordinated to be capable of loosing them. It was time to interview the Arnows' daughter, she decided. Norah was not as interested in ferreting facts as she was in getting a feel for the emotional climate of the Arnow family. Impressions were most valid firsthand; she would go herself.

It was a fine, bright day in May, a day that would have done June proud. Driving across the Queensboro Bridge, Norah felt as though she were suspended between clear sky and glittering water. For the first time since officially taking over her new duties she felt confident. She was headed out to do the kind of work she felt comfortable doing, that she enjoyed. She found the address easily and parking was no problem. She got out of the car and took a few moments to look the house over. It was newly constructed, modest, two-family, brick, on the smallest plot in the area. She walked up the flagstone path and rang the bell.

The woman who came to the door was about thirty, gaunt and tired-looking. Once she had been pretty—maybe a month ago, maybe a couple of years. She wore baggy brown pants, a creased white shirt with the tails outside. A faded red bandana covered her hair; the wisps that escaped were as dispirited as the rest of her.

"Lieutenant Mulcahaney." Norah showed her ID. "I'm sorry to intrude on you at this time."

Julia Loeb sighed heavily. "I thought it was all over. I thought the autopsy . . . They said they had to do it because my mother died unattended."

"Yes, that's right."

"But then I thought it would be over."

"I'm not here about your mother," Norah told her.

The woman gasped. What little color there was in her face drained, leaving her an unhealthy gray.

"May I come in?"

After the brightness outside, the room seemed gloomy. Actually, it was a cheerful place. Norah admired the blue and lavender flowered slipcovers and matching drapes. A bowl of blue hyacinths and yellow daffodils on the center coffee table accented the scheme. Through the latticed windows Norah could see beds of flowers. Apparently Mrs. Loeb cared more about the appearance of her house than of her own person. The housekeeping and gardening could be therapy. Norah knew all about that—she'd used housework as relief plenty of times. She felt sympathy for the daughter bereft of both parents, one within a week of the other.

"I came about your father."

"Dad? He's dead. They're both dead. They both suffered and now they're at peace. Can't you leave them alone?"

"We need to fix the responsibility for your father's death."

"My father took his own life. He chose to die. It was his right. I don't care who made it possible. Or how it happened. I don't care who brought it about. I told the hospital that. I'm not interested in bringing charges."

"The hospital is concerned that it might happen again."

"Again? How could it? I don't understand."

"Mrs. Loeb, two basically similar incidents have occurred since your father's death. In one, the plug of the respirator was pulled; in the other, the breathing tube was dislodged." Julia Loeb shook her head in awe. "So if you know anything at all about what happened to your father . . ."

"I know he wanted to die. He indicated it to me clearly. There was no possibility of misunderstanding his intent. He had a right to make the decision," she reiterated firmly, and having done so, closed her thin mouth as though she had no intention of saying another word.

Norah had lost her father a little over a year ago. Patrick Mulcahaney had cancer and he'd wanted to die at home. The family thought he should stay in the hospital and continue to receive every treatment available. So Mulcahaney had taken matters into his own hands. One night, he'd got himself out of bed, dressed, and simply walked out into the middle of a February ice storm. He died of pneumonia, a direct result of exposure. "You visited your father the afternoon of his death, isn't that right?"

"Yes."

"Did you untie your father's hands?"

Julia Loeb seemed saddened by the question rather than surprised. She considered a long time, but Norah had the sense she was weighing not so much the answer but how Norah would receive it. Then, shrugging, she gave up trying to guess.

"No. I didn't have the guts."

Her sigh shook her whole being. "He asked me to. That is, he indicated it was what he wanted. The last time I saw him, he was strapped to the bed, hooked to all those machines. He wanted to tell me something, but he couldn't talk because of the tube down his throat. I thought he wanted a pad and pencil to write with. The nurse got them for him. She untied one hand, but when she put the pencil in it he held it like a knife and made a stabbing motion toward his heart—up then down, up then down, over and over, more and more violently. I was shocked. Horrified. I tried to bolster his courage. I told him he was going to be all right. I assured him. I told him the worst was nearly over. I said, 'You'll be out of here soon.' He looked at me with the saddest eyes I've ever seen. There was sorrow in them and pain and disappointment. The nurse tied his hand again and he turned his head away from me. I left. I walked out of there. I couldn't wait to get out of there." Julia Loeb sank slowly into the nearest chair, a drab, unkempt figure in the clean, cheery room. She began to cry desperately—for a duty shirked, a responsibility avoided.

"The nurse provided the pencil; she must have seen how he used it. Do you think she might have helped him later on?"

The tears continued to flow but they didn't heal. "No. I told Mom. I told her how it had been, in detail. He had asked *me*, but I transferred the burden. I put it on her. She visited him right after me, that night. Mom was so grateful for every little thing, every little concession, that people were willing to be kind to her. She was unobtrusive, so they let her stay late. Before leaving, she loosed the gauze binding on Dad's hands, but in such a way they would appear still tied."

"As you said, it was your father's decision."

"He asked *me*, not Mom! I should have done it. Now I'm responsible for both their deaths."

"Did your mother tell you she was going to do it, or had done it?"

"No."

"Then how do you know?"

"Because I know her and I know how much she loved my father. In their whole life together, Mom never once denied him anything he wanted or needed. And he never would have wanted her to get into trouble, that's why he waited so long. He didn't want to involve her. That's why he lay there and waited and picked his time to die."

Norah's next stop was the Fry apartment. It was well after four but she had no doubt Gus and Jordan were still working. When she rang, Gus came to the door.

Detective August Schmidt was heavyset, medium height, blond hair turned nearly silver. His square face was heavily lined. He squinted through the metal-framed glasses he wore well down on his nose. They were for close work only; Gus's distance vision still met department standards.

Facing him across the threshold and out of the familiar environment of the squad room, Norah was suddenly aware that he was old. Not middle-aged. Not anymore. In that brief moment of realization, Norah also acknowledged that he had made a difficult transition unusually well. There were two kinds of cops: street cops and desk cops. Mostly, it was the desk cops that got promoted. They studied and prepared for their exams largely on department time. There were lieutenants, even captains, raised to rank through civil service, who had never made an arrest or fired a gun except on a police range. These cops continued on "active" duty well into the second or third tour. The street cops, worn out physically and emotionally and nervously, couldn't take the boredom of inside work. When they got old, they retired. Gus was an amalgam. He had experienced the danger and the excitement, and the monotony too, of the street. Always working "by the book" and scrupulously attentive to detail, he discovered he enjoyed searching records and examining documents. He learned bookkeeping and discovered a flair for math. At last he was doing what he might have done when he was younger—studying for the sergeant's exam. But Gus was doing it on his own time. He'd make it, too, Norah thought, with years of useful service still ahead.

"Lieutenant." Gus beamed at Norah. Though he regarded her as a daughter, he was always very formal in their work relationship. Alone, he let his feelings show—a little.

"How's it going?"

"So far all I've got is a list of the clients whose records were left, no indication of what was taken." He led the way into Harriss's bare office. Beatrice Fry had restored order by putting everything out of sight. Gus had brought it all out again and organized it. Stacks of paper were neatly lined up on a long trestle table—where he had obtained it, Norah had no idea.

"I'm more or less auditing each account. So far I've found no indication of illegality in anything that's here."

"I see. Where's Jordan?"

"I sent her home. I didn't know whether you wanted her to log overtime."

"If you need her . . ."

"It's not that big a job."

Something in his tone was puzzling. "Whatever you say, Gus."

He hesitated. "The truth of it is, Norah, between you and me—Officer Jordan isn't suited to this kind of work. She's got a short attention span. She's restless."

Norah was surprised on two counts. First, it was unusual for

Gus to be critical, particularly of a rookie. Second, she'd been anticipating strong approval of Jordan. "She's been doing good work," she commented mildly.

"I'm not questioning that, Lieutenant."

Norah frowned at the shift back to formality. "What happened? Come on, Gus. I asked for Jordan particularly because I thought she'd be good on this. I thought she had promise. If I've misread her, I'd like to know."

"It was her attitude. I put her to work drawing up charts of individual holdings looking for an overlap. When I checked to see how she was making out, I found omissions and errors. Sloppy work. If there's one thing essential in this type of job, it's accuracy. Or in any police work for that matter."

"Right. Of course. But she's new."

"She didn't want to learn, Norah. She didn't try. She acted like it was beneath her. She said she wasn't feeling well, so I sent her home. I'm sorry. If I'd known you had an interest . . ."

Norah started to deny it, then changed her mind.

"In a way, I did. She reminds me a little of myself. She's having a problem, and I thought a change of duty and working with you . . . Apparently, I was wrong." She shrugged. "So. Let's take a look at that list."

Glad to be finished with an awkward subject, Gus handed it over. "Those are the names of the clients whose records were left behind. The name you want probably isn't on it."

"It wouldn't be," Norah agreed. "So what do we do next?"

"We check through Harriss's own accounts receivable."

"You mean whoever broke in didn't take it? Just pulled the client files?"

"Probably didn't even know enough about accounting to realize there is such a thing." Gus grinned.

"Fantastic." She grinned back.

"There's always the possibility that Harriss didn't keep honest books," Gus cautioned. "But fortunately, he was in the process of transferring data to the computer. So he still had all his canceled checks, deposit slips—the works."

"Gus, you're brilliant!"

"That remains to be seen."

"So, where do we start?"

"Not you, Norah. You shouldn't be wasting your time on stuff like this. I can manage."

"It's no waste of time. I think Clark Harriss was killed for certain confidential information he had about one of his clients. He didn't appreciate its importance, not till later, after he was run down." Norah frowned, thinking back to her visit to the IC unit and the effort Harriss had made to communicate to a stranger—a police officer.

"The break-in took place after the alleged accident. The evidence was removed, but the witness still lived. Somehow the perpetrator found out Harriss had tried to talk to me and that I promised to see him again. I believe Clark Harriss was basically an honest man, that he kept honest books, and that we are going to find what we need—easily."

And they did. Going back six months, they came up with the name of a client who had been in arrears on his bill for half a year, then suddenly paid in full.

Walther Isserman.

CHAPTER TWELVE

From the morning when Walther awoke to find Christina's eyes open and on him, he was never far from her side. What sleeping he did, was in the chair beside her bed. During the first few days he left her to shower and change and even took fifteen or twenty minutes for a walk in the park across the street. Then he gave up the walks. He had his meals served in her room. He slept in his clothes and didn't bother to change.

He accepted calls from his office, no others. Not even from Lucine. When Sarah Hoyt came, he refused to let her see her sister. He physically blocked her way up the stairs to the second floor.

"I'll get a court order to remove Christie from your care. I'm taking her out of here," Sarah railed.

"Why don't you talk to her doctor first? Find out what kind of care she's getting? He'll tell you Christina's getting the best care. The best. She's on her way to recovery."

"Recovery!" Sarah Hoyt was patently unbelieving.

"Full recovery."

"Then why won't you let me see her?"

"Because you're a disturbing influence. Because I don't trust you. Because I don't trust anybody."

Within the week he fired all three nurses. Alone, without the help of even May Wrede or McCullough, Isserman cared for his wife. He bathed and dressed and fed her. He moved her from the bed to the chair in the morning and returned her to the bed at night. She was eating well, putting on weight. When the doctor came for his regular visit, Walther turned him away.

"Your services are no longer required," he informed Orin Lomason, the physician he had personally selected to replace Jeremy Kuhn.

"He can't be forced to have a physician attend his wife," Lomason explained to Sarah Hoyt when she appealed to him for help. "Nor can I in good conscience sign any kind of paper recommending she be removed from his custody. He's devoting himself to her care."

Sarah Hoyt licked her lips. "He says she's going to make a full recovery. Is that possible?"

Lomason sighed. "A week ago I would have said it was beyond possibility. Now . . . I don't know."

"Is she really that much improved? Is she fully conscious? Can she talk? Walk?"

He raised a hand. "Unquestionably, she's better. She responds to stimuli. She's taking regular food—a soft diet, of course. But consciousness in the sense you mean . . . I see no signs of it."

"Mrs. Northcott! Oh, ma'am, it's so good to see you."

May Wrede cried out, distress deeply etched on her plain face. The tears filled her brown eyes and were magnified by the thick lenses of her glasses.

As soon as she entered the foyer with its Italian marble floor and the graciously curving staircase she had herself designed, Lucine felt all her vague worries and unnamed fears intensify. On the surface, everything appeared normal—at least the place was clean, dusted, the chandelier sparkling, the wall sconces lit, fresh flowers on the console. Yet a sense of desolation pervaded it all. No, worse than that. Instinctively, she looked upstairs to the gallery. She was so familiar with it. She had selected the paintings, every chair and ornament; she would have noticed immediately if a single thing were out of place.

The rigid order only added to her dread. A miasma of decay seemed to seep from the upper floor, as palpable as smoke from a smoldering fire.

Lucine broke into a cold sweat. Her teeth chattered. Willing herself to stop shaking, she put a hand on the banister and started up.

"No! No, Mrs. Northcott! No. Don't go up there," the housekeeper cried out.

"Why not?"

"Nobody's allowed. He won't let anybody go up there. We're not even permitted up there to clean or to take the meals up." The dumpy little woman was actually trembling.

"Go back to your room, Wrede. Leave everything to me."

"Please be careful, ma'am. He's . . . Mr. Isserman . . . he's not himself."

"What's going on down there?"

Both women looked up. Wrede cringed in anticipation of a tirade. Lucine Northcott gasped, first in shock and then in anguish.

The change in Walther Isserman was appalling. He had a heavy dark beard—matted, unshaped, unkempt. His hair was greasy; his clothes rumpled and dirty. His trousers were soiled. He smelled. From where she stood, Lucine could smell the rancid body sweat. But worse than all of that were his eyes— his dark, red-rimmed, haunted eyes.

Her heart ached for him. She took a step up. "Walther . . ."

He ignored her. He was standing a mere half dozen steps above her, but he looked past her as though she weren't even there and spoke directly to the housekeeper. "I told you not to let anybody in."

"I'm sorry, sir."

"What good does that do?"

"It wasn't her fault, Walther," Lucine intervened. "I insisted."

It was as though she hadn't spoken. "Sorry doesn't mean a damn, Wrede! I told you *no one*. I told you I didn't want to be disturbed. I told you nobody was to come upstairs. Nobody. That doesn't mean you're to exercise judgment. I'm not

interested in your opinion or McCullough's. You work for me
and you'll do what I order or find yourselves other jobs.
Understood?"

"Yes, sir."

"Now get back to your quarters." He turned and started up
the stairs.

"Walther!"

He kept going.

"Walther . . ." Lucine ran up far enough to reach out, but
something told her to stop before actually touching him. "Let
me help you, Walther," she pleaded. He turned then and
looked down at her. At least, she thought, he's not screaming at
me. With a quick look over her shoulder, she whispered. "Go
to your room, Wrede. Go on."

She waved May off, then looked up to Isserman standing
just two steps above her. He hadn't moved, but he raised his
arms at the side to bar her way. What should she do? How
should she handle this agitated man obviously on the edge of a
breakdown, perhaps already over the line?

"Darling, why don't you come downstairs with me? Let's go
into the study and have a drink. I think you could use one. I
know I could."

Slowly, he let his arms drop. There was recognition in his
eyes, but something else too that her presence hadn't dispelled,
not yet. "Christina's getting better, Luci. She's coming out of
it."

"That's good news. Very good news."

"Yes. She's able to walk—with my help. And she's able to
feed herself."

"It's hard to believe."

His eyes flamed wildly. "It's true."

"Of course, of course it's true. It seems like a miracle. You
deserve a lot of credit."

"No. She did it herself, all herself. She came to me in the
night to show me she could get well. But she needed me beside
her. Just me. Nobody else. She didn't want anybody else
around, not the nurses, not the doctors. And she forgave me."

"For what? Neither one of us is to blame for what's
happened. You say she's curing herself, but she's also the one

who got herself into this condition. You know that. She's responsible. She was drinking before you ever met her and she was on drugs before you and I became close." Lucine put out her hand. "Come on, darling, let's go get that drink and you can tell me all about it." He didn't respond, so she placed her hand lightly on his arm. When he didn't repel her, she dared to take his hand into both of hers and squeeze. Gently then, she started to draw him toward her. She must get him down those stairs before he lost himself again amid his phantoms.

But it was too late.

For a moment, just a moment, Lucine thought she had won. At her touch, Walther's contorted face had eased, his eyes engaged hers and he seemed almost normal. Then, all at once, he stiffened. His eyes left hers and turned up toward the door at the top of the stairs. "I'm sorry. I can't. She needs me. She's calling me."

"I don't hear anything."

"I do."

"Oh, Walther, darling, you can't go on like this. Let me help you."

"I don't need your help."

"Let me help you both. Let me come up and see Christie."

"No!"

He shook her off. "You'll have to leave now."

Again he fixed on her, and this time there was no doubt that he knew her. He was quite lucid. "Don't come back, Luci. I'm sorry, but it has to end between us. If you come again, I'll refuse to see you."

She offered no more arguments. She didn't plead. She did wait till he turned from her and climbed to the landing. She waited until he opened the door of his wife's bedroom.

"Walther . . ."

The voice floated light, high, sweet . . . demanding. Was it Christie's voice? Lucine Northcott didn't recognize it.

"Walther . . ."

He slipped inside and the door clicked softly shut behind him.

"Walther . . ."

Had she really heard it? Was she imagining things? In the

last exquisite agony of loss, was she the one who called out his name?

Norah called Walther Isserman's office several times, only to be told he wasn't in and wasn't expected. Now that a connection had been established between him and Clark Harriss, Isserman must be considered a suspect—not only for the attempted murder of his wife, but also for the murder of the accountant. While Gus continued to investigate Isserman's financial position, Norah assigned Arenas to check out Walther's alibis for the time of the hit-and-run and the incident in the IC unit that ultimately resulted in Harriss's death. She put Wyler on Lucine Northcott. Could the two of them, husband and mistress, have been working together to eliminate the wife? A classic situation. Each could even have handled certain incidents alone, giving the other an alibi for any particular event. A standard variation.

Meanwhile, as head of Homicide Fourth Zone, Norah had to keep current. Four new cases had fallen within her jurisdiction during the past weeks. Two were family quarrels—one ended in a knifing and the other a strangulation. Both were quickly cleared. The third was drugs-related. She had the cooperation of the Narco squad on that; they were doing the canvass and interrogation of known pushers and addicts. In the fourth, there was no obvious suspect. It was the kind of crime the police referred to as a "mystery" and which required a full investigative effort. Brennan was carrying. She had no excuse to put off her paperwork.

It was the same old thing, Norah thought, her mind wandering—she didn't have enough outside interests. She got through the holiday weekend by working. Now it was quitting time and she knew she would stay on because she had nowhere in particular to go. She was alone too much. She thought of Gary. Maybe she should call Gary Reissig. Her hand was on the phone. What would she say? The last time they'd seen each other he made it clear he wanted a commitment. She wasn't any more ready to give it now than she had been then. Nothing had changed.

There was a knock at her door.

"Come."

Audrey Jordan entered. She approached diffidently a couple of steps, then stopped. She was wearing her blues. The uniform was clean, pressed, but not worn as it should be, Norah thought—with pride. Jordan slumped. Her lower lip was thrust forward. She was wan, listless.

"Can you spare a few minutes, Lieutenant?"

"Yes. As a matter of fact, I've been wanting to talk to you." She didn't offer a chair.

"Yes, ma'am." Jordan licked her lips nervously. "I came to thank you for selecting me for special assignment with Detective Schmidt and to apologize for the mess I made of it."

"Detective Schmidt is the one you should apologize to. He had to review your work and do it over."

"Yes, ma'am, I know that. He told me I should come to you because you chose me and I let you down."

Norah's eyebrows arched. "What got into you, Jordan?"

"I don't know, Lieutenant. I just don't know. I was sitting there going over those names and those columns of figures and I thought: What am I doing here? This is the kind of work I joined the force to get away from. I'm not a clerk. I'm not a bookkeeper. I'm a cop. And then I thought: But I'm too scared to do a real cop's job."

Norah sighed. "We've been over this before, Audrey."

"Yes, Lieutenant. I know you were trying to show me there are many sides to police work. I appreciate that, but the thing is, I don't want help. I don't mean to be ungrateful, but if I'm going to make it, I want to do it on my own."

"Assuming you overcome your problems and stay on, just what is your goal in the department?"

"Well, I'd like to make detective." She swallowed. "I want to be like you."

That was totally unexpected, and for a moment Norah didn't know what to say. "I didn't do it alone, you know. I had plenty of help."

"You mean because you married a cop?"

"I wasn't thinking of Joe specifically." Norah's stern look eased and the hard line of her jaw relaxed. "I learned from him, of course, as much by his example as what he taught me specifically. But there were others. So many others. I can't begin to tell you the people who showed me the ropes, gave me tips, covered for me when I messed up. Cops at every level gave me a hand. They were willing to teach me as long as I was willing to learn."

Audrey looked down. "I guess I don't make friends easily."

"Are you an only child?" Audrey nodded. "What's it like for you at home?" Norah thought of her father's early disapproval of the job. "Is your family supportive?"

"My mom and dad are on the coast. They're actors. I live alone."

"Actors?"

"They wanted me to go into the business, but I don't have any talent. I don't really like it. I don't know what I like."

Norah smiled for the first time since the conversation began. "You just haven't found yourself yet. You're brooding too much. Get out of yourself. Get a roommate. Take up tennis, skiing, bridge . . ." She stopped. The prescription was for herself as much as for the young woman standing in front of her desk. "You know what? I have an idea." She hesitated, then plunged. "Why don't you move in with me?"

Audrey Jordan stared.

"I've got a big apartment. Too big." Norah ran on, a bit stunned by what she'd started and afraid to stop. "I have an extra bedroom. My niece uses it occasionally, but Toni's off to a summer camp job in a week or so, and then she'll be going back to school. So it's empty and going to waste. What do you say?"

Jordan made a couple of false starts. "How would it look?"

"What do you mean, 'how would it look?'"

"You're a lieutenant."

"What's that got to do with it?"

"People would talk."

"About what?" Norah snapped. "I don't see that your rank or mine has anything to do with it. If you would feel uncomfortable, that's something else. Forget it." She was already regretting the suggestion. She'd acted on impulse, always a mistake. "Forget it."

Audrey didn't move. "We could try," she said finally.

Norah said nothing.

"See how it works."

By now Norah had decided she'd made a big mistake. She was annoyed with herself for getting into the situation and looked for a way out. "You're not going to offend me by saying no."

"I was just concerned for you, Lieutenant."

Norah believed her and her spirits lifted. "If you're going to be my roommate, you'd better call me Norah."

Audrey's smile barely got started before another qualm turned it off. "I want to pay my fair share of the rent."

"I expect you to," Norah replied. It was going to work, she thought. She was excited.

Repeated calls to Isserman's office brought the same answer. Norah tried the apartment and was told by May Wrede that Mr. Isserman wasn't taking any calls. Norah insisted the housekeeper inform him it was the police. Still, he refused to answer. What was going on?

She went to see his secretary.

Elsie Schubart was in her early fifties. Her dark hair was completely clear of any gray. Her full face was almost unlined—if the secretary hadn't been so conservative Norah might have suspected a face-lift. She had the calm look of one who has control of her own destiny. A graduate of Katherine Gibbs School, Elsie Schubart was proud of her proficiency and, as a member of a prominent Boston family, she considered herself the social equal of her boss. She had never married and lived with her mother, but she showed none of the spinster's bitterness. She gave every indication of being satisfied with the arrangement of her life.

Her reluctance to answer Norah Mulcahaney's questions was a matter of principle, for she was impressed with the lieutenant. Obligation to Isserman dictated caution; admiration for Norah and identification with her as a successful career woman made her want to cooperate. Sensing the witness's struggle, Norah chose a roundabout approach.

"I'm concerned about Clark Harriss's death. You've heard about it? Good. I need to learn something about him as a person as much as about his association with Mr. Isserman. I understand Mr. Isserman was a private client. Where did they transact their business—at Mr. Harriss's residence or here?"

"Mr. Harriss came here."

It appeared the secretary felt no constraint on this subject. "What did you think of him?"

"Competent. Enterprising. Pleasant."

"Was Mr. Isserman satisfied with his work?"

A slight drawing back. "He never said otherwise."

"Did Mr. Harriss also handle Mrs. Isserman's accounts?" She already knew the answer to that.

"They kept their financial affairs completely separate. Mrs. Isserman's personal account is handled by the same firm that keeps the books for Sexton Industries."

Norah sensed disapproval and judged it was for the wife rather than the arrangement. "How did Mr. Isserman come to select Mr. Harriss?"

"I don't know."

"Why go to Harriss direct rather than to the firm for which he worked—Fuller, Yankiver, Selden?"

"I don't know, Liuetenant."

"In going through Mr. Harriss's records we find that Mr. Isserman was in arrears by nearly six months, then suddenly paid in full. Can you explain?"

Ice crystals formed.

"You're the one who makes out the checks, aren't you? I assume it's part of your job."

She couldn't deny it.

"So Mr. Isserman must have given you instructions."

"You're putting me in a difficult position, Lieutenant."

"I'm investigating murder, Miss Schubart. Was Walther Isserman broke?"

The elegant secretary made a face at the term. "He had a cash-flow problem." With a gusty sigh and a turning outward of her beautifully cared-for hands, she indicated surrender. "As you say—he was close to bankruptcy. He owed rent and utilities; I was in doubt that he could keep this office going much longer. To tell the truth, I'd started to put out job feelers. I told him, regretfully, that unless he could pay me some of my back salary I would have to leave."

"Apparently he did pay you."

"Oh yes."

"And the rest of his creditors?"

"All of them."

"Where did the money come from?"

Elsie Schubart merely sighed.

"Could he have got it from Mrs. Isserman?"

"No." Her lips closed in that tight, immutable line.

"Where did he get the money to go into business originally?
You don't start a shipping line without considerable capital."

"Mrs. Northcott was his principle financier, but he didn't
need all that much at the start. You've heard of the 'Cruise to
Nowhere'? That was Mr. Isserman's concept. He was the
originator. He was able to charter a liner that would otherwise
have been out of service during the winter, and he began
modestly. It caught on quickly."

"Yes."

"His next idea was to fly passengers to a southern port,
giving them added time in the sun and sparing them days of
cruising in cold waters. He worked the tie-in with the airlines
to offer reduced fares to passengers booked on his ships. He
had three ships plying the route between San Juan and Trinidad
from October through March."

"Surely he made money."

"Oh yes, but he wasn't satisfied. He wanted to go a step
farther. It was his dream to restore transatlantic travel by ship.
Transatlantic passenger travel had been a family business and
tradition. He wanted no more charters. He swung a big loan
with a California bank and bought a ship—the old *Conte di
Parma*. He refurbished it to the tune of three and a half million
and renamed it the *Re Umberto* after one of Italy's kings."

"That was Isserman's ship?"

Elsie Schubart nodded. "You know what happened."

Everybody knew. It was a modern saga of the sea,
combining tragedy and heroism, disaster and miracle, on a par
with the sinking of the *Andrea Doria* off Nantucket. But this,
Norah remembered, happened much farther from home.
Somehow (it was never discovered how) the *Re Umberto* lost
control of its rudder just off the shore of Brittany. It is a coast

whose dangers cannot be charted; there are too many rocks, crags, reefs, islets impossible to spot till white water, and then, of course, it's too late. The *Re Umberto* struck and went down with the loss of thirty-four. The rest were saved by a flotilla of rescue craft, mostly from the nearby Scillies. Inevitably, cries of negligence arose. Isserman Shipping was sued. Design, maintenance, operation, and repair of the steering gear were blamed. In the end the damages were relatively minimal and the insurance company covered them, but the investors were wiped out and the bank lost its security when the ship went down.

"Mr. Isserman was absolved of any blame. Sexton Industries even offered him his old job back. He refused," Elsie Schubart told her.

He had been both proud and stubborn, Norah thought. "Have you any idea when he'll be coming in?" she asked.

"No, Lieutenant." The secretary let Norah see her concern. "I can't reach him. He won't take my calls. It really isn't a bit like him."

"Oh, Lieutenant, thank God you've come!" May Wrede cried out. Though she was as neatly dressed as ever, there was a frowsy look about her. There were heavy shadows under her eyes and she trembled slightly.

"What's the matter?" Norah asked as she entered the main floor of the duplex.

"It's Mr. Isserman. He hasn't come down in three days. He hasn't come down since Mrs. Northcott was here. We haven't seen him. He hasn't picked up the food, not his tray and not hers. Neither one of them has had anything to eat for three days. Oh, Lieutenant, we didn't know what to do, Mrs. McCullough and me."

"Are you sure he's still up there? He could have gone out using the upstairs entry."

"I never thought of that." May Wrede's distress was eased only momentarily. "No, ma'am. He wouldn't leave her. He couldn't. If he left her . . . if she's been alone all this time . . ." She began to shake.

"Now, Mrs. Wrede, easy. Take a couple of deep breaths. Go

on now, breathe slowly . . . deeply . . . that's right. Now, start again."

"Yes, ma'am." Wrede gulped. "He fired all the nurses and he's been taking care of Miss Christie by himself. He said it was the only way he could be sure there'd be no more accidents. He won't let anybody near her—not me, not Mrs. McCullough. He doesn't trust anybody. He won't even let us up there to deliver the trays. I'm supposed to put the tray at the foot of the stairs." She indicated a small table. "When nobody's around, he sneaks down and gets it. He brings the dirty dishes back when they're finished. He said Miss Christie was getting better. He said she was out of the chair and walking and getting stronger. But he hasn't picked up a tray in three days. We don't know what to do, Maggie and me. We called up, but there was no answer. We don't know what to do."

"It's all right, Mrs. Wrede. I'll go up."

"He'll be angry. He gave strict orders."

"Don't worry. I'll tell him you tried to stop me."

There was no doubt that, having shifted the responsibility, the housekeeper was relieved, but she was still afraid. "Be careful, Lieutenant," she warned. "Be careful. He hasn't been himself; he could be violent."

Norah climbed the sweeping stairs to the second floor of the duplex. Reaching the landing she had a faint whiff of the sweet smell of decay. It confirmed her own fear. She crossed over to the first door, which she remembered was Mrs. Isserman's room, and knocked as a matter of form.

"Police officer," she called out. When there was no answer, she tried the handle and it turned easily.

The shades were drawn and the lights on. The first thing Norah looked at was the stately canopied bed. It was empty. The coverlet was thrown back, the sheets rumpled. Certainly, it had been slept in, but how long ago?

The place reeked of neglect. It hadn't been cleaned in weeks. There was dust everywhere, soiled linen strewn on chairs, plates of partially eaten, spoiling food stacked on every available surface. Flies buzzed over it. The sour stench of urine mixed with that other, ominous odor. Norah noted the array of expensive medical equipment installed behind the bed; it was as dusty and neglected as everything else. Where was the wheelchair? With a deep sigh, she turned to the bathroom. The door was closed. Before opening it, Norah got out a fresh handkerchief and covered her nose and mouth. Then she went in.

Christina Isserman was in the tub, her head under the water. Her long blond hair floated around her like a mermaid's but couldn't hide her naked, wasted, and bloated body. The Jerry chair stood beside the tub, a mute witness. It suggested the victim had been wheeled in and the chair tilted to dump her over the side. On the peg back of the door hung a pink satin nightgown and the matching pink velvet robe. Apparently the perpetrator had undressed her before drowning her.

So, finally, after three attempts, he had killed her, Norah thought.

A wave of nausea brought on by the accumulated gases of putrefaction sent Norah to the bathroom window, to fling it wide and gulp the fresh air. From the very first time she had seen Christina Isserman, unconscious and on the respirator, Norah believed she was dealing with attempted murder. She hadn't been able to stop the killer, but she was determined to get him. She took another deep supply of clean air, then passed through the connecting door into the adjoining room.

She saw his feet first, clad in brown loafers with brown and yellow argyle socks. Her eyes traveled up the creased and stained cream linen pants to a dirty knit shirt, then finally to his unshaven, dirty face. She barely recognized him.

Walther Isserman hung from the ceiling light plate, suspended by a braided drapery cord. The vibration of her steps and the draft from the open windows set him swaying.

CHAPTER THIRTEEN

Murder and suicide, Norah thought as she looked up into the distorted face of the hanging man. The lividity was on one side, the side of the knot. The markings of the cord around his neck were soft with purple swollen borders. The chair he must have stood on was overturned about two feet to the side. All the indications supported suicide. Why had he done it? Norah asked herself. After having attempted again and again to kill his wife in a way that would pass as accidental, what had happened to make him do it in a manner that was so obviously murder and then hang himself?

According to May Wrede, Isserman had fired the nurses and devoted himself exclusively to his wife's care. He had refused visitors, had allowed no one upstairs, not even the servants. Was it because he was planning the murder? Or had he already killed his wife? A cold chill passed through Norah. How long had he been up there alone with her body?

How long after he drowned her did Walther agonize before taking his own life? What desperation drove him to make a noose, place it around his neck, step on the chair, tie the other end to the light fixture, and finally—to step off? It was difficult at best to estimate the progress of decomposition; since one body was immersed in water, comparing the condition of the

152

two was beyond Norah's expertise. She would have to wait for the medical examiner. A stirring of the tainted air brought on another wave of nausea and she ran out into the hall.

After recovering, she went downstairs to use the phone in the study. The double crime had to be reported. She called Communications, which would alert the various departments, then called her own squad direct. Arenas picked up. From those he named as available she chose Wyler. It was time she observed him in action.

Then she went back upstairs. The air had cleared enough so she could take a further look around, but it wasn't till the radio-patrol officer arrived and threw down ammonia crystals to dispel the remaining fumes that Norah felt well enough to make a thorough examination. By then, Acting Chief Medical Examiner Phillip Worgan was there.

Worgan, thirty-two, medium height with thick brown hair and small brown eyes that peered with darting glances from behind aviator-style glasses, had had a difficult period of adjustment when he joined the New York office. In Syracuse he had been the chief medical officer. In New York he was one of a large staff. Asa Osterman, legendary head of the department, took excellence for granted. Worgan learned to tone down his arrogance, even to accept that others might be equally capable. He learned not to bark out orders—and that sometimes detectives could actually make valid observations. From the first, Norah Mulcahaney recognized Worgan as a forensic scientist in the fullest sense—a medical man extremely sensitive to the circumstances of a crime. She had always shown him respect.

"Sorry, I was delayed," he said.

"I'm glad you came yourself."

He caught the anxiety in her voice instantly. "Where are they?"

She led him to the bathroom first.

Worgan stood at the side of the tub and looked down. "Clumsy way to commit murder," he commented. "Unnecessarily so."

The thought had occurred to Norah, but other priorities had pushed it to the back of her mind. Phil was right, of course.

Why drown a near comatose woman when there were other, simpler ways? For instance, the perpetrator could have put a pillow over her face and with little or no resistance from the victim, held it until she expired. That method was not only easy but had the additional advantage of possibly passing for natural death. There would have been no need for Isserman to hang himself.

Norah also noted stains on the tile floor, pinkish outlines, dry now but suggesting blood diluted by the bathwater. The bathwater was not stained, and nothing in the bathroom was broken. On a hunch, she looked in the hamper. There was a fluffy pink towel rolled into a ball. When she opened it she found fragments of a broken perfume bottle and more bloodstains.

"Looks like there was a struggle, after all."

"We'll examine both bodies for marks of violence," Worgan said. "Naturally we'll do an analysis on the stains."

"Why should he clean up afterward?" Norah wondered aloud. Then she put the question to Worgan. "If he intended to commit suicide, why bother?"

"You know it's too soon to ask that question. It's too soon to speculate."

"You're right."

In the next room, the photographers were still working. Worgan and Norah stood to one side till they were through and it was time to cut Isserman down.

"Not there, higher." Worgan indicated to the orderly where to sever the cord. "I want a good length to preserve the direction of the fibers."

Worgan wasn't missing a trick, Norah thought as she watched the body being carefully placed on the gurney so he could begin the preliminary examination.

"Well?" she asked after he straightened up and gestured that he was through.

"I can't even give you a ballpark figure, Norah, I really can't. There are too many variables. All right, all right . . . I'll estimate they've been dead at least two days. That's the absolute best I can do."

"Both of them?"

"Yes."

"How much of a time gap between the two?"

His straight, bushy eyebrows peaked slightly. "Very little. In fact, it may not be possible to say which one died first."

"But she had to be the first to go," Norah protested. "It couldn't have happened any other way."

"Why not?"

"You can't have the suicide before the murder. Unless . . ." She joined the medical examiner to take a closer look at the length of rope from which Walter had hung. The fraying would be in the opposite direction from the pull. If he'd stepped off the chair, the pull on that part of the rope over the fixture should be up. It was.

"So, you're right," Worgan conceded. "It was murder first, then suicide."

Norah walked the few blocks from Fifth to Park. She wanted to reach Lucine Northcott before the news of the two deaths was made public, before the media could turn it into a sensation, though this time, Norach conceded, they could hardly over-dramatize the facts. It was just six when she arrived and rang the socialite's doorbell.

Mrs. Northcott herself answered. She was swathed in a floor-length white bathrobe and her hair was wrapped in a towel, turban-style. "Excuse my appearance, Lieutenant. I was just getting dressed to go out."

"I'm afraid I have bad news."

"Oh?" Lucine Northcott stiffened.

Norah hesitated. Usually when she had to announce a death she'd found it best to speak straight out. For some reason, at some unexplained prompting, she went at it piecemeal. "Christina Isserman is dead."

"Oh." There was little surprise, some sadness, mostly relief. "I'm sorry. I'm very sorry, of course, but maybe, under the circumstances, it's for the best. It's for the best for every-body." She sighed. "Poor Walther. Would you mind . . ." She gestured toward the phone indicating she'd like to make a call.

"Walther Isserman is dead too."

She stood absolutely still. Her face was graven. Only her color changed—the year-round tan turned to ashes. "Dead?" she repeated, unbelieving. "Walther? How? What happened? Was there an accident?" Her voice was lower than usual, harsh, rasping. "What happened?" she demanded.

"We're not sure yet."

"What do you mean you're not sure? You must know how he died."

"We're waiting for the autopsy. We do know that he was last seen three days ago."

"You mean he was dead and lying somewhere unattended for three days? My God!"

"Actually, you were the last one to see him alive and talk to him."

"But that was last Saturday. That was four days ago."

"That's right. Meal trays were put out for him and Mrs. Isserman. They were picked up Sunday for the last time."

A cloud passed, darkening the room.

"I'm sorry to have to press at a time like this, but I'm sure that you want to help. How was Mr. Isserman that last time you saw him? What was his mood, his attitude?"

"Walther was disturbed, very disturbed. He was under a terrific strain."

"Because of his wife?"

"Of course."

"Why did you go to see him?"

"Because I loved him and he hadn't come to see me!" she cried out. "He didn't call me; he wouldn't take my calls." Abruptly, she turned and strode to the portable bar, where she poured herself a generous brandy and gulped a large portion of it.

"And Mrs. Isserman? How did you find her?"

"I didn't see her. He refused to let me go up."

"Did you know he had fired the nurses and wasn't allowing anyone to go up?"

"Yes. Wrede told me."

"Didn't you think that was strange?"

"Of course I did. My God! I was upset. I thought it was bad for him to be shut up alone with her like that. I wanted him to come away with me for a few days at least. I thought we could go to St. John. I have a house there. It would have done us both good."

"But he wouldn't?"

"I never even got around to suggesting it. The first thing he said to me was that he couldn't leave Christie. He claimed she was getting better, that she was conscious. Even that she could talk."

The servants had said the same thing. "Did you believe that?" Norah asked.

There was a long pause. Lucine Northcott fixed her brilliant dark eyes on Norah. "I didn't know what to believe."

"She had recovered twice before," Norah pointed out. "Twice before she had been in a coma and come out of it. Why not a third time?"

Lucine Northcott gulped some more brandy. "This one had lasted longer than any of the others."

Norah nodded. "You never mentioned that you had made Walther Isserman a substantial loan."

The abruptness of the change of subject startled Lucine. At the same time, by stimulating her pride, it helped her regain self-control. She spoke in the familiar elegant drawl. "I told you, Lieutenant, I was one of several investors, and that is so."

"According to my information you were the principal investor, and the company went bankrupt. You didn't get a cent of your money back."

She didn't dispute it, but she did attempt to excuse it. "It wasn't Walther's fault. It wasn't anybody's fault. He could hardly have foreseen the disaster. He could hardly have anticipated the ship would go down."

"You take the loss very lightly."

"No, I don't," the socialite retorted with a touch of annoyance. "It's not the first time I've had bad luck with an investment. If you want to make money, you have to be prepared to lose it. Anyway, it's not important, not now. I want to know what happened to Walther. How did he die? I have the right to know, and I don't intend to say another word until you've told me." Her eyes flashed.

The anger was too controlled, Norah thought. It could be a way of protecting herself, a hard shell over real pain. It could be a way of keeping Norah at a distance: the rich don't want pity from inferiors. "He died by hanging."

There was a long silence, then slowly Lucine Northcott shook her head. "I can't believe it. I can't believe it. Why? Why should he do such a thing? His finances weren't all that bad. He had good prospects, high hopes and ambitions."

"He'd also recently transacted a substantial loan."

"I didn't know that. Anyway, Walther wouldn't kill himself over money. If he survived the *Re Umberto* disaster, he could survive anything."

"Perhaps he was driven by guilt over his wife's condition."

"But he wasn't responsible. And she was getting better."

"You've already indicated you don't believe that. You've made it plain that you didn't believe it when he told you she was conscious, even talking. From what I've heard, Isserman was wavering at the edge of sanity. Having tried to kill his wife with drugs and alcohol, he was hounded by guilt and alleviating it with hallucinations of her recovery. Doesn't it make sense that he wouldn't let anybody go upstairs to see her because then he'd be forced to face the truth."

"I don't know. I just don't know."

"Surely if he really believed his wife was recovering, he wouldn't kill himself?"

Lucine Northcott finished the rest of her brandy, but it didn't help. "I'm sorry, Lieutenant, I don't think I can go on with this anymore. You'll have to excuse me."

But Norah didn't get up to leave. "How would you have felt if Mrs. Isserman had really been getting better?"

"I never wished Christina any harm."

"But you wanted her husband."

"Yes. I've admitted that. I've been honest."

"You've been waiting two years."

"I was prepared to wait as long as necessary."

"As long as there was a chance. As long as you were sure of his love. That situation changed: Isserman became obsessed with his wife. He was dedicating himself to her and shutting you out. He sent you away. You told me that. The housekeeper, Wrede, heard him."

"He was beside himself. He didn't know what he was saying. He was temporarily unbalanced."

"There have been instances of persons remaining comatose for years, for a lifetime. You realized he would never abandon Christina."

"Walther would never have turned his back on me either."

"You would have been satisfied with such a situation?"

"Not satisfied, of course not. I would have preferred to marry Walther, to be his legal wife. But if Christie did remain in a coma, I didn't expect him to divorce her. How could he? On the other hand, in such circumstances our relationship would be accepted by our friends and society in general. I could have lived with that. I would have lived with that."

"I find it difficult to believe," Norah said.

"You don't want to believe me." Lucine Northcott shrugged and, reaching down, helped herself to a cigarette from the silver box on the coffee table. "You've been trying to implicate me from the very beginning. Everyone who knows Christie will tell you she was addicted to alcohol and drugs and was slowly and inexorably destroying herself. We could only stand by and watch—and be saddened. As far as the attempt on her life while she was at Chazen-Hadley is concerned—I have no idea who might have done it. I didn't visit Christie that day; I wasn't on duty. I can only tell you what I heard—there's a mercy killer loose." Her voice, though hard and flat, was beginning to quiver slightly.

"I have to ask you, as a matter of routine, Mrs. Northcott, what did you do when Walther Isserman sent you away Saturday night?"

"It was late afternoon," she corrected. "I came home."

"And you stayed here? How about Sunday and Monday, Memorial Day?"

"Now you're trying to blame me not only for Christie's death but for the death of the man I loved. My God, Lieutenant, have you any idea what losing Walther means to me? Have you any conception of what loving a man and losing him—suddenly, violently—means?"

Norah thought of Joe. She thought of how he had been shot, run over, dragged through the streets. 'Yes,'' she said. "I do."

"Have you any idea how I feel knowing that he killed himself?" Lucine Northcott demanded, her voice rising. "I went to him. I wanted to help. I begged him to let me help. But he sent me away. He chose suicide. I failed him. Obviously, I failed him. But how? Where did I go wrong?" Turning her head aside, Lucine Northcott began to sob, quietly at first, and then in jagged bursts.

Norah made no move to soothe her, nor to cut short the crying jag.

Lucine did that herself soon enough. "I thought I could talk to you as one woman to another. I thought you would sympathize," Mrs. Northcott said bitterly, and ground out her cigarette. "But I suppose it's your job to badger and prod and irritate. All right, I did consider going to St. John on my own without Walther. I decided against it mainly because I didn't want to be alone. But I did need to get out of New York. I thought of my aunt, Mrs. Cynthia Dyson. She lives in Westhampton and was recently widowed. I owed her a visit but I'd kept putting it off because of the way things were here. So I called and asked her if it would be convenient for me to come out. She was delighted. I went Sunday morning. I wish now that I hadn't. I should have stayed here. I should have gone to see Walther again. Got him out of that place somehow."

"You drove up to your aunt's?"

"No. I don't keep a car in the city. It's expensive and an encumbrance, and I'm not that keen on driving. I went by limousine. It's a regular service, runs back and forth from the Hamptons a couple of times a day. I use it frequently. We all do. On summer weekends, Joseph—Joseph Moseby—the owner-driver, practically operates a shuttle."

"How long did you stay?"

She sighed. "I had intended to come back late Monday night, but we were having such a good visit. We spent every minute together, talking late into the night. I stayed over till Tuesday and got back here about two in the afternoon."

So she has an alibi, Norah thought. She'd get somebody to contact Joseph Moseby and Cynthia Dyson, but she had little doubt that it wouldn't check out. She got up. "I'm sorry to have intruded on your sorrow, Mrs. Northcott. Thank you for your time."

"Lieutenant . . . just a minute. You haven't told me how Christie died. Did she just slip away?"

"No. She drowned in the bathtub."

Lucine Northcott gasped. "Christie nearly drowned once before. It happened years ago at the lake. Sarah pushed her under."

CHAPTER FOURTEEN

Some of Lucine Northcott's color returned. Though still haggard, her face was composed. She walked over to the bar and poured herself another brandy. "Sure you won't change your mind, Lieutenant?"

"All right. I'll take a Coke, if you have it."

"Certainly." She fixed the drinks and brought them over, then sat down opposite Norah. "Walther knew about the incident, of course. Finding her in the tub, he would immediately have made the connection."

"Tell me about Christie and Sarah."

"When we were children we used to spend our summers together up at Paul Smiths, that's a small village near Lake Placid in the Adirondacks. I think I've already mentioned it. The Sextons had a lavish estate, Hilltop. My family had a place nearby, but I spent most of my time over at Hilltop, as did the other neighboring children, because everything was there. Mr. Sexton even imported sand to make a regular beach." She frowned. "He didn't have the lake bottom dredged. I suppose it didn't occur to him. Anyway, on this particular morning everybody was in the water laughing, splashing, tossing the beach ball around in our version of water polo. Christie was a timid swimmer, and one thing she didn't like was being dunked. We all used to tease her about it and made wild grabs for her. She screamed but it was all in fun, of course. Sarah particularly used to go after her. On the morning in question Christie was trying to elude her sister, swimming as hard as she could, but Sarah caught her and pushed her under. She came up spluttering; Sarah pushed her down again. And again. She held her under for a long time. When she let go, Christie didn't come up.

"At first Sarah laughed and called for Christie to stop fooling. But still Christie didn't surface. Then Sarah got frightened and she started screaming for help. She dove down a couple of times but couldn't get Christie. It seems that somehow Christie's foot was caught among the roots of a dead tree mired in the lake bottom. Apparently, she'd swum a distance under water to get away from Sarah and gotten tangled. The boys on the float finally realized what was happening, and one of them, the gardener's son, dove down, extricated Christie, and brought her up. He towed her to shore and gave her mouth-to-mouth resuscitation. He saved her life."

"The gardener's son? The boy Christie eloped with?"

"Mario . . . yes . . . I can't remember his last name."

"What was Christie's attitude when she recovered?" Norah asked.

"You mean, did she blame Sarah? No. She accepted it for what it was—an accident. We all did. There was no suggestion of anything else. Sarah was beside herself, of course. She didn't get over it for months. She certainly never teased Christie in that way again. In fact, her attitude toward Christie moderated. There had always been a rivalry between the girls, but after that Sarah seemed to accept being second, to step back even. I think that when Theo Sexton died, though he divided the estate, money, and shares in Sexton Industries equally, Sarah felt an obligation to sell out to Christie. It was almost as though she were compelled by her dead father's unspoken wish."

An interesting story, Norah thought. Another well-prepared family anecdote from Lucine Northcott. The history of sibling rivalry and the manner of Christina Isserman's death did point to Sarah Hoyt. Sarah's concern for her sister's safety and welfare, her insistence that Christie was in danger from her husband had to be reconsidered. It had appeared genuine; it could have been a cover-up. However, if Sarah Hoyt did drown her sister in the bathtub, there had to be a new and urgent motive. And how to explain Walther Isserman's suicide? Had he become so emotionally unstable that the death of his wife could drive him to kill himself? If not, how could a small, delicate woman like Sarah Hoyt have managed to string him up?

How had anyone—without leaving telltale signs on the rope?

Norah waited for the autopsy results.

Despite his best efforts, Phillip Worgan couldn't make a precise determination of the time of death of either victim. The condition of the bodies indicated death had not occurred less than sixty hours prior to discovery, that is, not before Sunday midnight. The last tray had been picked up for the Sunday evening meal. Most likely, Isserman had fed his wife first, then he had eaten; the progress of digestion was about equal in both. Without knowing what time they had eaten, the information was useless.

Worgan called Norah to prepare her for the official report. "Based on the available medical evidence and supported by the physical evidence at the scene, specifically the fraying of the cord from which Isserman was suspended, I'm calling it murder and suicide. Incidentally, Mrs. Isserman was alive when she was placed in the tub."

"I see. How about the bloodstains?" Norah was not surprised by his conclusion.

"There was a deep gash at the back of Isserman's head. The blood on the floor and on the towel is his type."

Had he slipped and fallen, smashing the perfume bottle and cutting himself while trying to tip over the Jerry chair? Or had the woman in the chair struggled? Had the semi-conscious woman been aware of her danger? Had Christina Isserman made a last vain attempt to live?

"I can't accept it, Phil," Norah said. "It's psychologically wrong. He was caring for her. He set himself apart from his own world, shut himself up with her, obsessed by the determination to make her well. How could he suddenly make a complete reversal and kill her? And why in that particular way?"

"Have you got new evidence?"

"I've got some new information. I don't know where it will lead. It would help if you could narrow the probable time of death."

"If we assume the food was ingested within an hour of the time the maid set it out at the bottom of the stairs on Sunday night, then we might fix it at somewhere between two and four A.M. Monday. That's for your guidance. It won't stand up in court."

"I understand. Thanks. I appreciate your help."

She had barely hung up when there was a knock at her door. Gus Schmidt and Audrey Jordan came in. Both were smiling. "You look like you've got something," Norah greeted.

Their grins broadened. "Some interesting facts," Gus said. He nodded to Audrey. "Go ahead."

"It was your idea."

"You did all the work."

"Somebody tell me something."

One more look passed between them, then Gus began. "Justin Hoyt was a client of Clark Harriss. His file was one of those taken. We found records of his payments in Harriss's cash receipts ledger. We got a court order to examine the books of his Alliance Depository Company. Part of the assets were shares in his wife's sportswear business. These had been turned over to East-West Investments Corporation three weeks ago. On May 18, fifty-one percent of his own holdings in Alliance Depository were also transferred to the same East-West Investments."

Norah riffled through the calendar she was keeping on the case. "That's when Harriss's home office was broken into."

"Right." Gus's eyes gleamed. "Naturally, we were curious about East-West. Then Audrey remembered it had been one of the shareholders in Re Umberto Shipping. Isserman's company," he added unnecessarily.

It wasn't like Gus to stress the obvious. He was excited. So was Audrey. They were getting along. "Good work," Norah said for both of them.

"There's more," Audrey, flushed with pleasure, volunteered, then once again deferred to her partner.

"East-West is a front for gambling interests based in Puerto Rico."

This time Gus didn't underscore. "Well, well, isn't that interesting?" Norah commented. "I assume you can document all this?"

Both nodded.

"There's more," Audrey said. "The head of the syndicate is a Mario Raffanti. His father once worked for Theo Sexton. When they were very young, he and Christina Sexton eloped."

Norah leaned back in her chair. "Okay. I think you and I should pay Mr. and Mrs. Hoyt a visit," she told Gus. "But first things first; let's find out how they spent their Memorial Day weekend." She flipped the switch and spoke into the intercom. "Ferdi, Roy, would you come in for a minute, please?"

Audrey Jordan cleared her throat.

"Audrey, I won't need you on this. Report back to the sergeant for regular duty."

"Yes, Lieutenant. It's about the key. You were going to give it to me."

"Oh, sure. Here. I had it made yesterday. I'm sorry I can't give you a hand, but you go ahead and I'll be home as soon as I can." She looked around to find Gus frowning. "Audrey's moving in with me."

"I didn't know that."

"We only decided a couple of days ago."

Sarah and Justin Hoyt lived in Sands Point on the north shore of Long Island, a stretch sometimes called the Gold Coast. Both commuted by helicopter to the Thirty-fourth Street heliport on the East River, or if the weather was bad, by their own chauffeured limousine, so a Manhattan apartment was considered unnecessary. As the bodies of Christina and Walther Isserman had yet to be released, the wake and funeral were in abeyance, and the Hoyts could be expected to be available. Norah called in advance to make sure.

Just after eleven on a fine June Sunday morning, Norah and Gus drove past the fretted iron gates and up a long wooded stretch of private road. The grounds were a happy blend of the wild and the cultivated. A clearing had been cut to accommodate the house and a sweeping lawn of Kentucky bluegrass, across which a pheasant paraded. An ornamental pond, serpentine in shape, was on one side of the road, a pair of swans regally presiding. On the other side the waters of the Sound could be glimpsed through a stand of pines. The house was in the style of an Italian villa, large yet suggesting comfort. Norah parked in the drive, then she and Gus mounted a shallow flight of steps to the terrace. The door was promptly opened by a houseman who ushered them along a spacious passage running the length of the house out to another terrace at the back. This one was paved with random-sized flagstones interplanted with grass and a creeping ground cover of small violet flowers—conceived to look natural, but undoubtedly planted and maintained at considerable cost and effort.

"Lieutenant Mulcahaney and Detective Schmidt from New York, sir," the houseman announced, and then withdrew.

Justin Hoyt was on his knees with his back to them, staking a bed of tomatoes. He got up, brushed the loose soil from his dungarees, and turned around. Tall, fit, auburn-haired, with liquid hazel eyes, he could have been arrestingly good-looking, but he had chosen to play down his looks. In dress and manner he was studiously low-key. His work pants were properly worn and faded, his madras shirt washed often enough for the right degree of "bleeding." The Adidas sneakers were muddy from the soil in which he had been digging, yet the effect was of money. He was a member of the American aristocracy, Norah thought, and there was no way he could disguise it. It was the grooming, she decided, the sense of cleanliness starting deep down in the pores. Justin Hoyt III wore his dark red hair just short of the collar, and not one single strand strayed past that arbitrary line.

He smiled engagingly. "Sorry I can't shake hands." He turned palms out to display the dirt that clung to them. Clean dirt, Norah thought wryly. Then he waved them to multistriped lawn chairs. "How was the drive? Not too much traffic early Sunday, I should think. Can I get you something cool to drink? Something to eat?"

"Nothing, thank you," Norah replied for both. "We won't take much of your time. Is Mrs. Hoyt not at home?"

"She's still in bed." He cast a glance up toward the second floor as though to indicate the location of her room. "She's deeply disturbed and anxious to see Christie put to rest. This whole affair is bad enough without the added trauma of the autopsy and the interminable waiting." He frowned, as close to expressing displeasure as he ever allowed himself to come.

"The autopsies have been completed, and I believe that both Mr. and Mrs. Isserman will be released to you very soon. Maybe later today."

"Thank God for that." Justin Hoyt sighed. "Well? What did they find out? What's the result?"

"Nothing conclusive, I'm afraid."

He raised thick, perfectly shaped eyebrows. "I'm not surprised. What happened was glaringly obvious, and we could have been spared the indignity to Christie and the strain on the family. On Sarah particularly. Well, it's finally over. We can bury them and put it all behind us."

"There are a few points . . ."

"What in God's name? What points?"

"I wanted to talk to Mrs. Hoyt."

"I'm sure I can answer your questions."

Norah looked to Gus; talking to each of them separately might be useful. They both sat down.

"One of the things we find puzzling is the manner of Mrs. Isserman's death," Norah said. "It appears to echo a childhood incident that involved both sisters."

For a moment Justin Hoyt looked blank. "You mean at the lake? That was an accident. You can't seriously suggest a connection."

"If Mrs. Isserman had been drowned while swimming in a lake or pool or at the shore, perhaps we could have accepted it as a coincidence. But to drown in her own bathtub? Particularly since she couldn't have been taking a bath on her own."

"Who knows why Walther chose that particular way? Who knows why he killed her and then himself? Obviously he was unbalanced. Surely his behavior in shutting himself up with Christina, allowing no one to see her, surely that is proof enough of his instability."

"It's not the answer we're looking for."

Justin Hoyt's perfect eyebrows went up again. "It may not be, Lieutenant, but it's the only one I can offer."

As quietly as he, and with the same determination, Norah persisted. "It must trouble Mrs. Hoyt that her sister died in that particular way."

"It devastates Sarah that her sister was murdered. She anticipated it and she tried very hard to prevent it—as you, Lieutenant, very well know."

Norah did not respond to the implied rebuke. "You all grew up together—you and your wife and her sister. You were part of the same group; you went to the same schools and spent your summers together. You were all present when Christina Sexton was pushed underwater and nearly drowned. It was a long time ago, and by mutual accord the incident appears to have been set aside and nearly forgotten. Walther Isserman was an outsider. He wasn't there when it happened."

"Obviously he knew about it. He'd heard the story."

"From whom? Why should anyone bring it up?"

Hoyt shrugged. "Maybe Christie told him herself. Understandably, she was less than enthusiastic about swimming after that. Walther probably wanted to know why. Maybe he thought that by killing Christie in that manner he could implicate Sarah."

"Then why commit suicide?"

"Trying to make sense out of the tortured reasoning of a disturbed mind is futile, Lieutenant. Besides, what does it matter? They're both gone now. It's over and done with." He stopped just short of being curt, but it was plain he intended the interview to end.

Norah did not. "There's the murder of Clark Harriss."

Hoyt scowled. Carefully making sure not to get mud on his clothes, he reached into his shirt pocket and pulled out a small ostrich-leather cigarette case. Politely, though perfunctorily, he offered it around before lighting up.

"He was your accountant," Norah continued.

"That's right."

"Harriss's home office was burglarized. Files were stolen, yours among them. Detective Schmidt worked long and hard to reconstruct the missing accounts."

"That's an invasion of privacy."

"Not in a murder case." Before he could protest further, she added, "We did get a court order, Mr. Hoyt. What Detective Schmidt found was a transfer of shares in Sarah Hoyt Sportswear to the East-West Investments Corporation without equivalent moneys or other considerations." At her nod, Gus opened his briefcase and produced photocopies, which he laid out on the garden table.

Justin Hoyt made no move to examine them. He kept very still, the cigarette smoldering between his fingers.

Norah continued. "Shares of your Alliance Depository were also transferred to East-West Investments without any recompense that we could discover. Would you care to explain?"

"No."

Just that and no more.

"Then I'll tell you how Detective Schmidt and I interpret the transactions." Norah paused to give him one last chance to speak. He didn't avail himself of it. "East-West Investments is the front for a gambling syndicate. The head man is one Mario Raffanti, owner of The Alhambra Hotel and Casino in San Juan. Of course, you know him well. He's the gardener's son who saved Christina Sexton's life and who later eloped with her."

"It's a small world."

"You are one of Raffanti's regular clients. You are what is known as a 'credit player,' a high roller who comes and gambles for two or three days at a time, drawing against an established line of credit. I suggest that those shares of your wife's business and your own company were your line of credit."

Slowly, deliberately, Hoyt snubbed out the cigarette. He unfolded his lanky frame from the chair, stretching to the full six feet two inches of his height and looked down on Norah and Schmidt. "This has no connection with the murder of my sister-in-law and the suicide of her husband. Therefore, I have no comment." He started for the house.

"You lost a great deal of money gambling, Mr. Hoyt. You are in danger of losing a large part of your wife's company and all of your own. That gives you a very strong motive for murdering your sister-in-law and her husband. With both of them dead, your wife inherits the Sexton fortune."

He stopped short of the door.

"The money would come in handy."

"Money usually does," he admitted with astonishing equanimity. "Aren't you supposed to show means and opportunity?"

His arrogance was almost convincing. "The means were at hand," Norah replied. "As for opportunity . . ."

"I was out of town."

"Can you prove that?"

For the first time Justin Hoyt looked distinctly uncomfortable. He worked his lips in and out a couple of times. "If I must," he said finally.

The appeal left her unmoved.

"I was in San Juan for the entire Memorial Day weekend. I took the red-eye back on Tuesday night."

"There seems to be some doubt."

"How can there be? I have my canceled airline ticket."

"You were missing from the tables for an extended period."

"My God, everybody has to eat and sleep, even gamblers." His voice rose in frustration.

"No gambler leaves when he's losing, not willingly. Gamblers take black coffee, uppers, whatever—but they don't leave," Norah retorted. "And you were losing. Yet you left the tables at about ten Sunday night. You didn't resume play until Monday afternoon."

"That doesn't mean I was in New York."

"Where were you?"

He sighed. "All right. I was trying to raise money to go on playing. But I stayed in San Juan. I never left the island."

"The maid went into your room at the Alhambra on Monday

morning. The bed hadn't been slept in. She went in again on Tuesday and it had."

"That indicates I was up all night, not that I was in New York."

"You were seen, Mr. Hoyt. You were seen on Fifth Avenue." She had saved this for the last. "You were seen by a neighbor of the Issermans who says you were coming out of their building a little after four A.M."

"What neighbor? Who?"

"He was returning a day early from what should have been a long weekend upstate. He was surprised to see you—there and at that time. He knows you very well."

"Who? Who knows me so damn well? I demand to confront him. Let him say what he has to say to my face."

"If that's what you want, I'm sure Frank Veloney will agree."

Patently that was a chock. Now Justin Hoyt parried. "All right. I was in New York. I went to talk to Walther. To ask him for his help."

"Just a minute, Mr. Hoyt," Norah broke in. "I have to advise you of your rights."

"No, never mind. It's not necessary. I want to tell you."

Norah held up her hand. "We are obliged by law to read you your rights, Mr. Hoyt." She indicated for Gus to go ahead.

"Now," she said when he was finished. "What did you want from Walther Isserman?"

"I wanted him to get my stocks out of Christie's safe."

CHAPTER FIFTEEN

"I borrowed money from Christie and put up the stock for collateral."

She'd required collateral from her brother-in-law? Despite all she'd learned about the very rich that still surprised Norah.

"I couldn't blame her. She knew what the money was for."

And Hoyt took it for granted, even forgave her. "At least she made sure the business stayed in the family."

From then on he told his story without prompting. He sat up with perfect posture in the lawn chair that was meant for reclining, his lean face drawn but still haughty. He told it straight out, as though divesting himself of a burden, and dealt with the questions that followed as requests for elucidation, never attempts to discredit. It didn't occur to him that he might not be believed; certainly not that he could be in any jeopardy.

"As you discovered, Lieutenant, I was losing heavily in San Juan. I needed more money. I had nothing left to offer Raffanti as security. I had already turned over to him a block of my shares in Alliance, my last holdings in fact, as security for an earlier extension of credit. The only way I could get them back was to win them back. If Christie had been herself, of course, I wouldn't even have thought of going to her. She wouldn't have listened to me. But with her in a coma, well, I thought I could appeal to Walther. He had access to Christie's safe-deposit and I thought he might be sympathetic and get them for me."

Norah looked to Gus. She wanted him to take part so the pressure would come from two sides—also to remind Hoyt that Gus was the expert who had examined Harriss's books and reconstructed Hoyt's file.

Gus nodded and picked up from her. "This block of shares that Mrs. Isserman held had been turned over to her before you gave shares to Raffanti?"

"It antedated that transaction by sixty days."

"How do you know the shares were in the vault?"

"Because that's where she kept her valuables."

"Why should Walther Isserman help you out?" Norah asked.

"I thought he might feel for me since he was in a similar situation himself."

"Walther Isserman gambled?" Gus asked, surprised.

"No, no. What I meant was he knew how hard it was to try to raise money from Christie. Besides, I intended to offer him ten percent. He was back in business by then, but I was sure he could use it."

Norah's next question was automatic. "Does your wife know about your gambling?"

"She doesn't know the extent of my losses." He seemed annoyed at being forced to admit that much.

"Of course. Go on."

"That's it, really. I arrived at the apartment. I rang the doorbell, but there was no answer. I waited . . ."

"You're going too fast, Mr. Hoyt. What time did you land at Kennedy?"

"Oh, one-thirty or so. There wasn't any traffic so I got into the city in less than an hour. I entered the building using the side door. After midnight, the doorman only monitors the main entrance and the elevators are all self-service." He paused, waiting for comment, and when there was none, continued. "I rang and there was no answer. I tried the door. It was open."

At this, Norah raised her eyebrows.

"I thought it was odd, but I was tired from the trip, keyed up, and anxious to get what I'd come for. So I went in. I tapped at Walther's door first; there was no response. I thought he might be sitting with Christie, so I went to her room. Nothing.''

"Excuse me," Norah interrupted. "Were the lights on or did you have to turn them on?"

"No, they were on. They were on in the hall and in her room when I looked in. But she wasn't there, not in her bed, or in the chair. I didn't know what to make of that. I wandered around as though she might be hiding from me," he remarked with irony. "Then I looked in the bathroom." Cold sweat filmed his brow.

"She was in the tub, under the water. I was transfixed. I don't know how long I stood there. There was no doubt in my mind she was dead. I didn't make any attempt to raise her or resuscitate her." He turned first to Norah, then to Gus for reassurance.

Neither was in a position to give it.

"I looked around. Everything seemed normal—except for Christie, of course. Something, I don't know what, told me to go into Walther's room. I tell you in all honesty, Lieutenant Mulcahaney, Detective Schmidt, I never imagined Walther could or would do such a thing. I couldn't believe what I saw. My first instinct was to go to the telephone and call the police, then I remembered why I had come. I knew that for all her business sense Christie was careless with her jewels. I was sure I could find enough jewelry and loose cash around the house to put me back in the game. And I did." He sighed. "If I'd called the police I would have given up my chance to go back and try to recoup my losses."

"Also, you would have had to explain what you were doing in the apartment with two dead bodies."

"Yes."

"And your wife would have found out that you had gambled away part of her company."

"Yes."

He offered neither justification nor regret. Norah believed Justin Hoyt III felt both, but his pride would not permit him to admit either.

"Unfortunately, the facts are open to a different interpretation," she said. "You were desperate to make up your losses and to keep your gambling activities secret from Mrs. Hoyt. So you flew to New York and went to the Isserman apartment. You rang. Walther Isserman admitted you. You appealed to him, but he turned you down. You quarreled. It came to blows. You knocked him unconscious. Maybe you thought he was already dead. In either case, it occurred to you that if Christina were also out of the way, if they were both gone, then your wife would inherit. Sarah Hoyt would come into the entire Sexton fortune. The money would be hers and your credit would be almost bottomless."

"No. It happened as I told you."

"By this time it was generally known in your circle that Walther Isserman was deranged," Norah continued. "Anything he might do could be explained in that context. You decided to kill your sister-in-law and make it look as though Walther had done it and then killed himself. Murder and suicide."

They didn't know she was there till she cried out, "No! The fact that Christie drowned clears Justin."

Sarah Hoyt stood framed in the French doors that opened onto the terrace. Her feet were bare; her dark hair tangled; her face puffy and without makeup. Her white linen slacks were wrinkled; over them she wore a rumpled navy shirt. She looked as though she'd just awakened and thrown on whatever was handy. There was no trace of The Smile.

"Justin would, at all costs, avoid the one method of murder that would draw attention to me. Everybody knows you can't profit from murder."

Deliberately Norah turned back and continued the questioning of Justin Hoyt. "You said that when you went upstairs you found the door of the Isserman apartment unlocked. That door is self-locking. It is possible that it was adjusted not to lock— for some reason—but how did you get into the building? If you bypassed the doorman at the front and Isserman was already dead, then he couldn't very well buzz you in. I don't imagine you rang a stranger's bell in the middle of the night. If you had, you wouldn't have got an answer. So how did you get in, Mr. Hoyt?"

Justin Hoyt's eyes fixed on his wife. He stared at her across the terrace. He hesitated a long time before answering and then spoke quietly to her and only to her.

"I had a key. Christie gave it to me. I'm sorry, Sarah."

She held his gaze without moving or speaking.

"It was a long time ago. A very long time ago," he pleaded. "Before we were married."

Still silent, she turned and went back into the house.

"It was over!" he cried after her. "I swear, Sarah. It was over."

According to Captain Jacoby the manner of Christina Isserman's death had no real relevance. The way Manny Jacoby saw it, the crime was unpremeditated. Hoyt killed Walther Isserman primarily out of frustration at being denied his securities. It was unintentional. Hoyt's first instinct was to get out. Certainly the idea of inheriting all the Sexton wealth must have been in the back of his mind for a long time. Now, suddenly, with Walther dead and Christina unconscious in the next room, he had the opportunity of turning fantasy into reality. All he needed to do was finish off Christina—not a big obstacle since she could hardly be said to be truly alive.

Manny Jacoby set out the rationale with complete confidence. It was his contention that once Hoyt had made his decision, the next concern was how to cover his tracks. He settled on a murder/suicide scenario—Isserman kills his wife and then himself. According to Jacoby, Hoyt never thought back to the childhood incident. It was all extemporaneous.

Norah argued that the fraying of the rope pointed to Isserman's having hung himself. Jacoby dismissed it. Hoyt was tall and strong. He could have stood up on the chair and held his victim up with him. When he let go of the unconscious man, the slack would have been taken up in the same way as if Isserman had himself kicked the chair aside.

Reluctantly, Norah had to admit it could work. Given the emotional stress, however, she found the method too contrived.

Jacoby lost patience.

"Either Isserman killed his wife and committed suicide, or

somebody killed the two of them. Take your choice. One or the other."

Norah frowned. It was twenty-nine hours since she and Gus had brought Justin Hoyt in for further questioning and ultimate arrest. Gus had made the official collar and had seen Hoyt through the sixteen hours of arraignment while Norah waited in her office, ready to go down to the court when advised the case would be coming before the judge. She had returned to the precinct to run interference with the press.

"I know, Captain, but there's something missing. No, it's there, but we're not seeing it." The glare of the setting sun made her squint and cover her eyes. She realized how tired she was.

So did Manny Jacoby. "Go home, Lieutenant. Get some sleep. You'll see it all clearly in the morning."

But she didn't. The next morning, she had, if anything, even greater qualms. She could accept Hoyt's guilt for the deaths of Walther and Christina Isserman in their apartment Sunday night. Captain Jacoby's theory was logical, but it didn't take into account the preceding events. Somebody pulled the plug on Christina Isserman's respirator and Hoyt's alibi for that period was impregnable. It also covered the night before— when Clark Harriss was run over. Nobody was giving the accountant much thought, Norah realized with a sudden pang. He was all but forgotten. Whatever happened, however the rest of the case was resolved, Norah promised herself she would find the person who had crept into that IC unit and ripped the tube from Harriss's throat while he lay helpless. She would not forget again.

According to the papers, the DA apparently had resolved any doubts he'd had about Hoyt. After all, the circumstantial evidence was strong and so was the motive. Finally, the privileges of class that has worked for Justin Hoyt all his life turned against him. The prosecutor did not want to be perceived as extending special consideration because of the wealth and position of the suspect, and so Hoyt was charged with the double murder. On Wednesday, seventy-two hours after he had been apprehended, Justin Hoyt was brought before the grand jury, which handed down the indictment.

Officially, as far as the NYPD was concerned, the case was closed. But Norah couldn't leave it alone. It occurred to her that everyone she'd interrogated regarding the near drowning at the lake were friends of the Sextons. Not one had strayed from the accident theory, the harmless prank. They stood fast by their own. There was one outside the group though, not bound by the code, the one who had gone down and extricated Christina Sexton's foot from the tangle of roots and saved her. Norah contacted a friend on the Organized Crime Force for a background on Mario Raffanti.

Lieutenant Charles Ombrusco informed Norah that Raffanti was opening a new branch of the Alhambra in Atlantic City. It was scheduled to open on the coming weekend, but the New Jersey Casino Control Commission had not yet granted the new license. Test operations were to be conducted that week using play money. State gambling inspectors would monitor. The next day building inspectors would enter and give a certificate of occupancy. Then the doors would open to the public.

Any hint of scandal between now and Friday would kill a thirty-four-million-dollar investment.

Charlie suggested that the morning after the test operations and before the formal opening would be as good a chance of finding Raffanti off guard as she was likely to get. And that wasn't very good. Raffanti was known to be shrewd and cool. He was also considered legit.

Norah and Gus stood on the outside of the massive plate-glass door and held their open shield cases for the guard on the inside to see. He took a good look before letting them in.

For all the vaunted luxury and lavish appointments, for all the touted decor, these places were all the same, Norah thought as she and Schmidt entered the vast lobby of the Alhambra Atlantic, the biggest and newest hotel-casino on the East Coast, offering 152 table games and 1900 slot machines. Yet in spite of herself, Norah was impressed. The lobby was enormous and, as it was empty, its proportions were all the more striking. An attempt had been made to establish a Moorish theme, but it was tempered for modern comfort. Vaulted arches fronting the waters of the bay were glassed in to make temperature control possible. The walls were tiled in brilliant mosaic colors and patterns traditional of the Arab style, but the floor was thickly carpeted wall-to-wall. Massive lanterns hung from the three-story ceiling at varying heights; of course, they were electrified. Exotic plants and the rush of a fifty-foot waterfall both cooled the air and soothed the senses. When the public, heated by gambling fever, crowded into the immense space, who would notice any of it?

"He's expecting us," Norah told the guard.

Nevertheless he called upstairs for instructions. Then he led them to the last rank of elevators, reached to insert a special key in the lock marked "Penthouse" and stepped back to allow the doors to close. The car shot up, its movement so smooth as to be imperceptible.

The doors opened directly into Raffanti's office. Sky and water was all anyone would be aware of at the first moment, even before stepping out. It was an overcast day, the sky brooding and the sea sullen, yet the vista offered by the immense picture window was overwhelming. Both Norah and Gus stood stock-still.

"It's something, isn't it?" Raffanti came out from behind his desk grinning like a schoolboy. "It changes all the time. I never get tired of looking at it."

"I can believe that," Norah said. Though the decor was purposely understated so as not to detract from the spectacular display of nature, the office was impressive in its own right. Contemporary, a studied contrast to the public rooms. Nothing in it masqueraded as something it was not. It told her a great deal about Mario Raffanti.

In his person Raffanti was not at all prepossessing. He wasn't even handsome. Agreeable would describe him best; five foot eight, slight, face smooth and hardly lined. Yet judging by the receding hairline and the clear beginning of dewlaps, Norah put his age at close to forty. Raffanti's ears stood out from the sides of his head, and his pale blue eyes, inherited from his Irish mother, were wide as though in permanent wonder at finding himself the master of so much splendor. Genially he waved them to chairs.

"Can I offer you anything? The kitchen isn't open yet, but I can get you sandwiches if you're hungry."

The chairs were even lower than they looked, and more comfortable. One sank into comfort so deep as to be out of control. Shrewdly planned. "I'd like some coffee, if it's available," Norah said, and pulled herself forward to the edge of the cushion where she could perch erect.

"Coffee for me too, please." Gus followed her example.

Apparently delighted that he could do something for them, Raffanti picked up the phone on his desk, pressed the appropriate button on a small console, and gave the order. Then he leaned on the outer edge of the desk and faced them both. "So, Lieutenant Mulcahaney and Detective Schmidt, how can I help you?"

He had put the right name to the right person. He was engaging, disarming. Look out, Norah thought.

"We're investigating the deaths of Christina and Walther Isserman."

"Yes." He sighed slightly. "Have you contacted the local police?"

"We informed Chief Walsh we were coming to see you. It's a courtesy."

"Yes." He grimaced. "This comes at a bad time for me. I'm sure you're aware of that." He shrugged. "It's been a lot of years since I had contact with the Sextons."

"But you were once very close to Christina."

"You could say that." He grinned. "Childhood romance. First love for each of us."

"You grew up with the girls."

"No." This time the smile was tinged with bitterness. "I was one of the children permitted to play with them during summer vacations so that they might 'expand' their social horizons. Mr. Sexton liked to appear democratic, but he couldn't help condescending. I was the gardener's son and nobody ever forgot it. Including me."

"I was told he was very good to you."

"In his way, yes."

"You haven't returned the kindness.."

"What do you mean?"

"Justin Hoyt is deeply in debt to you."

"Justin came to my place to gamble. If he'd won, he wouldn't have thought twice about walking out with my money. Why should I feel any differently about his?"

"You could have refused to extend his credit line."

"Why? Then he would have gone to someone else. Justin is a compulsive gambler. He can't stop. Why should I let him lose his money at another establishment?"

"What about Walther Isserman? Your East-West Investments Corporation put money into his shipping business."

"And lost every damn cent when the boat went down."

"You must have known that Christina didn't want him to go into business on his own."

"Why should I care? That was between him and her. It looked like a good deal, and I bought into the action."

"Where were you over the Memorial Day weekend?"

Now they had come to it. He knew it. Though he remained apparently relaxed, the easy affability was gone. "Right here. I was right here."

"Not in San Juan."

"No. We had hoped to open the Alhambra Atlantic by Memorial Day but we were delayed. Every extra day into the season we don't open costs money. I was here to speed things up and, believe me, I was never alone."

"I didn't ask you for an alibi, Mr. Raffanti."

"I thought you did. Though I don't understand why; you've already got the killer."

"Maybe not." Raffanti's blue eyes showed their surprise. "Christina Isserman was drowned in her bathtub. Why should Justin Hoyt choose a method sure to draw attention to his wife, and very likely to put her inheritance in jeopardy?"

"I have no idea. I would have said Justin was too smart for that."

"You were at the lake when Sarah pushed her sister under. Christina's foot got caught in a tangle of roots and you dove down and freed her. You saved her life," Norah pointed out.

"I dove down and got her, yes, but she was already free."

Well-schooled in not revealing her reactions, Norah had a

hard time covering her surprise. Even Gus Schmidt's stolidity cracked.

"That's right," Raffanti went on. "She could have come up on her own. She was free and perfectly capable. She was staying down to cause a commotion, a big scare, particularly to make trouble for Sarah."

Norah shook her head.

"You don't believe that? I don't blame you, but that's the way it was. Everybody was trying to curry favor with the old man, even his daughters. And the old man liked it that way. I did bring Christie up to the surface and she told everybody I had saved her life. Mr. Sexton accepted it; whether or not he believed it is something else. But why shouldn't he? Anyway, Christie made a hero out of me and I . . . well, I went along with it. It would have been a lot harder not to. Besides, I enjoyed it. As a reward, Mr. Sexton put me through school. I took courses at Cornell in landscaping and club management. When I graduated I had a couple of really good job offers from big clubs in California, but Mr. Sexton topped them. Naturally I went to him, and it turned out that I was head gardener, or groundskeeper if you prefer, like my father before me. When I put it to him that I wasn't using the education he had given me or even earning the money he paid me, that I wanted to actually manage his properties, he slapped me on the back. He said he'd been waiting to see what I was made of and gave me the job.

"The big bust-up came when Christie and I fell in love and decided to elope. The old man found out and came after us. He stopped the marriage and he fired me. I was good enough to send to college, to manage his estates, but not to be his son-in-law. Theo Sexton wasn't democratic enough for that."

"How about Christina? How did she react when her father broke you up?"

"Christie knew how to wheedle and cajole the old man, and she did—when he was in the mood to be wheedled and cajoled. But to oppose him outright? No way."

"You haven't married, Mr. Raffanti."

"Now, Lieutenant, don't try to make a romance of broken hearts and undying love out of this. We were a couple of kids,

Christie and me. She was my first love and so I'll always remember her with tenderness, but she wasn't my only love. I haven't got married because I've had too many other things on my mind. Someday I'll find the right woman, and then she'll be the only thing I have to think about." He shrugged and grinned, back to the old engaging lassitude.

"How do you suppose Mr. Sexton found out you and Christina were running away together?" Norah asked.

"Somebody told him. He had a nice little spy network among the servants."

"But he found you. How did he know where to look?"

The gambler shrugged. "Maybe Christie told somebody. Maybe she told her sister."

"Would she?"

"Probably. She'd want to brag. She'd want to be one up on Sarah. Then Sarah snitched to her father to curry favor. The girls were at it all the time."

There was a knock at the door and the coffee arrived. It was served and no one said anything till the waiter withdrew.

"It seems to me, Mr. Raffanti, that you've been biding your time to pay the Sextons back—the father for stopping your marriage, Christina for not loving you enough to defy her father, and Sarah for betraying you."

He started to laugh, and the laugh seemed genuine. "You think I'm carrying out some Monte Cristo style vendetta? Cutting down the Sexton women and their men? You really are a romantic, Lieutenant. That kind of thing is out of style. What's the line? 'Living well is the best revenge.' That happens to be true. The old man treated me as fairly as he knew how. According to his lights, I was the traitor for running off with his daughter. As for Christie, she never had a chance to find out what it might be like to think and feel on her own. Maybe if we'd managed to get past the ceremony she might have found the strength to be independent, but with the old man showing up at the Justice of the Peace, bursting in with his private security people, literally snatching her away, she didn't have a chance. I'm not angry at her. I'm sorry for her.

"As for Sarah—the truth is that she was the one I was sweet on at the beginning. Maybe that was why Christie made out as though I'd saved her life. It certainly brought us together. I don't know whether Sarah ever figured it out. Maybe Christie told her; I wouldn't put it past her. As far as I'm concerned, it's all over and the score is even."

"What about Clark Harriss?"

"Who's he?"

"He was the accountant for both Isserman and Justin Hoyt. His private office was burglarized and a portion of his files stolen. It was through the reconstruction of the missing documents that Detective Schmidt uncovered the connection between Hoyt and East-West Investments as the holding company for the two Alhambras."

The mild blue eyes turned cold and pale as ice on a mountain. For the first time Norah was allowed a glimpse of the man who headed a vast gambling syndicate, who commanded millions of dollars, who could order a death or a maiming as casually as he ordered up their coffee. "I inquired about you, Lieutenant Mulcahaney, and I was told that you're a competent, even thorough, police officer. But you're spinning fiction here. You think I invested in Walther Isserman's ship with the express purpose of sabotaging her? Expensive. And difficult. You think I enticed Justin Hoyt to gamble? To get in so deep he had to turn over Sarah's company and finally his own? Maybe that might have been a little easier once he turned up at my tables, but he still had to have the desire to come the first time.

"The investment in Isserman Shipping was offered to me through the usual channels. The fact that Isserman was Christie's husband didn't enter into my decision. The money wasn't mine alone; I represented a group. I wasn't about to put money belonging to associates into a losing proposition—not on purpose. I knew Christie was against the venture; naturally I researched why she herself wasn't investing and why Sexton Industries stayed out. When I discovered there were personal motives involved and that no weakness in the scheme was indicated, I was satisfied.

"So, Lieutenant Mulcahaney, you haven't a single piece of evidence to tie me into any of these deaths. I'm not responsible for the alcoholic, drug-addicted woman Christie turned into. If you want my opinion, her father was at the root of her dependency. He was her anchor, and after he died she was without direction or purpose."

He picked up his cup. "Drink up, Lieutenant, Detective Schmidt." He pointed to the cups no one had touched. "There's nothing worse than cold coffee."

There was silence while the coffee was obediently consumed.

Raffanti set his cup down first. "I did not go to New York at any time during the Memorial Day weekend. I had no contact of any kind with Christie or Walther. I was here. I can parade witnesses that will swear to my whereabouts for every hour of every day from the time I left San Juan to the time I went back."

And he could, Norah thought, and got up. "Thank you for your time."

He hesitated. There was the merest race of tension in the way he slanted his shoulders, the right leading slightly. "Will you be seeing Chief Walsh?" he asked.

"I don't think that's necessary."

The shoulders eased, straightened. "May I offer a comment?"

"Of course."

"It looks to me like someone's out to frame Sarah."

With Gus doing the driving on the way back, Norah had plenty of time to think. Up to now everyone Norah had talked to had characterized the near drowning at the lake as a prank that had got out of hand. According to Raffanti's version—and Norah had no reason to doubt it—the act had been an expression of deep hostility between the girls. Suppressed, the antagonism had grown over the years. Walther Isserman had certainly been aware of it. In the hospital, across Christina's bed, he had openly accused Sarah of wanting her sister dead. She had turned the accusation back against him. Her almost hysterical attempts to remove her sister from his care, her insistence that she wanted to save Christina's life, could have been either a desperate attempt to quell her own hate before it went out of control, or a cover-up. Maybe she was the one who had been introducing the Valium into her sister's drinks all along. Maybe she had pulled the plug on the respirator. Of all the suspects, certainly she had the best opportunity, and if, after having lost young Mario to her sister, Sarah had learned of her husband's affair with Christina, that could have pushed her over the edge.

The money didn't matter to Sarah, Norah thought. As for the MO, she had been psychologically driven to accomplish what she had come so close to accomplishing all those years before. This time there was no one watching. She didn't have to pretend to be horsing around. She could hold Christina under water for as long as it took.

Captain Jacoby was right about one thing, Norah decided, sliding low on the end of her spine, head back against the seat, as they drove past the dreary landscape of factories and warehouses bordering Pulaski Skyway. He was right about the deaths of Christina and her husband being linked. It was easy to accept Sarah's ability to handle her sister and tumble her into the bathtub, but how had she managed to hang Walther? First of all, she had to render him unconscious. Well, that wouldn't have been so hard to manage. But . . .

"She's small," Norah said aloud. "She can't be more than five foot three and a hundred five pounds. How could she have hoisted Isserman into midair? How could she have rigged it to look like he did it himself?"

Gus stole a glance at her. She was drawn, tired. He wished that she'd accept Hoyt's guilt, but he knew she wouldn't, not as long as she had the slightest doubt, as long as there was a single unexplained aspect. She was more determined than ever on this one—because she was in charge, of course, but also because she was alone without Joe to make her ease off. He understood that Norah needed company, someone to talk to, a friend. Nevertheless, Gus had reservations about her having taken Jordan in as a roommate. It didn't seem to be doing her much good. Not yet, anyway.

"Two people working together could have done it," he suggested.

"I know. Physically, it works. It explains the method. Psychologically, emotionally . . ." She sighed. As she had earlier considered the possibility of shared guilt between Walther and Lucine in the murder attempts on Christina, Norah now examined how a conspiracy between Sarah and Justin Hoyt might have worked in the accomplished deaths. Justin's trip to San Juan would have been for the express purpose of providing an alibi. While there, he'd gambled; he couldn't resist. He'd lost again, and that had merely strengthened his determination to help Sarah get the Sexton money. Justin was taking the full accusation alone to spare her and, of course, to preserve her right to the inheritance. The defense could lean heavily on the implausibility of choosing drowning as the MO, and with the kind of legal talent the Hoyts could afford, he had a good chance of being acquitted.

As for Sarah, her alibi wasn't much better than her husband's. On the night in question she had attended a charity theater party followed by a late-night supper at Tavern on the Green. She was driven home to Sands Point in her own limousine, arriving at approximately two A.M. She could easily have waited till the chauffeur was in his own quarters, then taken her Jaguar and driven herself back to the city. Justin himself had commented on how little traffic there was at that hour. They could have met at the Isserman apartment . . .

"No!" Norah exclaimed.

"What? What's the matter?" Gus asked, but Norah's answer was drowned out by the echoing roar of traffic as they entered the Holland Tunnel.

By the time they exited on the New York side, Norah was close to bursting. "It doesn't work," she said. "If Justin and Sarah had planned the murders together, they would have planned how to get into the apartment. Justin would not have needed to admit that he had a key. He would not have been forced to confess the affair with Christie."

CHAPTER SIXTEEN

It hadn't taken Audrey long to move in. Her possessions were few. The adjustment, on the part of both the rookie and Norah, wasn't as quick or as easy. During the first week they worked different shifts so they hardly saw each other. Audrey was still sleeping when Norah left. When Norah returned, she had already gone on duty. It was when they were both on the eight-to-four that the awkwardness began. Who used the bathroom first? Who cooked? For herself or for both? If for both, who did the marketing? Going back to the time she had lived with her father and run the house for him, Norah was used to her own ways. Audrey had been a loner since childhood. They were both straining to conform to the other's wishes. After dinner was a particularly difficult time. They did the dishes together, then Audrey retired to her room pleading personal matters— laundry, letters, even a headache. Norah wanted her to feel the whole apartment was hers and to make use of it. She kept urging Audrey to come and watch television with her. It resulted in their sitting in front of the set, bored and afraid to admit it.

Since Norah had stopped seeing Gary Reissig, she'd had no one with whom to discuss the job. Roy was now a dedicated family man and rushed home after work. Ferdi had a girlfriend, and it looked as though he might at last be able to set aside his guilt over the death of Pilar Nieves. Gus was a good friend, as lonely as herself, but not a contemporary. Certainly she didn't talk shop when she went to visit the family, so it was good to be able to make casual allusions to Audrey without having to explain. It was comfortable. Audrey was shy about recounting the events of her day—they were inconsequential compared to what Norah had done. But Norah's remarks did ease her shyness and the girl began to respond. Common interests and the inescapable give-and-take of daily living began to forge a bond. Norah even began to think aloud, to bounce ideas off her roommate, to use Audrey as a sounding board.

"Every time I think I've got an answer, I'm faced with another contradiction," she complained. They were sitting at the table after a stuffed-cabbage dinner cooked by Audrey from a recipe of her grandmother Erminia Jarembowska—Jordan being her parents' stage name.

"There must be a reason why the perpetrator chose drowning," Audrey observed. She was still not sure whether she should remain strictly a listener. But it wasn't her nature to remain passive for long—any more than it was Norah's.

"I'm not forgetting that," Norah replied. "I have this nagging feeling not only that I'm missing something, but that's it's right there for me to see. Something in the apartment. I have a feeling there was something at the scene."

They were silent for a while.

"Maybe if you went back there?" Audrey suggested. "Maybe if you went there alone, without all the confusion and distraction . . ."

Norah thought about it. The two domestics at the Isserman place had been dismissed with generous severance, but the apartment and its furnishings awaited settling of the estate, which in turn was in abeyance till the outcome of Justin Hoyt's trial. In fact, the place was still posted as a "Crime Scene."

"Why not?" she said. "I've tried everything else."

Norah unlocked the door and stepped inside. She remained in the dark for a few moments to get a sense of atmosphere. As her eyes adjusted, she could make out the limits of the circular foyer with the massive octagonal table in the center and the sweeping staircase beyond. Listening, she tried to break down the silence into its components, but instead of the usual creakings and settlings, she heard a soft sighing. No, it was more like a thin, high wail. As she strained to hear, concentrating on the sound, a gust of frigid air passed over her. She shivered.

Then she shook herself. It was a draft. Someone had left a window open somewhere, that was all. Resolutely, Norah felt along the wall and found a panel of light switches. She flipped the first one and the chandelier overhead glittered. Blinking in the pool of light, Norah had to shield her eyes to see the shadowed shores of the second floor. Another switch in the row took care of that and the gallery blazed. Firmly, she grasped the banister and began to climb.

What Norah wanted was a feel for the emotions of past events that still lingered in this place, but she must not let herself slip into fantasy. She must reconstruct on the basis of factual evidence. She must remain objective, Norah cautioned herself as she grasped the handle of the door to the master suite, took a deep breath, and walked in.

She put the lights on and looked around. It all seemed the same: the unmade bed, the drapes drawn over the closed windows. The air was musty but clean. Otherwise Norah could sense no change. Nothing suggested itself, but then she hadn't really expected that it would. Not after one quick look. She intended to go over each square foot of space. To make sure she didn't overlook anything, Norah took the original diagram she'd made on her first inspection of the scene out of her handbag and began to compare it to the bedroom. Had the position of anything changed? Had she left anything out? Almost instantly Norah froze in shock.

It had been there in plain sight all along, glaringly obvious. How could she have missed it? Norah groaned. She realized its significance now only because it was gone. All the medical equipment was gone. Wait . . . she strode quickly to the bathroom. Yes, the Jerry chair too had been removed. Returned to the surgical supply company, of course. It didn't matter. There were still plenty of gaps, but at least she knew how the crimes had been committed. Everything else would fall into place. Her heart was pounding. She felt like shouting. She locked up and hurried home.

When she got there, Audrey was already in bed. Norah was surprised at the depth of her disappointment, at how much she'd been counting on her new friend. She hesitated in front of Audrey's door. She wanted to share her elation, to talk, discuss, plan. No use keeping them both up all night, she thought. Sighing, she tiptoed quietly into the kitchen, poured herself a beer, and carried it out to the living room where she settled in her favorite chair—shoes off and feet up on a small hassock—to think. The glut of complications had to be cleared. The Bertram Arnow suicide, Norah now perceived, had served as a signpost to the killer. A suggestion. For now, Clark Harriss's death and the happenings related to it—the hit-and-run, the break-in of his home office, and the dislodging of his breathing tube—must be set aside.

What she had to do, Norah thought, was draw a direct sequential line of the events resulting in the death of Christina Isserman. Christina was the target. The rest were all distractions. Clear them away, pare the case down to the essentials. Sipping her beer, Norah went back to the beginning, the real beginning of the case, before the Rose Ball—the first time Christina Isserman went into a coma.

Norah got out her notebook and pencil. It shaped up like this:

Two episodes of alcohol and drug overdose. Result: temporary coma. Possibly self-inflicted. Possibly induced.

Third episode of alcohol and drug overdose. Result: irreversible coma. Possibly self-inflicted. Possibly induced.

Plug pulled on Christina Isserman's respirator. Result: no additional damage. First overt attempt at murder.

Immersion in bathtub. Result: death. Murder.

Hanging of Walther Isserman. Result: death. Murder or suicide.

The death of Walther Isserman was the only one inextricably linked to Christina's death; a clue leading to the solution of how he died must inevitably reveal her killer.

Norah considered the bloodstains on the bathroom floor and the blood-soaked towel in the hamper. Lab analysis had shown them to be the same blood group as Isserman's. He had, in fact, been cut on the back of the head—but it was a relatively small cut to have bled so profusely. The blood type, O, was the most common in the white race, occurring in forty-five percent of the population, so it could also be the killer's blood. That would explain why it had all been mopped up, but at best that was corroborative evidence.

Norah sat in the chair long after the beer was finished. She reviewed what she had seen in the apartment and what she now believed had happened there. By morning, she had a plan.

As soon as she got to the squad she called in Ferdi Arenas, gave him two names and sent him to check the blood group of each. Next, Simon Wyler was dispatched to Sands Point. Meantime, Norah herself contacted the surgical supply company to retrieve the medical equipment that had been in Christina Isserman's bedroom.

Wyler was the first to report back.

He came in slouching, his wide-brimmed fedora pulled low over the widow's peak of his wavy dark hair, his fists jammed deep into the pockets of his expensive tweed jacket, pulling it out of shape.

"Well?" Norah asked.

"The Jaguar was in the shop for repairs. The chauffeur is positive she didn't use the limo. His quarters are right over the garage and he had an upset stomach that kept him up most of the night. He's positive he would have heard anybody starting it up."

"Any other way Sarah Hoyt could have got back to New York in the early hours?"

Detective Wyler scowled. "Not unless she walked. Sorry, Lieutenant."

"Don't be. You've just eliminated one more suspect," she replied, and sent Wyler out again.

This time he came back standing tall at the full six foot two of his narrow frame, tweed jacket impeccable without a bulge or wrinkle. Smiling, he swept off his fedora in salute.

"The lady says she never slept better in her life."

"Really?" Norah grinned. "Does that mean she's not usually a heavy sleeper?"

"She hasn't been sleeping well at all since her husband died."

Norah called a strategy meeting.

Brennan, Arenas, Schmidt, and Wyler made up the nucleus of the team. They sat in Norah's office on a gray and drizzly morning tossing ideas back and forth, looking for the weak spots. Notes were consulted for the date of the first time Christina Isserman went into a coma: March 12, a little over a year before. On that occasion, she remained unconscious for close to forty-eight hours. It had been accepted as an accidental OD. It was now accepted as the first attempt at murder.

The second murder attempt took place on November 15 of the same year. It had also been considered an accidental OD and, as before, blood tests showed the presence of Valium. The coma lasted four days and it was during this period, Norah pointed out, that Walther Isserman's business received a sudden influx of cash and credit based on a new loan from the bank in California. The first collateral had been the ship, the *Re Umberto* itself. On this occasion there was no such surety and the bank had refused to specify what Isserman had put up. Norah had requested a court order for disclosure, though she had a pretty good idea what it was.

"It's also interesting to note that each time Christina Isserman went into a coma it was after a big night out—the Boys Town Benefit, the Black and Red Dinner, and this last time, of course, the Rose Ball," Norah pointed out.

"Except that the suspect did not attend the Rose Ball," Ferdi objected.

"Mrs. Isserman continued drinking after she got home," Brennan put in.

"From a fresh bottle," Norah pointed out.

"So, the only one who could have doctored her drink there

was her husband," Ferdi replied. "And we know he didn't do it."

"How do we know?" Norah asked. "Because he was killed along with her?"

They stared at her.

She allowed herself a smile. "Here." She pulled out her rough diagram of the suite, and they gathered around while she explained her theory of why Christina Isserman had been drowned and why Walther Isserman's death had been rigged to look like suicide. This time around she could show how Clark Harriss's death fit into the pattern.

There was a long silence.

Gus spoke up. "You've explained it, but how are we going to prove it?"

Norah grinned. "I thought you'd never ask."

She laid out the plan, then made the assignments: Ferdi was to check car rentals for the night of the accident; Gus was to do a detailed survey of the suspect's finances. If the information was as expected, Brennan would set up the stakeout.

"We're also going to need someone to leak the information to the suspect," Norah said. She looked around from one to the other of the detectives. "Who can put it over? Any suggestions?"

Art Potts put his head in the door. "He wants you."

Norah was deep in the planning and Potts had to repeat the summons.

"What's up?"

Potts was the buffer between the captain and just about everybody in the precinct from cops to cleaning people. Usually, he was more than willing to give a hint of the cause of Jacoby's displeasure, irritation, or concern to the unfortunate about to be harangued. Uncharacteristically, he held back. "It's about Officer Jordan," he admitted finally.

"What about her?"

"You've asked for her for special assignment."

"So?"

"Again."

"What's the problem?"

Potts was embarrassed. "You'd better ask the captain."

"Art . . ." Norah called, but he was already slipping out the door. Norah liked the small, pudgy detective with the fussy manner. She trusted him. So did everybody. Art Potts maintained a delicate balance between loyalty to his boss and friendship to the men and women under Jacoby. If he ever stepped over the line, it was to the side of the detectives. What could be so sensitive that he refused to confide it? He'd said it was about Audrey. Could Jacoby have gotten wind of the scheme Norah and her team had worked out? She hadn't cleared it with him. After all, she was commander of homicide detectives and in charge of the investigation. Manny Jacoby was precinct head and higher in rank. If he should give her a direct order forbidding the operation . . . Reluctantly, Norah left her desk and went next door.

"Oh, it's you," Jacoby scowled, even less pleased than usual to see her.

He leaned back in the swivel chair and folded his hands across his small but growing belly. It was a cool day; the office was comfortable yet his balding pate glistened with sweat.

Norah felt herself grow warm. "You wanted to see me, Captain."

"Yes. Right. Well, sit down, sit." He cleared his throat. "I'll get right to the point."

But he lapsed into another protracted silence. He took a breath. "It's about Jordan. This is the fourth time you've requested her for special assignment."

"The third, Captain," Norah corrected. "The first time, the toss of the Isserman apartment, she was assigned by the duty sergeant."

"Let's not quibble, Mulcahaney. The perception is that she's getting preferential treatment."

"Officer Jordan is intelligent, hardworking, and she has real aptitude for the job."

"She's also your roommate."

Norah sighed. She squared her shoulders, raised her chin, and looked straight at the captain. "That has nothing to do with it."

He met her look. "Then give the assignment to somebody else."

"That would be discriminating against Jordan because she's my roommate."

"Your people have to respect you, Mulcahaney. They don't have to like you, or admire you, or think you're smart, but they have to *know* that you're fair. They'll forgive everything else."

He was talking to her as an equal. His face was earnest; he was giving her advice he had learned through hard experience and disappointment. Norah was touched as well as grateful. "Audrey Jordan has got more than the usual share of breaks," she admitted. "But it happens that she's uniquely suited for this particular job. I need somebody to play a crooked cop and attempt to sell information to a suspect."

Jacoby started to speak, obviously to object, and Norah hurried on.

"It could be somebody who's case-hardened and venal, or else young, opportunistic, amoral. I go for the latter because . . ."

"No!" Jacoby exploded. "It's out. I won't permit it. There'll be no scams run out of this command."

"Captain," Norah pleaded. "It's the last chance we have of solving this case."

"The case is solved. An arrest has been made and we have an indictment."

"There are too many contradictions."

"The DA is satisfied."

"I don't think he is."

"Enough to go to trial."

"On the double charge. How about the other murder? How about Clark Harriss? I can't forget Clark Harriss, Captain."

Jacoby drew the open palm of his hand across his mouth.

Norah recognized that as a gesture of uncertainty and followed up. "Justin Hoyt has an alibi for the night of Harriss's accident and for the night the breathing tube was removed from his throat. Both are solid. There's no way we can tie him to Harriss's accident and ultimate death. That means the Harriss case is still open. I intend to continue the investigation."

Jacoby grunted, his face now well-oiled with sweat. "What do you have in mind?"

"A shakedown."

"What are you going to use for bait?"

"Jordan will offer to sell incriminating evidence."

"You can't do that."

"Not real evidence."

"That's entrapment."

"Not if the suspect doesn't buy it."

"I don't buy it." As far as Jacoby was concerned that was the end of it.

But Norah didn't leave. They both remained staring at each other, locked in silence.

That the scheme could be labeled entrapment had not escaped Norah. It worried her too. She did not lightly flout legal procedure, but it was an acknowledged gray area difficult for police and lawyer to interpret. "Captain, this isn't a matter of a decoy prostitute entrapping a john. Or an undercover cop making a buy from a pusher. We're dealing with a killer, and not an ordinary killer either. I've seen violence and cold-blooded disregard for human life, but never such complete lack of human compassion. My God, Captain, these victims were totally defenseless!"

Jacoby sighed deeply. "Assume the suspect takes the bait . . . Then what? How are you going to make it stick?"

"I'm looking for a confession."

He shook his head. "I don't know . . . They'll claim it's tainted."

"That will be for the jury to decide, won't it?" Norah pleaded. Then when she saw Jacoby still uncertain, she sat up straighter, thrust her chin forward with determination. "We have to do this, Captain. If anything goes wrong, it'll be on me. I'll take full responsibility."

He met her look squarely. "Not while you're in my command, you won't, Lieutenant."

"No, sir."

"Now, about Jordan." Jacoby was all business again. "She's too inexperienced."

Norah wanted to say thank you, but this was not the time.

"Sir, the cop who makes the approach should be someone who's been working on the case and can logically be assumed to have inside information. The cop has to convince the suspect that she's in jeopardy. We'll write the script, but the cop has to deliver the lines, put on a good show. Jordan's people are actors. She considered going into the business herself. Do we have anybody else with that kind of background and experience?"

She drove home the point with complete confidence in what the answer had to be. Up to now, Norah had been plagued by doubts in her own judgment and abilities, worried about how she was perceived by those she commanded and by those to whom she was accountable. She had been as concerned over her own performance as about solving the case.

"Jordan has one more qualification: because she is my roommate, the suspect will be convinced of her credibility."

In attempting to convince Jacoby of the plan and justify her intention to use Audrey, Norah had succeeded in sweeping aside her own uncertainties.

CHAPTER SEVENTEEN

Once again Norah stood in Christina Isserman's bedroom, this time in darkness, with the moon casting just enough light through the big bay window to silhouette the furniture and the life-support equipment. Audrey had made the call that afternoon, and a meeting had been arranged. Norah glanced at her watch: ten P.M.; it should be taking place right now. They had gone over the script, rehearsed and rehearsed, tried to anticipate every possible reaction. Now it was up to Audrey to put it over.

According to the theory they had all worked out together, the killer had a key to the apartment. Therefore Norah's concentration was on that first indication they were right—the sound of the key turning in the lock. Of course, there were lookouts posted down on the street at the front and side entrances of the building; they would alert her in plenty of time. She should relax. She couldn't. No matter how many times she'd been in similar situations, no matter how clearly she'd analyzed a case, the anxiety of the anticipated confrontation never eased. At this time, Norah thought, she carried the full responsibility for success or failure. No, she brought herself up short. Joe had told her that failure was the responsibility of the one in charge; success was shared by all.

Norah took up a position beside the canopied bed so she could face both entrances—the one from the adjoining bedroom and the door from the corridor. Her moves had all been planned in advance. There was nothing to do but wait.

Eleven o'clock. Twelve. Had Audrey failed? What had gone wrong?

The two-way radio crackled. "Norah? She's crossing Fifth Avenue."

Norah jumped. In the silence Simon Wyler's voice sounded as though it were amplified. Actually it was a hoarse whisper. Norah's heart pounded. The bait had been taken. Audrey had done it.

Low static indicated another transmission. "She's inside." It was Wyler again, and he sounded relieved.

Norah's blood tingled. She was supremely alert. Now the period of waiting seemed so brief she was almost surprised when she heard the click of the key. After that, another very short wait. Norah strained for other sounds that would indicate progress, but there were none. For a big woman she was light on her feet, Norah thought. And of course she knew her way around. Then the door to the corridor edged open. The moonlight didn't reach that far, but Norah didn't need it to see.

"Looking for something, Mrs. Northcott?" she asked, and reached to turn on the bedside lamp.

The two women blinked at each other.

Lucine Northcott wore gray slacks and a loose gray silk shirt with a discreet strand of pearls and matching earrings—not an outfit designed for illegal entry.

"I'm afraid you're too late," Norah told her.

"For what?" the woman retorted in her throaty, elegantly slurred disdain.

"For whatever you came here to do."

"I don't have to tell you my business."

"I'm afraid you do. This is a 'crime scene,' Mrs. Northcott. The sign is clearly posted on both entrances advising unauthorized persons to keep out. You ignored it." The socialite pressed her lips together. "By the way, where did you get the key?"

After a short hesitation Lucine Northcott decided to reply. "I've had it for a long time."

"From when you were employed to redecorate the apartment?"

The question was phrased to distract the suspect, to rankle her pride. She hesitated, then licked her lips. "Yes."

Norah was pleased. Answering the first question, no matter how innocuous it might appear, or how neutral the reply, signaled a lowering of defenses. It was a breach in the protective wall.

"That was after Christina was divorced from Ruthven Duveen, of course," Norah went on. "She wanted all trace and memory of him removed. Naturally you needed a key to let the workmen in and out, to come and go yourself. She never thought to get the key back. Probably you forgot you had it."

Lucine Northcott shrugged.

"Your decorating business wasn't all that successful, though, was it? You did a few jobs, mostly for friends, and when those ran out . . ."

"It wasn't a business. It was more of a hobby. I did it as a favor for special friends. Then I got bored with it."

"You considered Christina Sexton a special friend?"

"Certainly."

Norah shook her head. "I don't think so, Mrs. Northcott. I don't think you were ever Christina Sexton's friend, nor Sarah's either. You grew up with them, went to the same school, spent summers at their place, were invited to their parties—and resented everything they had and you didn't. You were always in the second rank, always behind the Sexton girls."

"That's not true. My family goes back a lot farther. My great-grandmother was a leader of society when theirs was still taking in washing."

"Poor but proud, right, Mrs. Northcott?"

"You keep harping on money, Lieutenant. I've told you it's not important."

"Then why did you say you were planning to go with Mr. Isserman to your place in St. John over the Memorial Day weekend? You don't own that house anymore. You sold it.

Over two years ago. In fact, you used the money from its sale to invest in the *Re Umberto*." Turning slightly to her right, Norah flipped a wall switch, and the various wall sconces were turned on. Lucine Northcott was startled. She looked around as though to hide.

But she recovered her equanimity quickly. "I sold the house to my aunt and I still have full use of it."

"I see. Well, it may have been a small lie merely to reinforce your status, but it had the unfortunate result of causing us to examine your financial situation very thoroughly. We discovered that you got rid of all your properties and invested the proceeds in Isserman shipping. You are deeply in debt, living on credit, and can't go on much longer."

"I have resources you know nothing about, Lieutentant." She drew herself up. "I don't care to discuss this."

"Are you leaving, Mrs. Northcott?"

"Do you intend to stop me?"

Each fixed her gaze on the other.

Lucine Northcott was smart and tough, Norah thought. Under the sophistication and elegance she was as hard as any street-smart woman. She was challenging Norah to state the evidence she had against her, and that was exactly what Norah planned to do, but in her own way and in her own time.

"You were already in debt, living in a style you couldn't afford when you met and fell in love with Walther Isserman. And he fell in love with you. That was the most wonderful thing that had ever happened to you. In addition, you were taking him away from a Sexton, from Christina. You couldn't help but savor that. You put everything you had into the relationship—emotionally and financially you invested in Walther Isserman. He promised to marry you, but he didn't leave Christina. The money tied him to her, of course, but you were afraid it might be something more."

Norah paused, but Lucine Northcott neither moved nor said a word. So far so good.

"So you decided to get rid of your rival." Norah picked up the tempo. "By this time Christina was drinking heavily and taking pills along with the liquor. It was simply a matter of using her own addiction against her. Getting a supply of the drug, Valium, was no problem. Any doctor will give a regular patient a prescription.

"Getting Christina to take the extra amount was simple too. You moved in the same circles, went to the same dinners, parties. All you had to do was slip a couple of extra tablets into her drinks. You did it on two occasions—at the Boys Town Benefit and at the Red and Black dinner, and each time she went into a coma and then recovered. You were getting desperate. The *Re Umberto* was a total loss. Isserman Shipping went bankrupt. It appeared that Walther couldn't establish credit to start again. You'd lost everything, and unless you could get him away from Christina once and for and all, you might lose Walther too. So you had to make one last try."

Again Norah gave the suspect a chance to parry, and she did. "I didn't attend the Rose Ball. If you'd done your homework, Lieutenant Mulcahaney, you'd know that." She was openly disparaging.

"Of course you didn't. It was Walther who spiked his wife's drink that night after they got home."

The socialite showed no reaction.

"About six months ago you convinced Walther to borrow certain bearer bonds his wife kept in their safe deposit. The bonds had belonged to her father, had been held by him and now by her as sentimental mementos of his first big investment. There was little or no likelihood she would ever dispose of them. Walther could take them and use them as collateral for a loan that would put him back in business again. Once the word was out that his credit was good, other investors would come in. He could repay the loan and replace the bonds. Christina would never know. She had no occasion to visit the vault, and even if she did, it wouldn't occur to her to check the securities. So he did it. And then, unexpectedly, Christina stopped taking the Valium. Oh, she went on drinking, but Walther wasn't ready to replace the securities. As she became more stable, he got more nervous. You suggested that he could keep her off balance a little while longer by getting her back on the drug, introducing it into her drinks a little at a time. You couldn't do it by yourself because you couldn't get close to her the way you used to. Anyway, it seemed that involving Walther in this manner would strengthen his commitment to you. You assured him it would look like Christina had resumed her old habit, that nobody would suspect. Finally he agreed. Only it didn't work out. The Valium didn't have the same effect. The alcohol had made her resistant.

"Walther was getting desperate. He was thinking of confessing everything to Christina and throwing himself on her mercies. You told him to increase the dosage. Even if it put her out, you argued, it would just be for a short time. Like before. You supplied the drug as usual, only this time you needed more than you could ask your doctor for, but you could help yourself from the supply room at Chazen-Hadley, couldn't you? The dose should have been lethal. But it wasn't. Christina seemed indestructible.

"At least this time the coma appeared irreversible. At least she wouldn't wake up. It might all have ended there, except that Sarah stepped in and accused Walther of attempted murder. If it should ever come out that he had 'borrowed' the bonds, Walther Isserman was as good as convicted. You couldn't allow it. Clark Harriss was Walther's accountant; he knew about the bonds. So you tried to run him down."

"I don't have a car, Lieutenant. Remember?"

"You rented. From Hertz. Unfortunately for you, you were required to show a driver's license, so you had to use your real name. It didn't worry you—you never dreamed anyone would be checking." Norah sighed. "You're a fine sportswoman, Mrs. Northcott, but you're not much of a driver. You ran Harriss down, but you didn't kill him.

"Walther agonized over his wife's condition. He never expected such a severe reaction to the spiked drink. He was riddled with guilt—for the theft of the bonds, the failure of the marriage, his affair with you, but most of all for having come so close to committing murder. The only way he could make it right was to take Christina home and get her well again.

"That was when you pulled the plug on her."

Norah waited for a reaction, but Lucine Northcott remained stoic, not even deigning to deny the accusation.

"The whole hospital was buzzing over the death of a patient whose hands had been untied and who had extubated himself:

Bertram Arnow. That was what gave you the idea. Christina was unconscious and couldn't pull out her own tube, but if there was a mercy killer loose untying the hands of dying patients it could be passed off that he had pulled the plug. So you went ahead and did it.

"Only she didn't die. She actually got better. And because of what had nearly happened, Walther become more determined than ever to get her out of Chazen-Hadley. Security around Christina became almost impregnable. You couldn't get at her so you really had no choice but to go along with Walther's decision to take Christina home. In fact you encouraged it. Maybe you even helped him get ready for her, advised him what equipment would be needed and where to get it." Norah paused, looking toward the bed and the array of machines at its head. Lucine Northcott's eyes followed hers. "With Walther preoccupied, you broke into Clark Harriss's home office and removed all papers and files pertaining to him personally and to Isserman Shipping. But Harriss himself was still alive. He couldn't be allowed to recover. Using your freedom as a volunteer, you slipped into the IC unit."

Norah thought of Harriss as she had last seen him—neat features bloated, bright and intelligent eyes closed, hands tied to the bedrails at either side. "Clark Harriss was at your mercy, and you had none.

"When you told me you would have been satisfied to live as Walther Isserman's acknowledged and official mistress while his wife remained in a coma for the rest of her life, I believe you meant it. You didn't foresee, how could you, the extent of Walther's remorse. When he finally brought Christina home you certainly didn't expect he would shut himself up with her. When he informed you she was recovering, you were beside yourself."

Till now the socialite had listened intently but betrayed little emotion. "I didn't believe she was recovering. I didn't believe it."

"It doesn't matter. It doesn't matter whether or not it was true. *He* believed it. Because he wanted to. Because he had to."

"I don't know anything about any alleged bonds," Lucine

Northcott went on, acknowledging at last that she must offer a defense. "Walther isn't here to speak for himself, but I don't believe he ever took anything that wasn't his. As for the rest of your . . . theory, that I behaved like a kind of Lady Macbeth, you're making it up out of whole cloth."

"You came here to see him and to get him away from the unhealthy atmosphere, the miasma of culpability and regret he had plunged himself into. You came to get him away from Christina. But he wouldn't leave. He wouldn't listen. It was too late. You'd lost him."

A tremor passed through Lucine Northcott.

"Maybe there was still a chance. Maybe something could still be done and the situation somehow salvaged. You had put everything into Walther Isserman, your fortune and your future. You would not accept defeat. You didn't have to. There was one way you could still win it all. Kill Christina. Kill her outright. See her dead. Let Walther see her dead."

Norah paused. The first phrase of the scheme had been to convince Lucine Northcott that she knew the forces that had motivated her, impelled her to plan and commit the murders. Now she must move into the second phase: the method of the murders.

"Last Sunday night, or to be accurate—in the early hours of Monday morning, when both Christina and Walther could be presumed to be sleeping, you came here and let yourself in. You crept down the corridor and entered this bedroom, just as you did tonight."

Again, for just a moment, the two woumen took their eyes off each other and looked toward the big canopied bed with its rumpled rose sheets.

"Christina was alone and sleeping quietly. Of course, you had no idea if what Walther had told you about her condition was true; she might have been as far along to recovery as he claimed and able to offer resistance or call for help. You brought a small bottle of chloroform with you, just in case." This was the delicate part, Norah thought. This should, must, throw her off guard. "But one look at the thin, wasted coma-tose figure in the bed and you knew that you wouldn't need it. You set the chloroform aside."

Some of the suspect's tension eased. Norah could see her strong, broad shoulders relax. She almost looked smug.

"You lifted Christina out of the bed and put her in the Jerry chair, then you rolled her to the bathroom." Norah looked to the open door, where the chair could be seen. "You filled the tub and then you tumbled her into the water. In this way you recalled the childhood incident and pointed to Sarah Hoyt as the killer. You leaned over Christina and pushed her under.

"Then Walther walked in on you.

"He was horrified. First, he pulled you off his wife. Then he tried to raise her. You wouldn't let him. You argued. You pleaded with him. You tried to make him face the reality of Christina's condition. You pointed out that she would never again be a conscious, functioning being. You told him you loved him. He didn't hear. He was impervious to your words, your touch, your tears. All he wanted was to haul Christina out of the tub. You struggled. Water splashed everywhere. A bottle of cologne was knocked off a shelf and smashed. You were cut on the fragments."

It was no more than a flicker of the eyelids and a reflexive hug of her right arm to her body, but Norah had been looking for some such reaction.

"Your blood type is the same as his, type O, and it was your blood that gushed over the tiles. While you attempted to staunch the flow with towels, Walther made another try at saving his wife. Cut, bleeding, you shoved him to one side and he fell, hitting his head on the edge of the tub.

"So now you had the added problem of what to do about Walther. He was no longer your lover, the man for whom you'd sacrificed; he was changed—unbalanced, an enemy. You hadn't planned for all this; you had to improvise. By this time Walther's emotional instability was known to his friends. The two domestics, Wrede and McCullough, would support accounts of his derangement. You could rig the two deaths to look like murder followed by suicide."

Norah took a deep breath, then slowly released it. She needed to ease her own tension and also to ready herself for the next and final phase—to convince the suspect she could prove what she charged, that the incriminating evidence did in fact exist. That was the purpose of the entire scam.

"You overdid it, Mrs. Northcott. You were too clever," Norah told her. "A simple murder, a pillow over the comatose woman's face might have suggested that she suffocated in her sleep. It could have been done quietly without disturbing Walther. You, would have got away with it." She stopped and waited.

"Is that it? Is that your case, Lieutenant?" the elegant woman drawled. "What am I supposed to do? Break down and confess? I'm sorry to disappoint you, but I didn't do it. Again, I have to remind you—I have an alibi. I was with my aunt, Mrs. Cynthia Dyson, in Westhampton. Ask her. She'll tell you."

"She already has. She's told us she's a light sleeper, but that first night you spent with her she had the best rest she's had in months. Since her husband passed away, in fact."

"What am I supposed to have done? Put Valium into her milk?" Lucine Northcott asked scornfully.

"Exactly."

She gasped, then managed a smile. "You've got an answer for everything, Lieutenant, but proof for nothing."

"We have your fingerprints on the chloroform bottle. You forgot to take it away with you."

Lucine Northcott laughed. She laughed too hard and too long. "That's been tried on me once already tonight, Lieutenant Mulcahaney. By your roommate, in fact. She offered—I really don't know what she offered—to sell me the bottle or to rub off the alleged prints." She shrugged. "Is this an elaborate backup for her pitch? Are you trying, as they say, to put the arm on me? Please don't bother. I didn't buy it from her and I'm not buying it from you."

"Then what are you doing here, Mrs. Northcott?" Norah asked quietly. "Why did you sneak in here in the middle of the night?"

For a second Lucine Northcott's eyes flashed, then dulled as though a curtain had been lowered over them. "I want my lawyer."

"Certainly. First, I'll read you your rights." From her

pocket, Norah took the worn plasticized card. Keeping her eyes on Northcott, she recited. "You have the right to remain silent. If you refuse that right . . ."

"I want to call my lawyer now."

Norah finished the reading, then pointed to the phone. "Go ahead."

Stony-faced, Lucine Northcott turned vaguely in the direction Norah pointed, as though she was uncertain where the phone was. Then suddenly, without any warning, she whirled and lunged toward the dressing table and snatched the marble-pedestaled face mirror. With the practiced pitch of a girl who had played on the boys' baseball team, she sent it hurtling straight at Norah's head.

Norah ducked just in time and the mirror crashed against the wall behind her, shattering and knocking plaster loose. Before she could recover, Lucine Northcott took two long strides and aimed a vicious kick at her jaw.

It sent Norah sprawling. She nearly blacked out. There was a fraction of a second's break in time when, like the break in a strip of film, nothing happened. When the gap was bridged and the film was running again, it seemed to Norah that she saw and felt everything with a greater sharpness and clarity, that her perceptions were abnormally acute.

The pain shot from her jaw to her temples, throbbing, but she managed to scramble to her feet.

"What are you doing here in the middle of the night, Mrs. Northcott, if you're not worried about fingerprints? Maybe not fingerprints on a chloroform bottle, maybe we were wrong about that, but on something else? Not something you could have taken away with you, but on something here that you used and forgot to wipe clean? You turned the faucets on and off. You wiped the floor and mopped up the glass and blood. What else did you handle that night?"

Anger flashed in Lucine Northcott's eyes, not fear and not despair. She backed up and then, in another sudden move, she swooped to the dressing table again. This time she grabbed a pair of antique barber's shears—slender and delicate but strong and wickedly sharp. They were at least six inches long.

All Norah had to do was pull her gun. It was, as always, in

her shoulder-strap handbag close to her left side. Once she went for it that would be the end of the confrontation.

"What did you touch that night?" Norah asked again. "What did you handle?" she probed. "The Jerry chair, of course, but the push bar doesn't take prints."

Holding the scissors clenched in her fist like a dagger, Lucine Northcott moved toward Norah with deliberation.

Norah fell back. "Even after the two of them were dead, you could still have left things as they were and walked out. It could have passed as a double murder during the commission of a robbery: Isserman is bathing his wife, he hears a sound, he turns to investigate and discovers the intruder. Walther is killed by a blow to the head and Christina, unattended, slips underwater and drowns. All you had to do was leave them and walk out. Instead, you took the trouble to clean up. Neither Walther nor a stranger would have done that.

"Then you dragged him into his room. You removed the drapery cord and put it around his neck. You sat him in a chair under the light fixture, then threw the other end of the cord over it. But, strong as you are, you couldn't pull him high enough, certainly not high enough to make it look as though he'd stepped off. You needed help. You found it. Mechanical help.

"It was right here in this room along with all the medical equipment—the lifter. That's what it's called and that pretty much explains what it is. It consists of a canvas seat or sling in which the patient is placed and a hydraulic pump that raises it up a central pole. You're a hospital volunteer; you're familiar with the device; you've used it many times to transfer bedridden patients from bed to chair or even up over the high side of a whirlpool bath. Christina was so light and fragile you hadn't needed it for her, but it was exactly what you wanted for Walther. You rolled it into his room and put him into it.

"He did die of strangulation, you know. Maybe you thought he was already dead, that when he hit his head the blow killed him. But it didn't. He was alive when you put the noose around his neck, alive when you raised him into the air. Alive still when you wheeled the support out from under him."

Lucine Northcott didn't flinch.

She had loved that man, Norah thought; there was no doubt that she had, yet she remained stony, as impervious as she had been to all the barbs, all the previous attempts to break her. What would it take? Norah wondered. How much longer could she hold off drawing her gun?

"So you put the lifter back where you'd found it, here, at the head of the bed." Saying so, Norah switched on one more light—a small standing lamp which was focused on the medical equipment. The pump handle of the lifter, a long bar, jutted straight out. The chrome glittered. "You came here tonight to remove your fingerprints from that handle."

Lucine Northcott raised the scissors high.

The two women circled each other. With a grunt, the kind of exhalation trained athletes use to prepare themselves for maximum effort, she drew back to deliver the blow. But Norah moved first and flung herself on her would-be attacker. Norah matched her opponent in size and strength; she was as well-conditioned and more skilled, but Lucine Northcott was fighting for her life. Both Norah's hands were clasped on her assailant's wrist, trying to force her to drop the weapon. The socialite tried to shake Norah off. After a few moments of intense effort by both, Lucine Northcott raised one knee and thrust it hard into Norah's groin. Somehow, Norah managed not to scream, but she let go, bending nearly double with pain. Waves of nausea passed over her. Her vision blurred. Slowly she sank to her knees. The killer stood over her, poised for the final strike. She had time; she took time. Meanwhile, still hunched over, Norah managed to look up. Desperate now too, she summoned all her resources and, clenching her teeth on the shooting agony between her legs, she pushed off in a low tackle that brought Northcott down.

Instinctively, as she tried to break the fall, Lucine Northcott dropped the shears. Norah grabbed for them and tossed them as far as she could. Scrambling on all fours, she straddled the prone woman and pinned her arms firmly at her sides.

"It won't do you any good to kill me," she gasped. "Your fingerprints have already been lifted and turned over to the lab."

Exhausted, spent physically and emotionally, neither woman

moved for several moments. The hiatus was so long Norah thought Northcott had finally given up.

"I don't believe it!" she cried out.

She began to writhe under Norah, to twist and heave in an effort to get her off. "You're lying. I don't believe it!" With the extraordinary strength of desperate emotion, she wrested one hand free and, curling her long, perfectly manicured hands into claws, raked Norah's face.

Norah put her hands up to protect her eyes. The blood stung. Was it from scratches or were her eyes injured? She rolled off Northcott and, fumbling for a handkerchief, wiped gently at the blood.

Lucine Northcott got up. She was not as quick as she had been. Her breathing was labored. Dazedly she looked down at Norah still on her knees. From her, Lucine Northcutt turned to the bed. It was unmade, the satin coverlet heaped on a chair, the rose top sheet turned back as she had left it when she carried Christina from bed to chair. Moving slowly, almost in a trance, she grabbed at the top sheet and yanked it free. Dragging it with her, she walked around the foot of the bed to the medical equipment on the other side. Using the sheet as a cloth she began to rub frantically at the shiny chrome of the lifter arm.

Lucine Northcott was sobbing when the detectives came running up from the fifteenth floor—sobbing and rubbing the metal handle.

The word was out that Norah was buying.

The whole squad, with the exception of the detectives working the shift, started to drift into Vittorio's right after four. Roy said he couldn't stay long because his mother-in-law was coming to dinner, but at five he called Grace and told her not to put the roast in the oven for another half hour. Ferdi had a date; at five-thirty he called Concepción and asked her to join him there. Gus's staid face was beaming. Simon Wyler made sure his hat and suede coat were properly hung in the coat room, and then prepared to make a night of it.

Audrey had been shy about coming, but she was there. She'd given a brilliant account of herself pretending to shake down Lucine Northcott with the chloroform bottle for bait, knowing that it was false evidence and at the same time enticing her with hints of the truth so she would return to the scene. It had been a professional performance. What had appeared spontaneous and subject to chance had been rigidly prepared, all actions choreographed, and every possible contingency taken into account. In spite of arduous preparation, Norah had not allowed Audrey to work alone. No officer ever should. The purpose of the backup was not merely to provide protection, but also for corroboration of evidence. Audrey had been wired, and her backup team, Detectives Lionel Rangel and Raymond Butas, were at the bar, paying a lot attention to their young partner.

Norah herself had not gone in alone. Roy, Ferdi, and Gus had worked the stakeout. They bugged the upstairs of the Isserman duplex and then monitored from downstairs.

Norah joined Roy at the bar. "You let it go awfully late," she told him. "I was beginning to wonder if you were going to show up."

"I counted on you to take her," Roy grinned. Then he became serious. "I'm sorry about your injuries."

"My eyes are all right, that's the main thing." Norah touched the long gash down her right cheek. "The doctor says there won't be any scar."

"Thank God. To tell you the truth, we were all getting pretty nervous downstairs. Until she started polishing that machine we didn't have a damn thing."

"I know. I was anxious myself, believe me. She just wouldn't admit she was guilty. She never did say it. I couldn't get her to say she'd killed the two of them, or admit any involvement with Harriss. I couldn't even get her to admit complicity with Isserman in doctoring his wife's drinks."

Audrey moved over. "Why did you need to? You had the fingerprints."

Norah and Roy looked at each other. "Actually, we didn't," Roy said.

"What?"

Art Potts joined them. "They didn't tell you because they thought you had enough of a selling job to do as it was."

"But . . ."

"The equipment in Christina Isserman's bedroom last night was not the original equipment leased by her husband when he brought her home from the hospital," Norah explained. "That was returned to the surgical supply company shortly after the murders. It wasn't practical to try to trace it and get it back."

Audrey gasped.

"By then the fingerprints would probably have been wiped off or smudged anyway." Norah paused. "If she had, in fact, left any that could be identified."

Wide-eyed, Audrey looked from one to the other of the detectives. "So the idea was to make her think she had. But . . . since she never admitted to the murders, never actually confessed . . . " Her eyes rested on Norah.

"We got it all on videotape," Norah told her.

Attention Mystery and Suspense Fans

Do you want to complete your collection of mystery and suspense stories by some of your favorite authors? John D. MacDonald, Helen MacInnes, Dick Francis, Amanda Cross, Ruth Rendell, Alistar MacLean, Erle Stanley Gardner, Cornell Woolrich, among many others, are included in Ballantine/Fawcett's new Mystery Brochure.

For your FREE Mystery Brochure, fill in the coupon below and mail it to:

Ballantine/Fawcett Books
Education Department — MB
201 East 50th Street
New York, NY 10022

Name_____

Address_____

City_____State_____Zip_____

TA-94

CONSPIRACY
INTRIGUE
MURDER

From Fawcett Books